DISNEP

Tangled

The
Series
...

Hair and Now

Facebook: **facebook.com/idwpublishing**
Twitter: **@idwpublishing**
YouTube: **youtube.com/idwpublishing**
Tumblr: **tumblr.idwpublishing.com**
Instagram: **instagram.com/idwpublishing**

ISBN: 978-1-68405-555-5   22 21 20 19   1 2 3 4

COVER ARTISTS
EDUARD PETROVICH,
ROSA LA BARBERA,
& MONICA CATALANO

COVER COLORIST
TOMATO FARM COLOR TEAM

SERIES ASSISTANT EDITOR
ANNI PERHEENTUPA

SERIES EDITOR
CHRIS CERASI

COLLECTION EDITORS
JUSTIN EISINGER
& ALONZO SIMON

COLLECTION DESIGNER
CLYDE GRAPA

Originally published as TANGLED: THE SERIES: HAIR AND NOW
issues #1–3 and TANGLED: THE SERIES: HAIR IT IS.

Chris Ryall, President, Publisher, & CCO
John Barber, Editor-In-Chief
Cara Morrison, Chief Financial Officer
Matt Ruzicka, Chief Accounting Officer
David Hedgecock, Associate Publisher
Jerry Bennington, VP of New Product Development
Lorelei Bunjes, VP of Digital Services
Justin Eisinger, Editorial Director, Graphic Novels & Collections
Eric Moss, Senior Director, Licensing and Business Development

Ted Adams and Robbie Robbins, IDW Founders

Special thanks to Stefano Ambrosio, Stefano Attardi, Julie Dorris, Marco
Ghiglione, Jodi Hammerwold, Manny Mederos, Eugene Paraszczuk, Carlotta
Quattrocolo, Roberto Santillo, Christopher Troise, and Camilla Vedove.

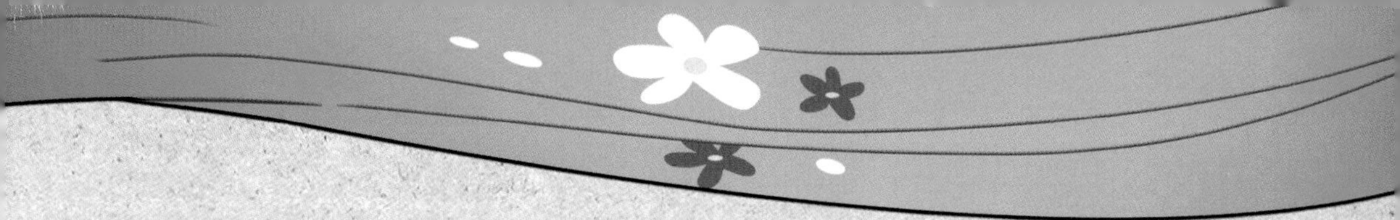

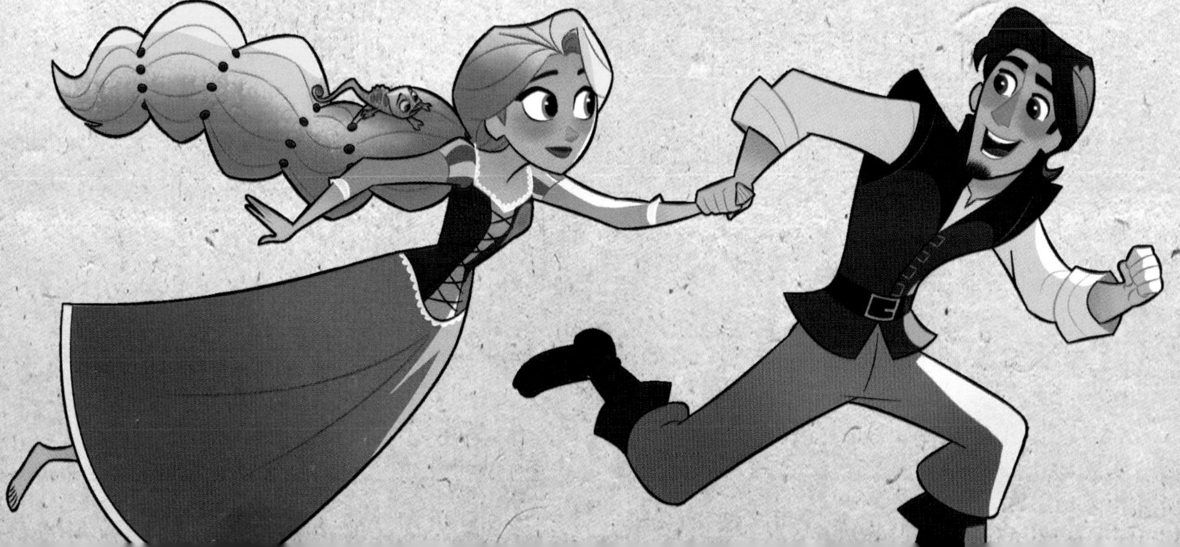

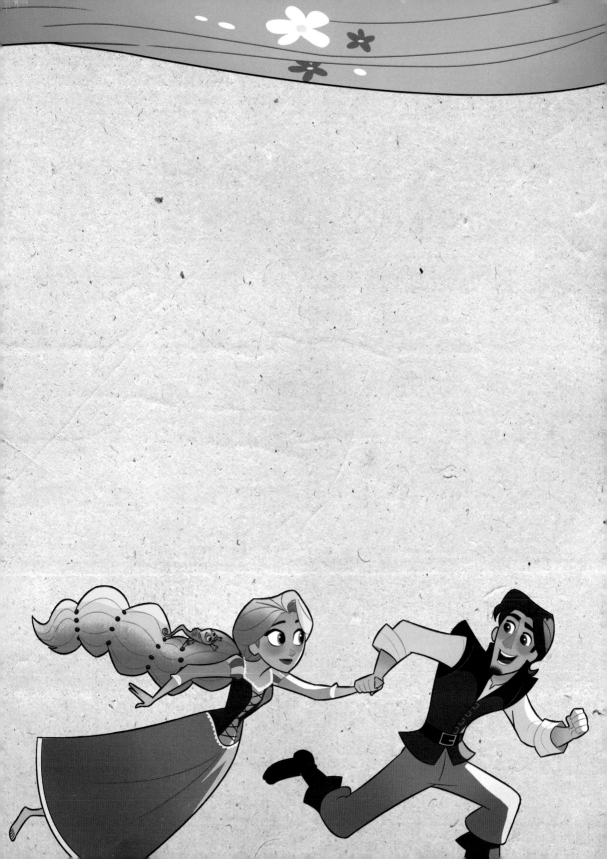

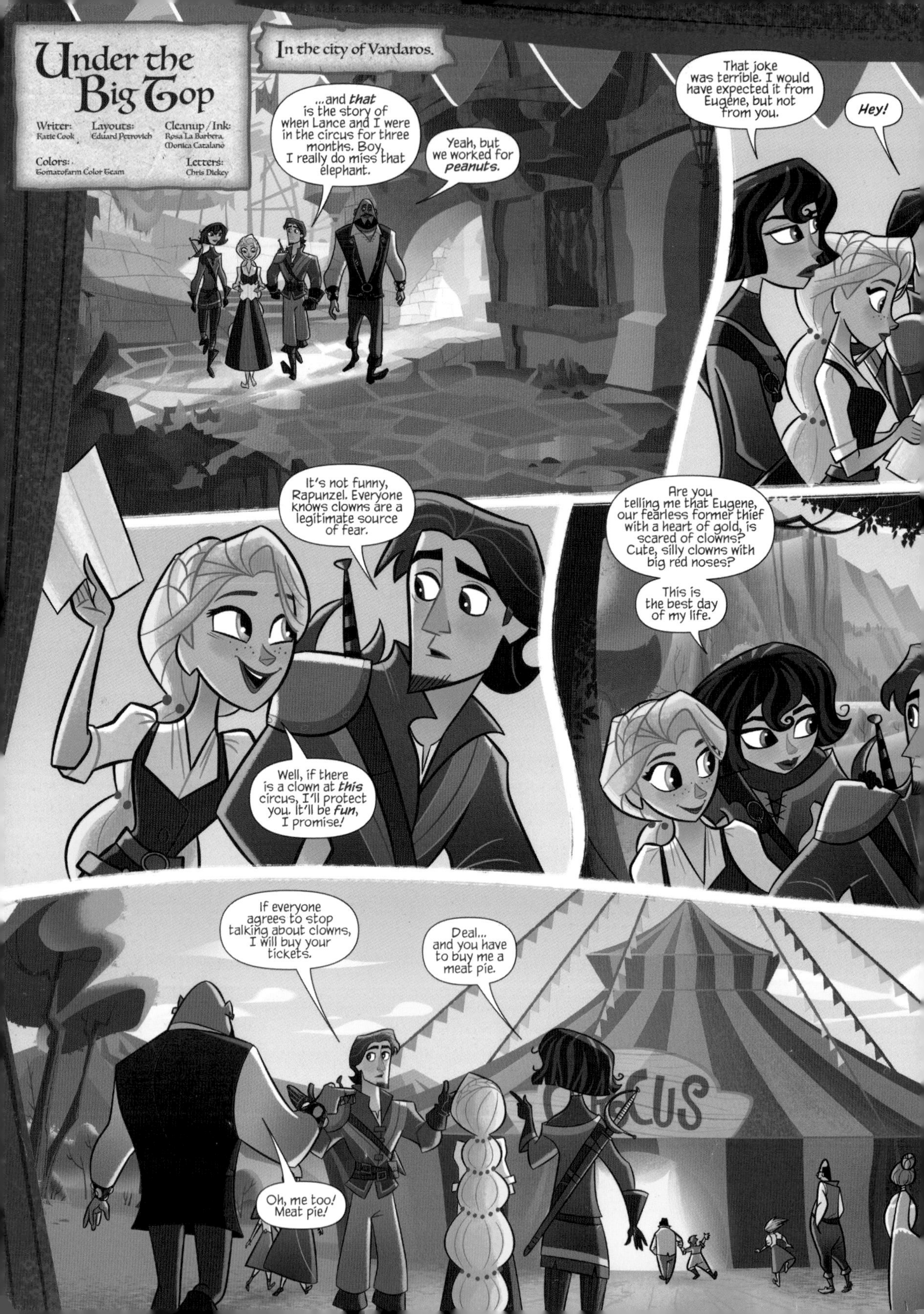
Under the Big Top
Writer: Katie Cook
Layouts: Eduard Petrovich
Cleanup / Ink: Rosa La Barbera, Monica Catalano
Colors: Tomatofarm Color Team
Letters: Chris Dickey
In the city of Vardaros.
...and *that* is the story of when Lance and I were in the circus for three months. Boy, I really do miss that elephant.
Yeah, but we worked for *peanuts*.
That joke was terrible. I would have expected it from Eugene, but not from you.
Hey!
It's not funny, Rapunzel. Everyone knows clowns are a legitimate source of fear.
Well, if there is a clown at *this* circus, I'll protect you. It'll be *fun*, I promise!
Are you telling me that Eugene, our fearless former thief with a heart of gold, is scared of clowns? Cute, silly clowns with big red noses?
This is the best day of my life.
If everyone agrees to stop talking about clowns, I will buy your tickets.
Deal... and you have to buy me a meat pie.
Oh, me too! Meat pie!
CIRCUS

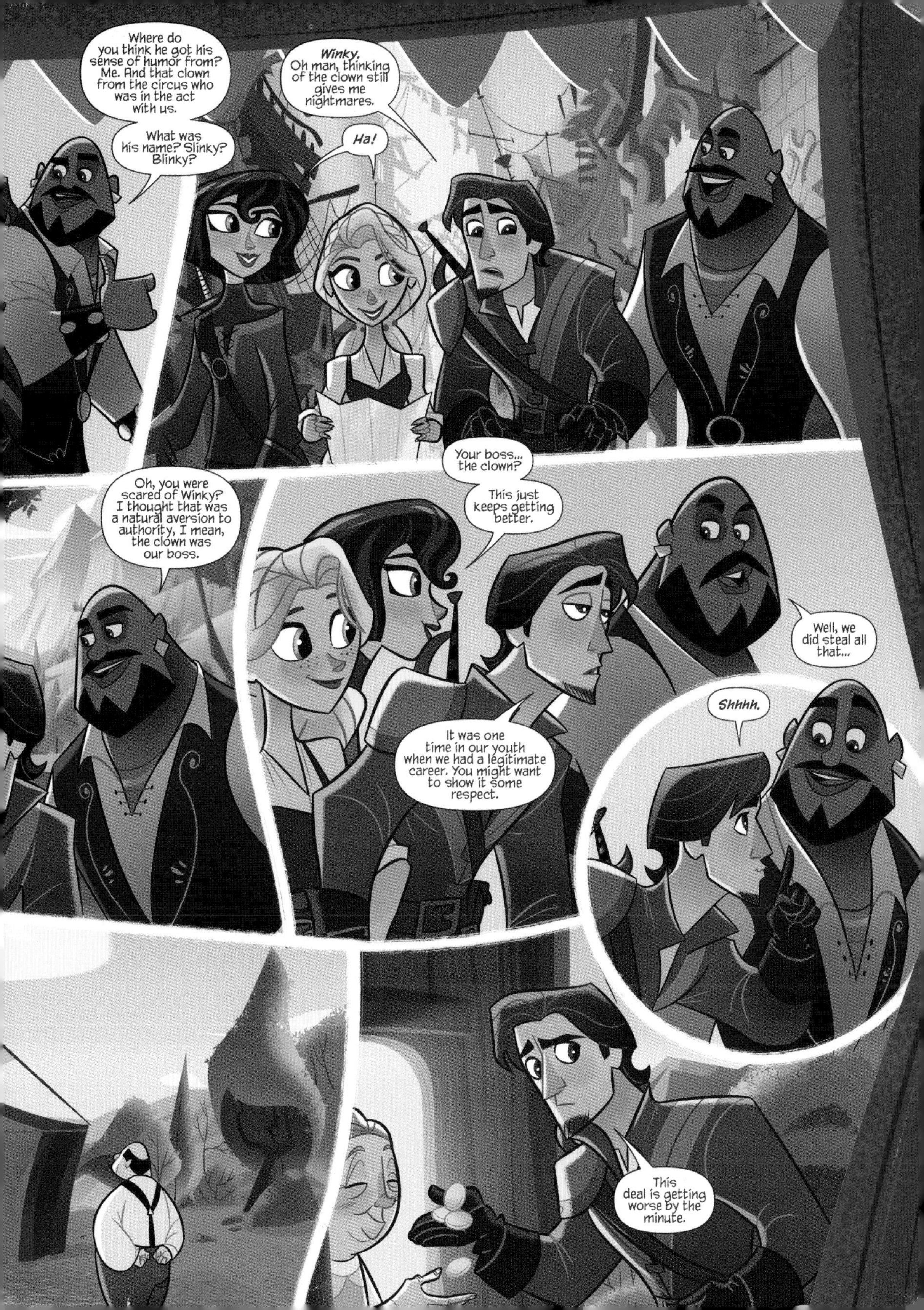
Where do you think he got his sense of humor from? Me. And that clown from the circus who was in the act with us.
What was his name? Slinky? Blinky?
Winky. Oh man, thinking of the clown still gives me nightmares.
Ha!
Oh, you were scared of Winky? I thought that was a natural aversion to authority, I mean, the clown was our boss.
Your boss... the clown?
This just keeps getting better.
It was one time in our youth when we had a legitimate career. You might want to show it some respect.
Well, we did steal all that...
Shhhh.
This deal is getting worse by the minute.

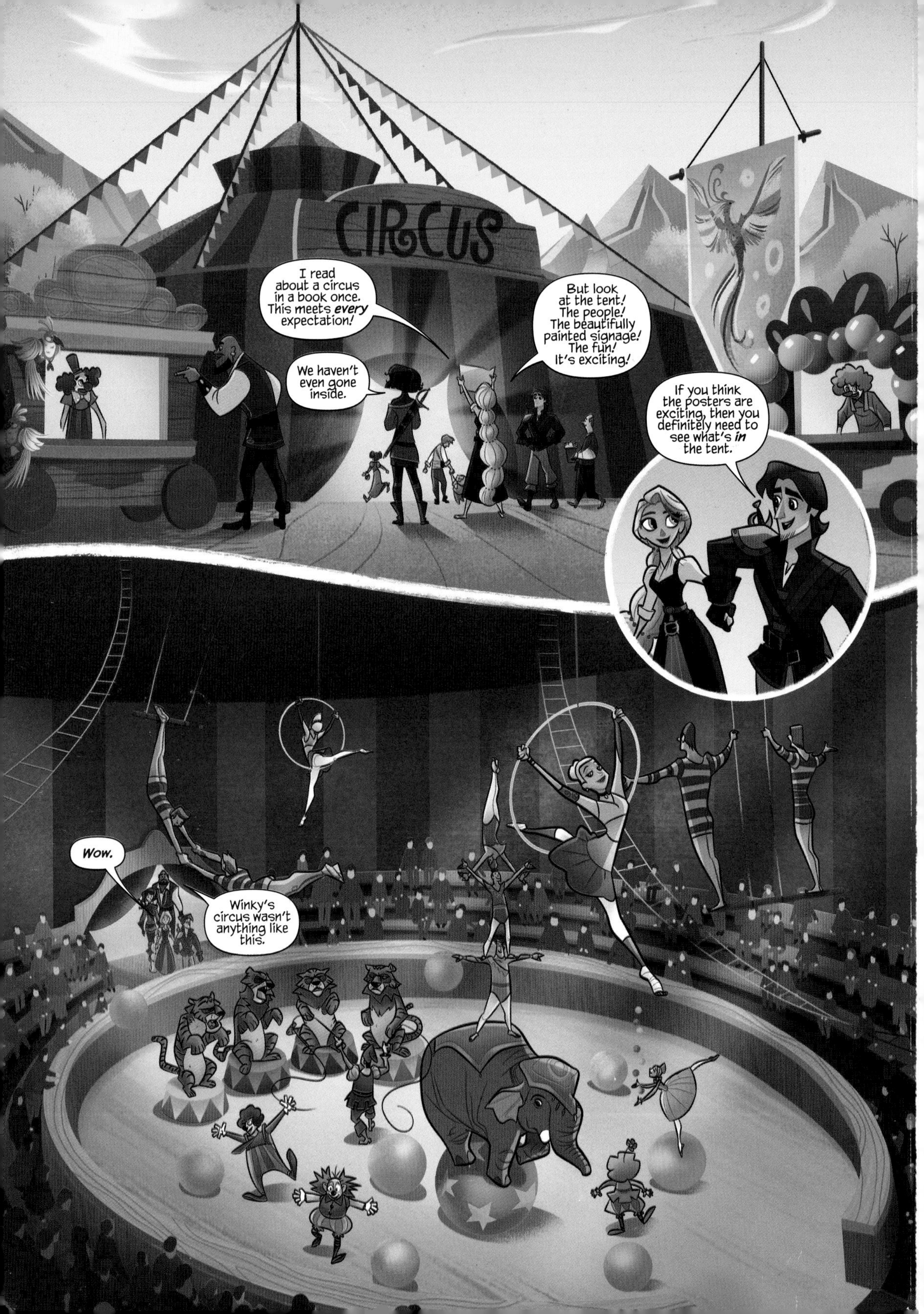

CIRCUS
I read about a circus in a book once. This meets *every* expectation!
We haven't even gone inside.
But look at the tent! The people! The beautifully painted signage! The fun! It's exciting!
If you think the posters are exciting, then you definitely need to see what's *in* the tent.
Wow.
Winky's circus wasn't anything like this.

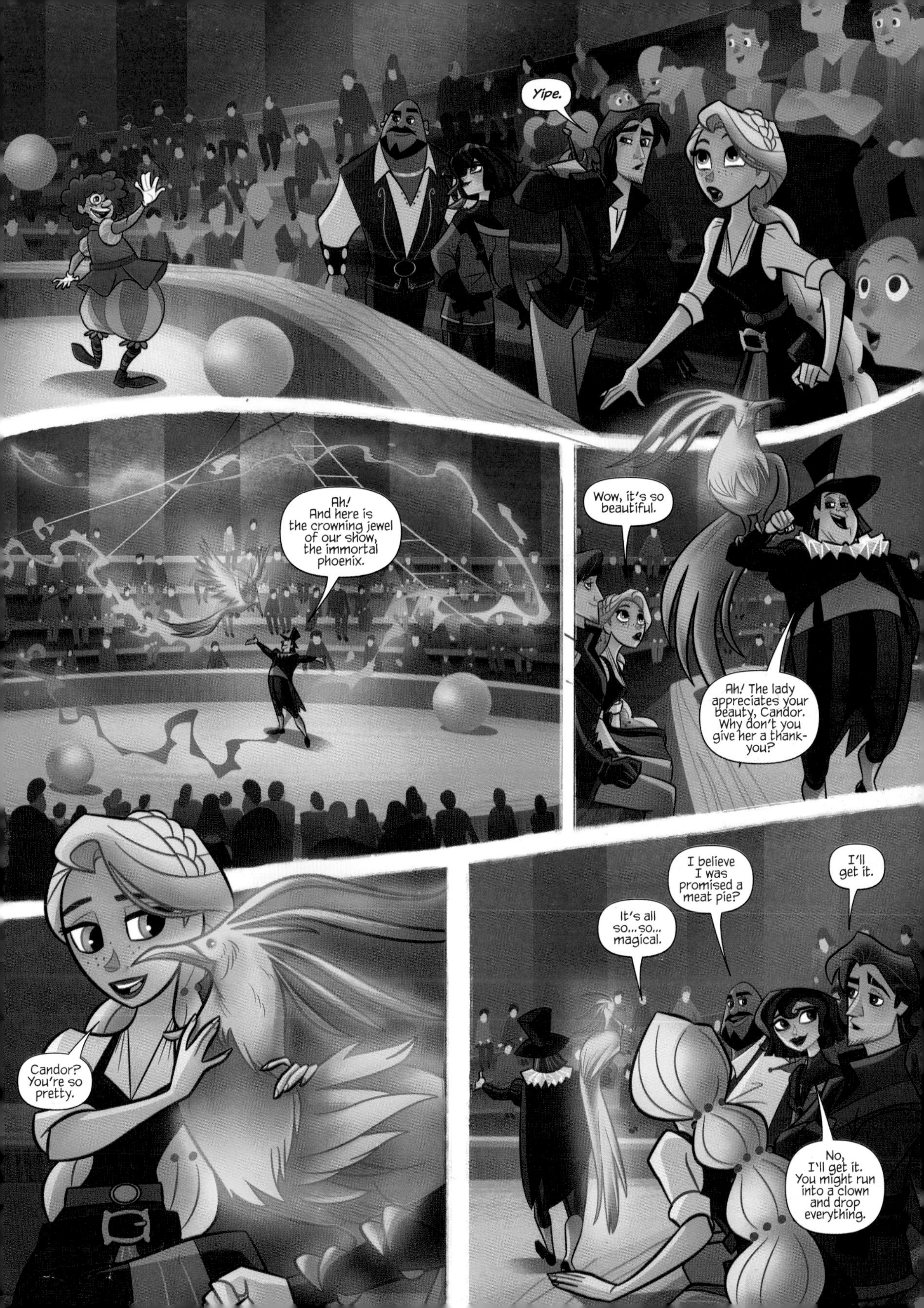
Yipe.
Ah! And here is the crowning jewel of our show, the immortal phoenix.
Wow, it's so beautiful.
Ah! The lady appreciates your beauty, Candor. Why don't you give her a thank-you?
Candor? You're so pretty.
It's all so... so... magical.
I believe I was promised a meat pie?
I'll get it.
No, I'll get it. You might run into a clown and drop everything.

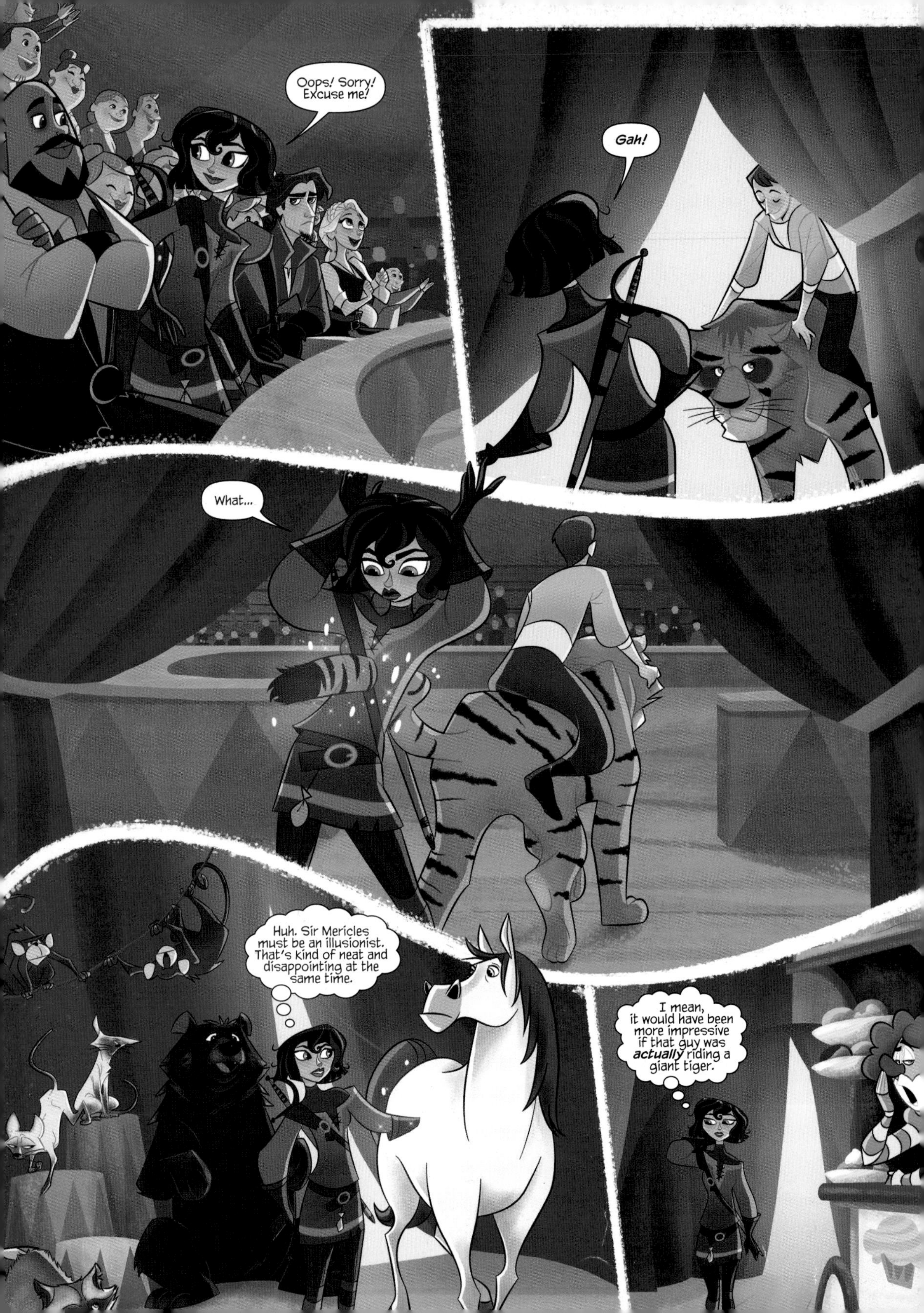
Oops! Sorry! Excuse me!
Gah!
What...
Huh. Sir Mericles must be an illusionist. That's kind of neat and disappointing at the same time.
I mean, it would have been more impressive if that guy was *actually* riding a giant tiger.

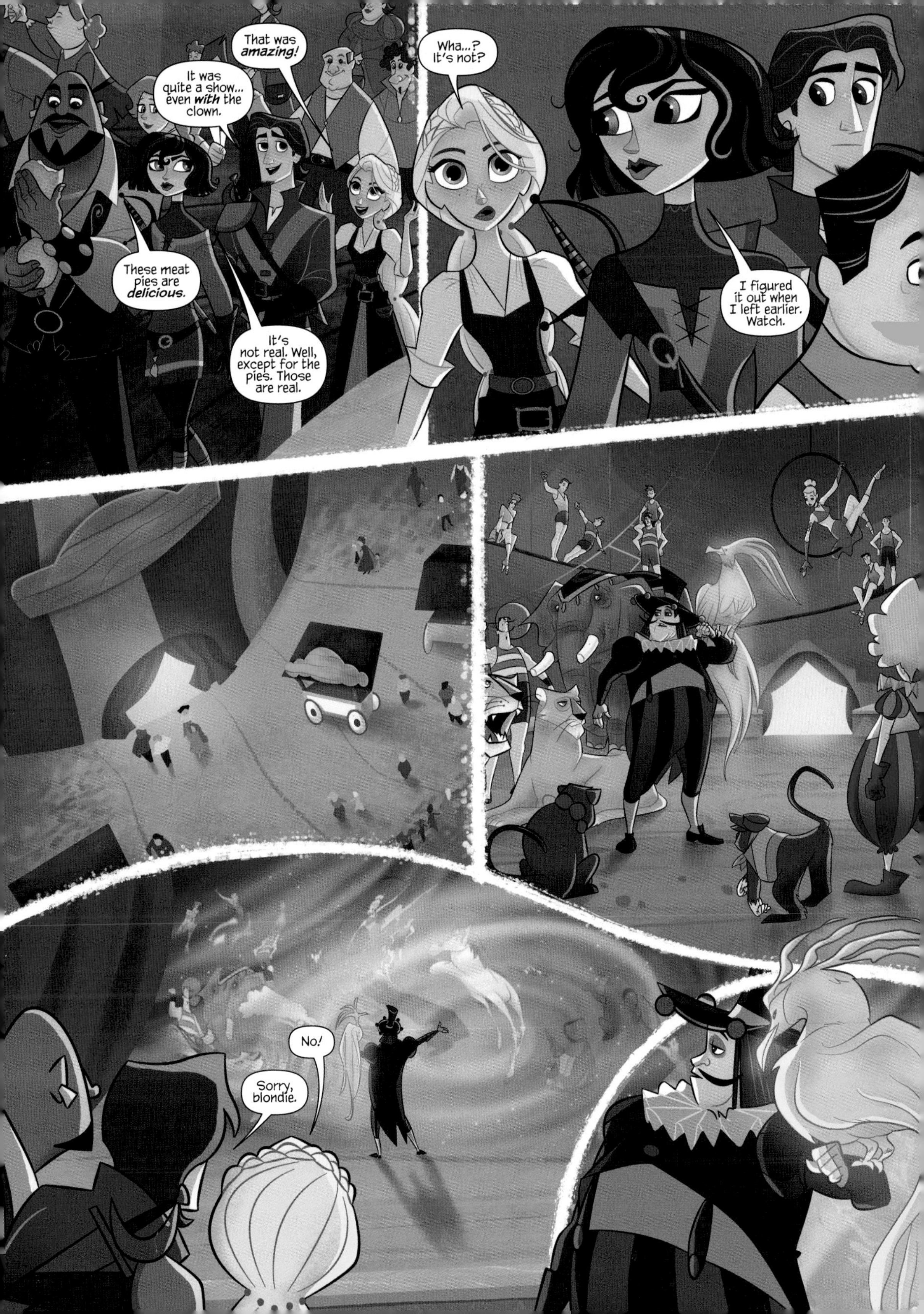
That was *amazing!*
It was quite a show... even ***with*** the clown.
These meat pies are ***delicious.***
It's not real. Well, except for the pies. Those are real.
Wha...? It's not?
I figured it out when I left earlier. Watch.
No!
Sorry, blondie.

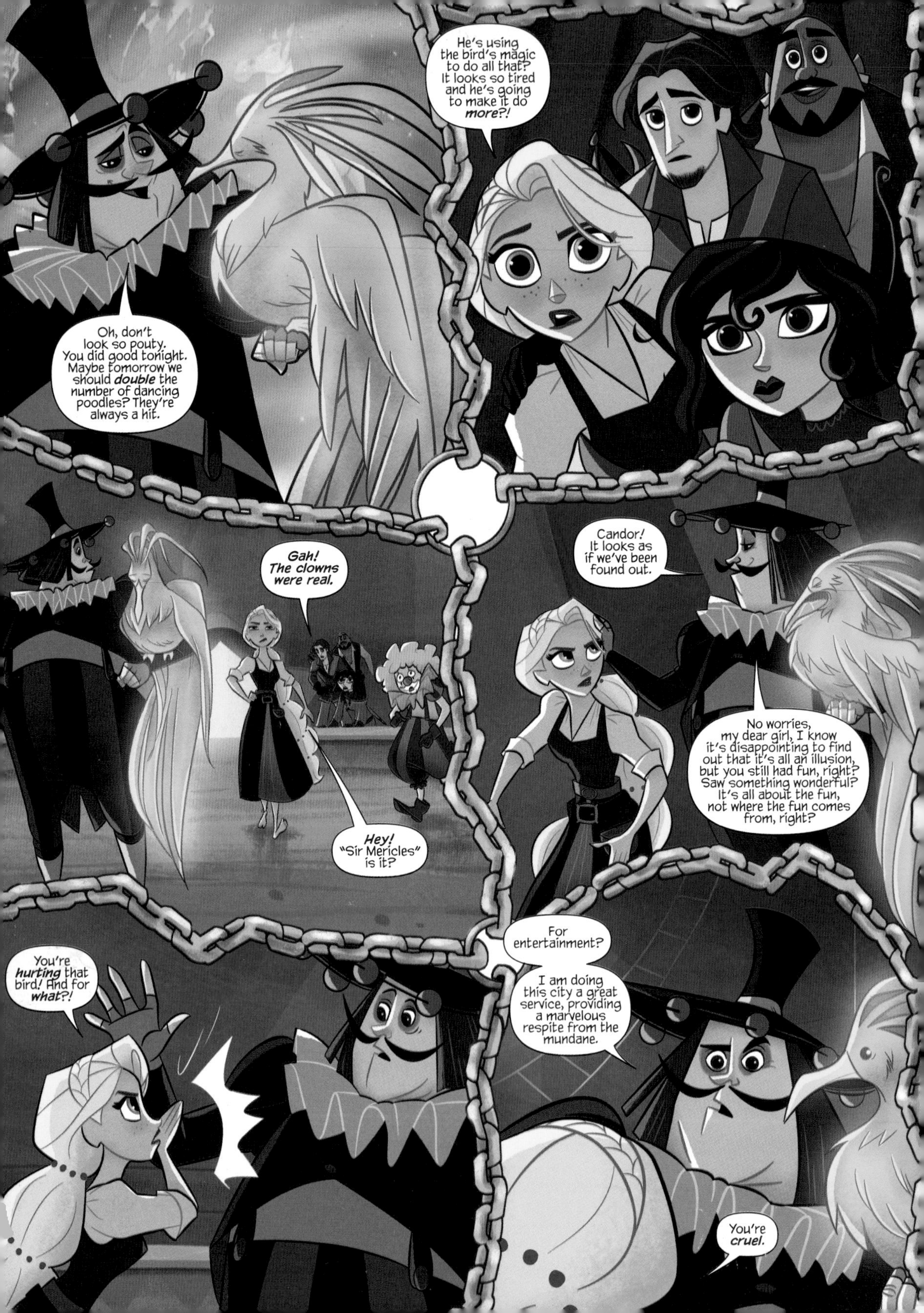
Oh, don't look so pouty. You did good tonight. Maybe tomorrow we should *double* the number of dancing poodles? They're always a hit.
He's using the bird's magic to do all that? It looks so tired and he's going to make it do *more*?!
Gah! The clowns were real.
Hey! "Sir Mericles" is it?
Candor! It looks as if we've been found out.
No worries, my dear girl, I know it's disappointing to find out that it's all an illusion, but you still had fun, right? Saw something wonderful? It's all about the fun, not where the fun comes from, right?
You're *hurting* that bird! And for *what*?!
For entertainment?
I am doing this city a great service, providing a marvelous respite from the mundane.
You're *cruel*.

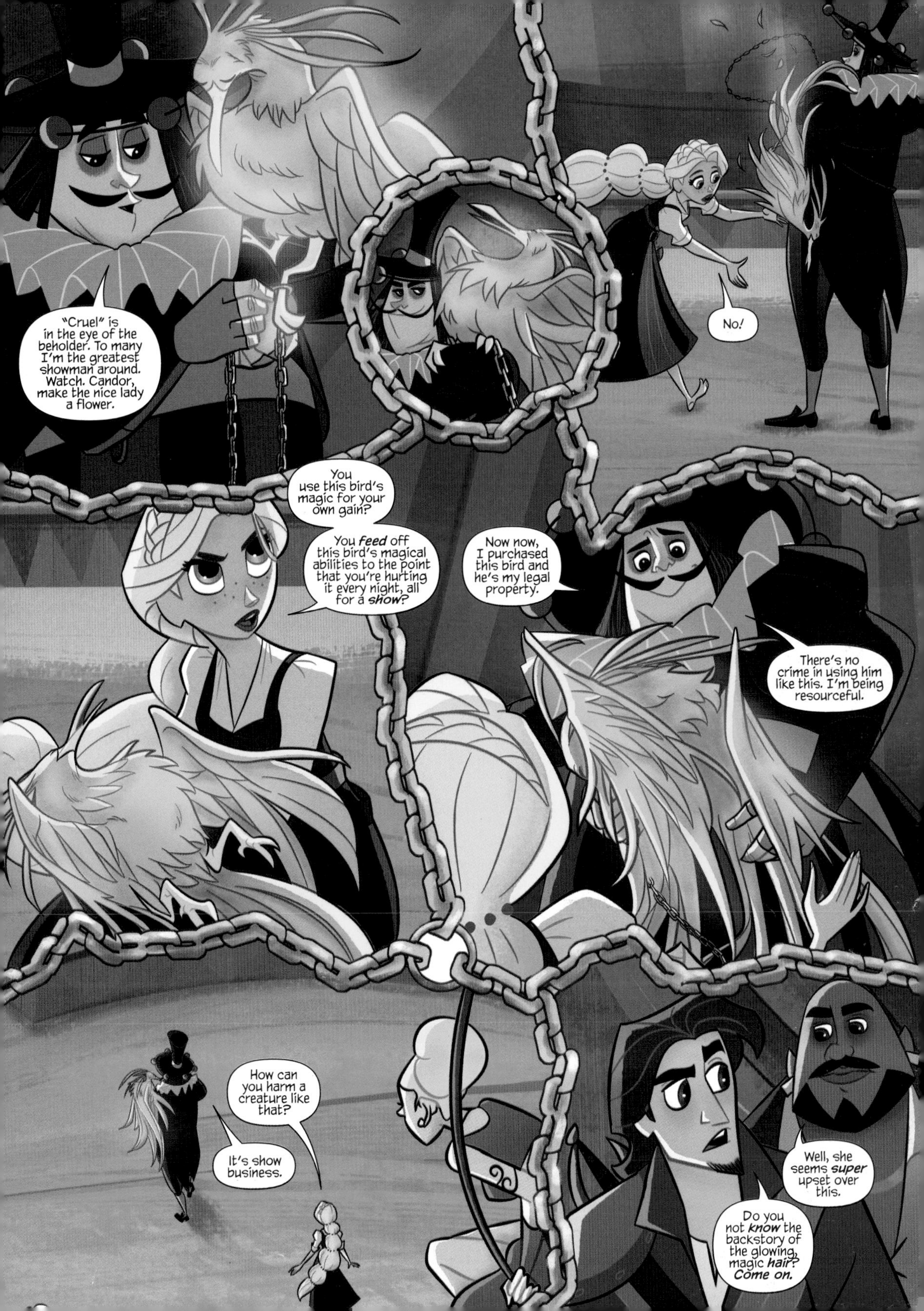
"Cruel" is in the eye of the beholder. To many I'm the greatest showman around. Watch. Candor, make the nice lady a flower.
No!
You use this bird's magic for your own gain?
You *feed* off this bird's magical abilities to the point that you're hurting it every night, all for a *show*?
Now now, I purchased this bird and he's my legal property.
There's no crime in using him like this. I'm being resourceful.
How can you harm a creature like that?
It's show business.
Well, she seems *super* upset over this.
Do you not *know* the backstory of the glowing, magic *hair*? **Come on.**

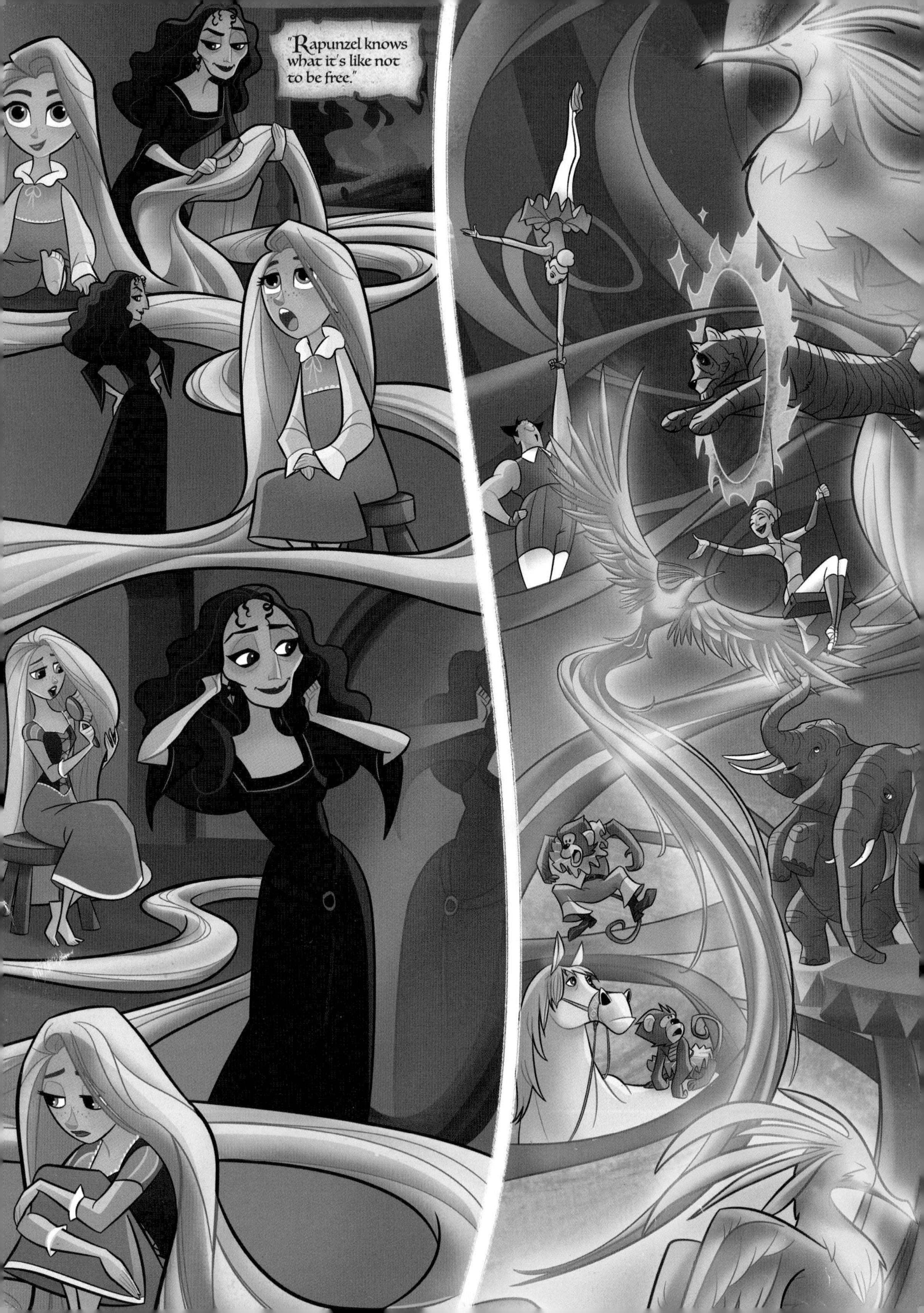
"Rapunzel knows what it's like not to be free."

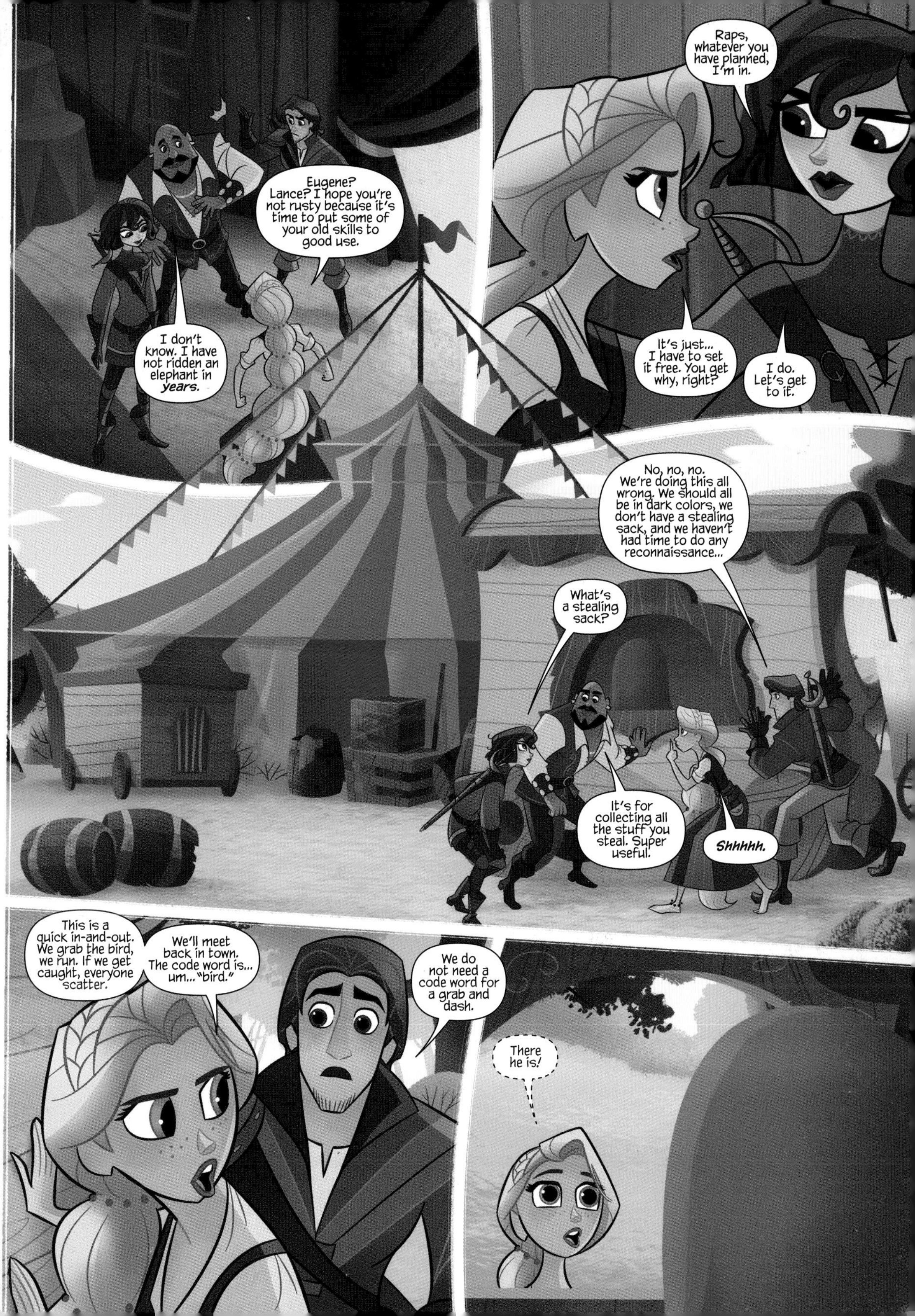
Eugene? Lance? I hope you're not rusty because it's time to put some of your old skills to good use.
I don't know. I have not ridden an elephant in *years.*
Raps, whatever you have planned, I'm in.
It's just... I have to set it free. You get why, right?
I do. Let's get to it.
No, no, no. We're doing this all wrong. We should all be in dark colors, we don't have a stealing sack, and we haven't had time to do any reconnaissance...
What's a stealing sack?
It's for collecting all the stuff you steal. Super useful.
Shhhhh.
This is a quick in-and-out. We grab the bird, we run. If we get caught, everyone scatter.
We'll meet back in town. The code word is... um... "bird."
We do not need a code word for a grab and dash.
There he is!

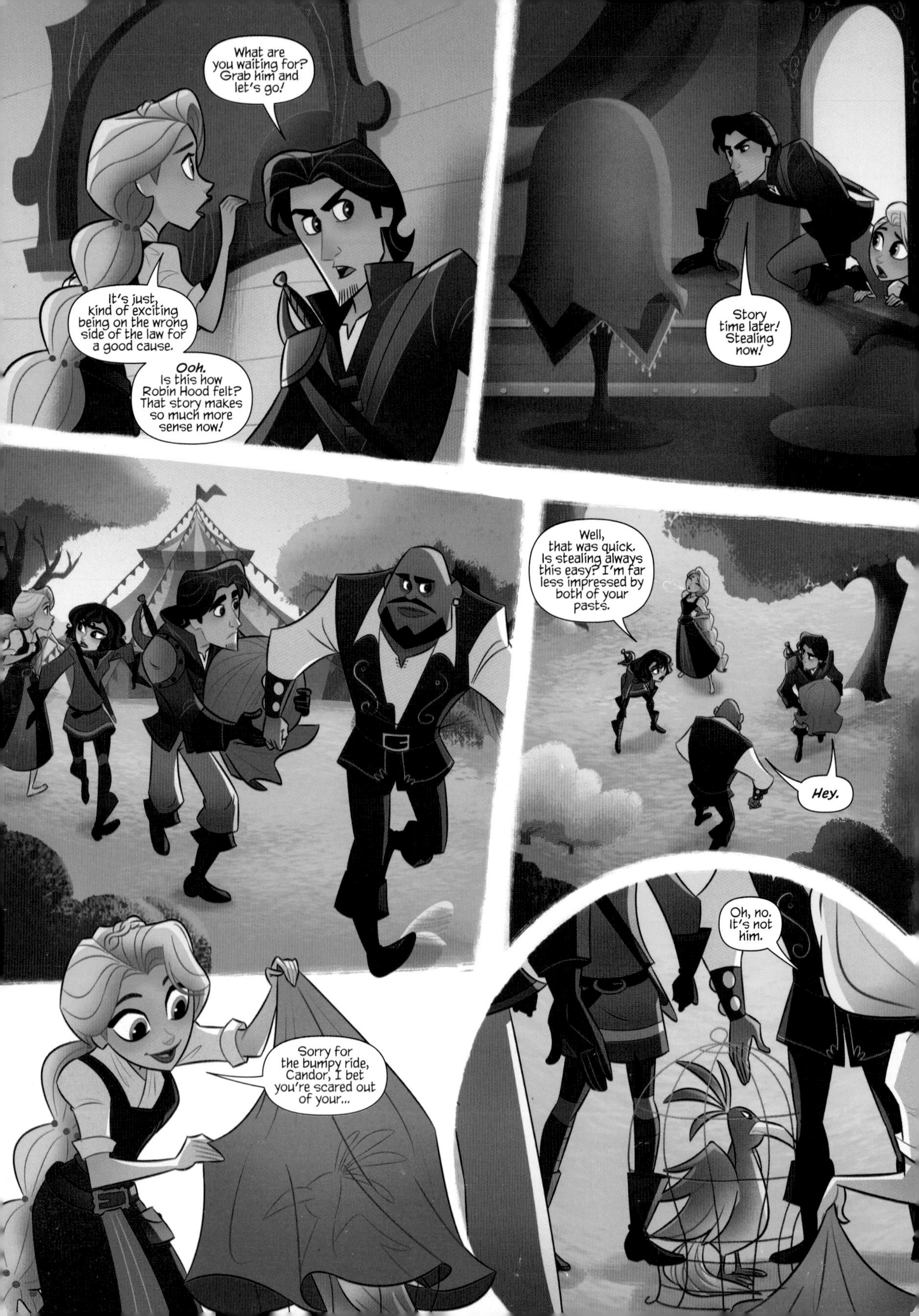
What are you waiting for? Grab him and let's go!
It's just kind of exciting being on the wrong side of the law for a good cause.
Ooh. Is this how Robin Hood felt? That story makes so much more sense now!
Story time later! Stealing now!
Well, that was quick. Is stealing always this easy? I'm far less impressed by both of your pasts.
Hey.
Sorry for the bumpy ride, Candor, I bet you're scared out of your...
Oh, no. It's not him.

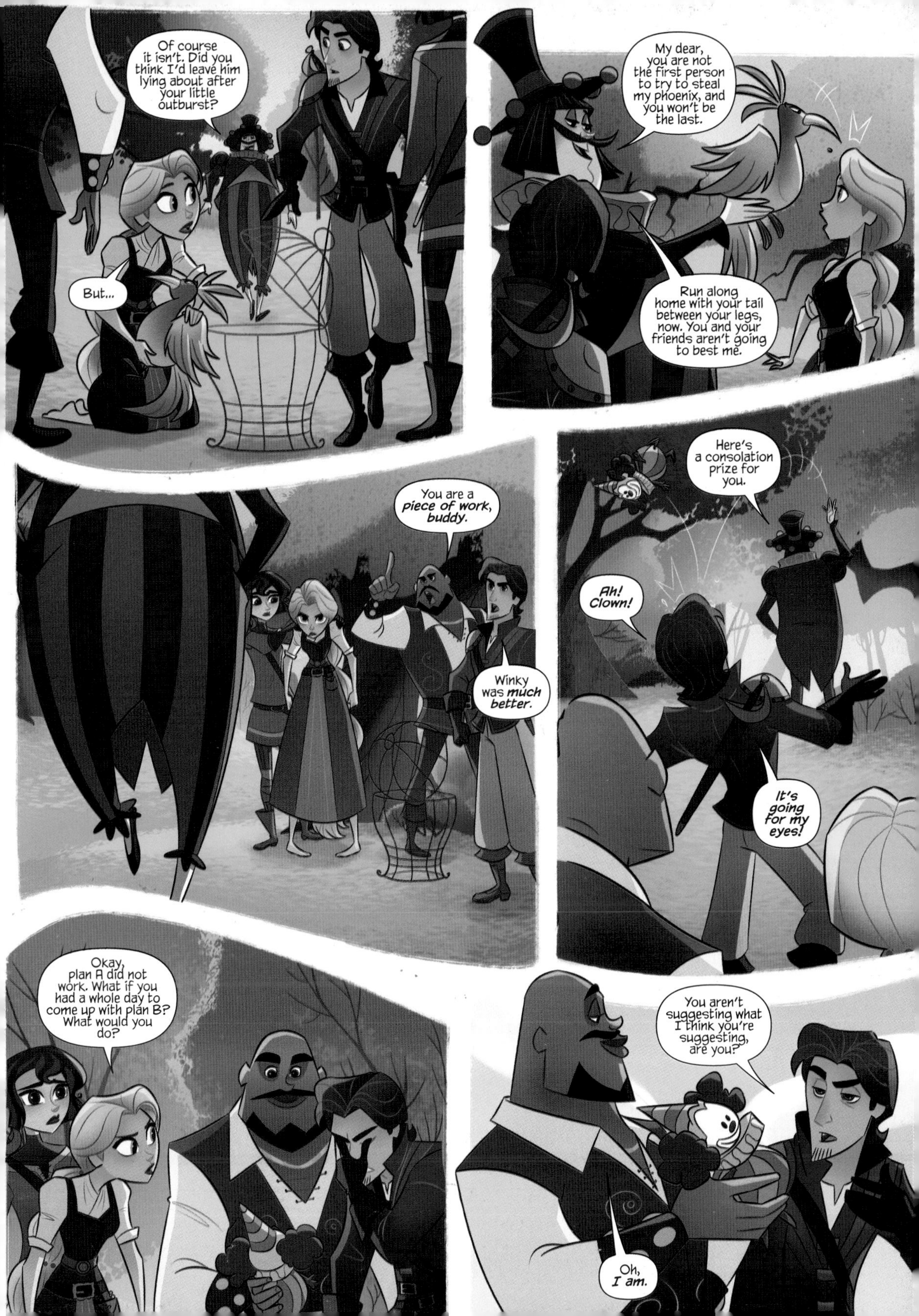
Of course it isn't. Did you think I'd leave him lying about after your little outburst?
But...
My dear, you are not the first person to try to steal my phoenix, and you won't be the last.
Run along home with your tail between your legs, now. You and your friends aren't going to best me.
You are a *piece of work, buddy.*
Winky was *much better.*
Here's a consolation prize for you.
Ah! Clown!
It's going for my eyes!
Okay, plan A did not work. What if you had a whole day to come up with plan B? What would you do?
You aren't suggesting what I think you're suggesting, are you?
Oh, *I am.*

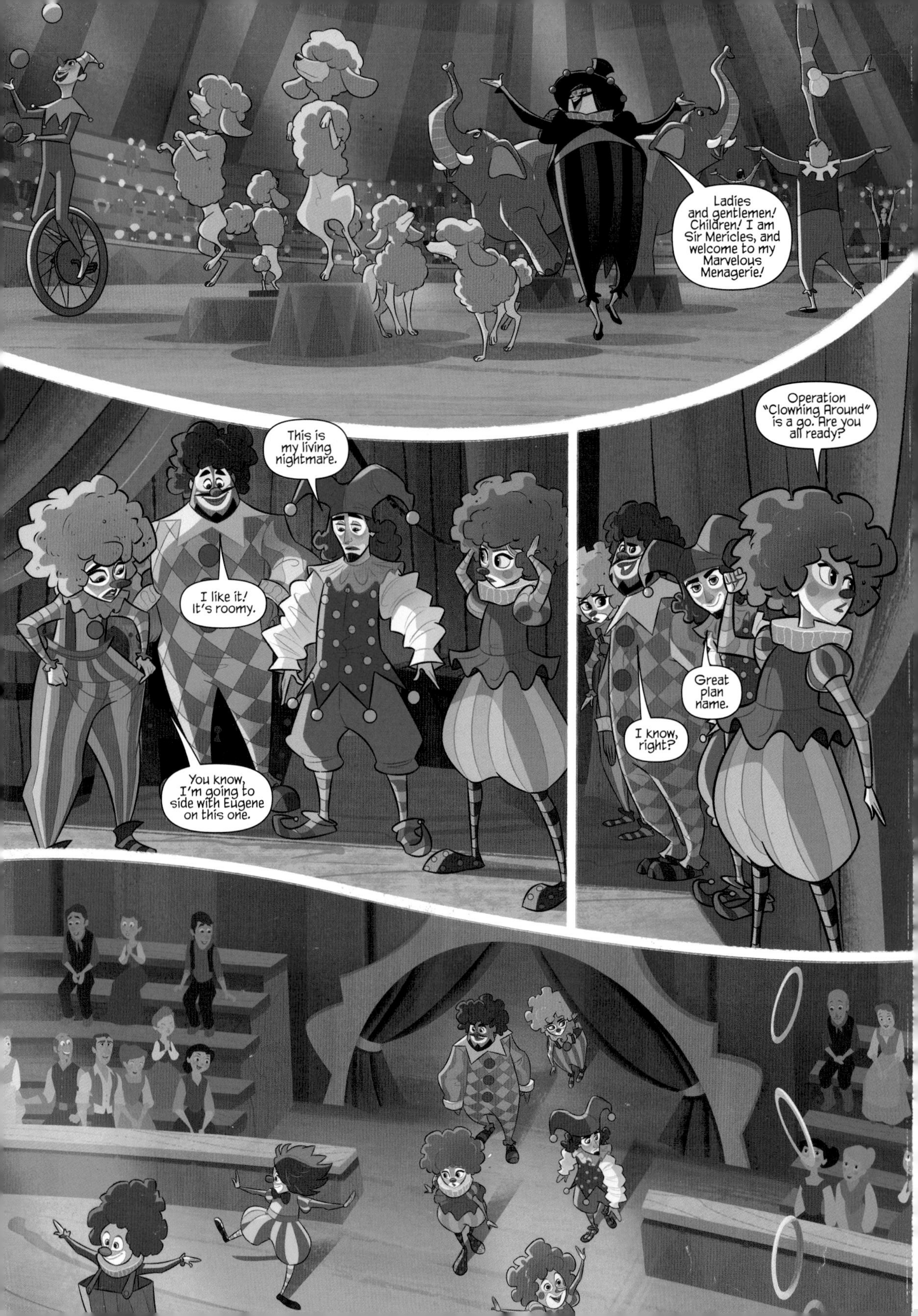
Ladies and gentlemen! Children! I am Sir Mericles, and welcome to my Marvelous Menagerie!
This is my living nightmare.
I like it! It's roomy.
You know, I'm going to side with Eugene on this one.
Operation "Clowning Around" is a go. Are you all ready?
Great plan name.
I know, right?

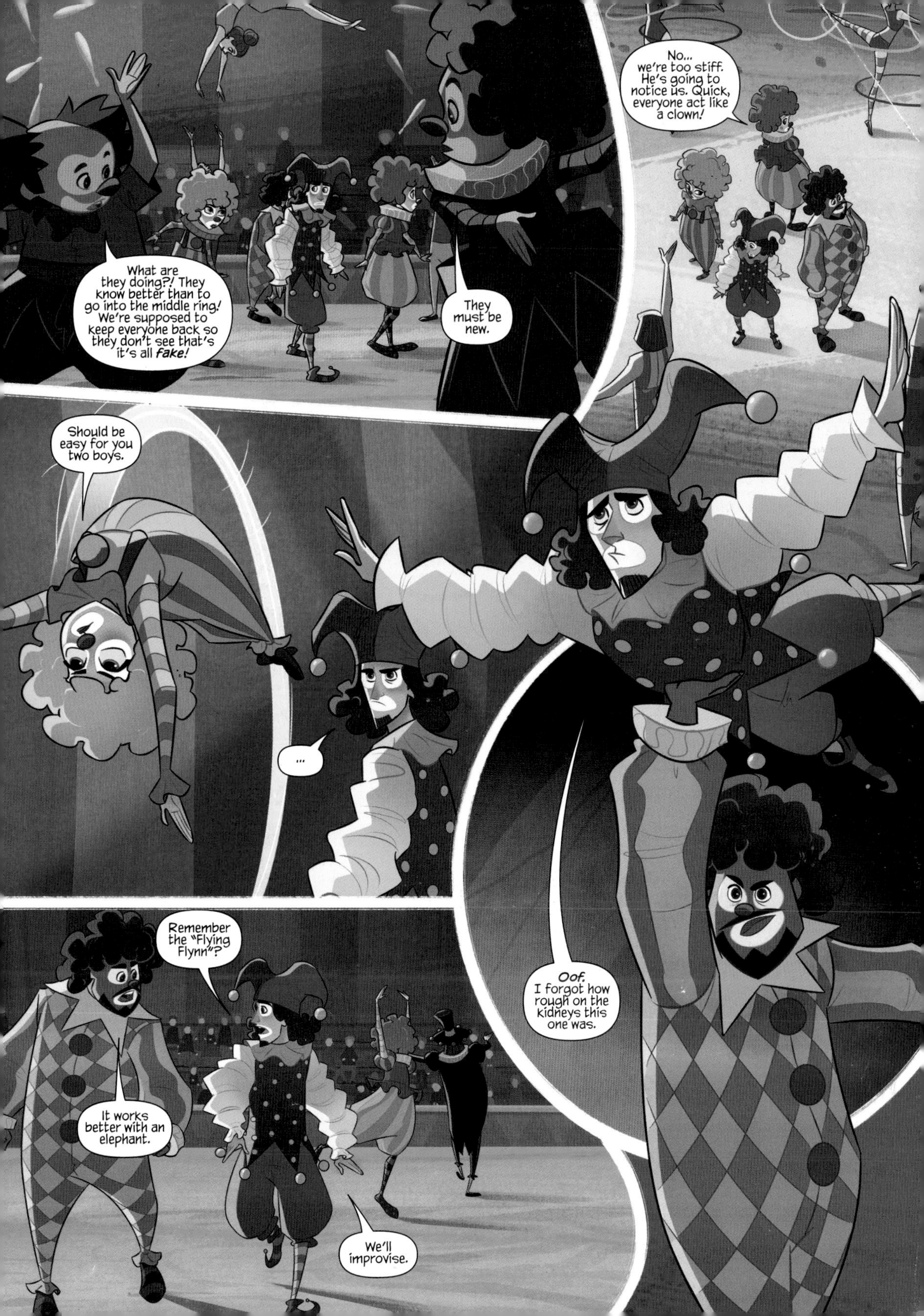
What are they doing?! They know better than to go into the middle ring! We're supposed to keep everyone back so they don't see that's it's all *fake!*
They must be new.
No... we're too stiff. He's going to notice us. Quick, everyone act like a clown!
Should be easy for you two boys.
...
Oof. I forgot how rough on the kidneys this one was.
Remember the "Flying Flynn"?
It works better with an elephant.
We'll improvise.

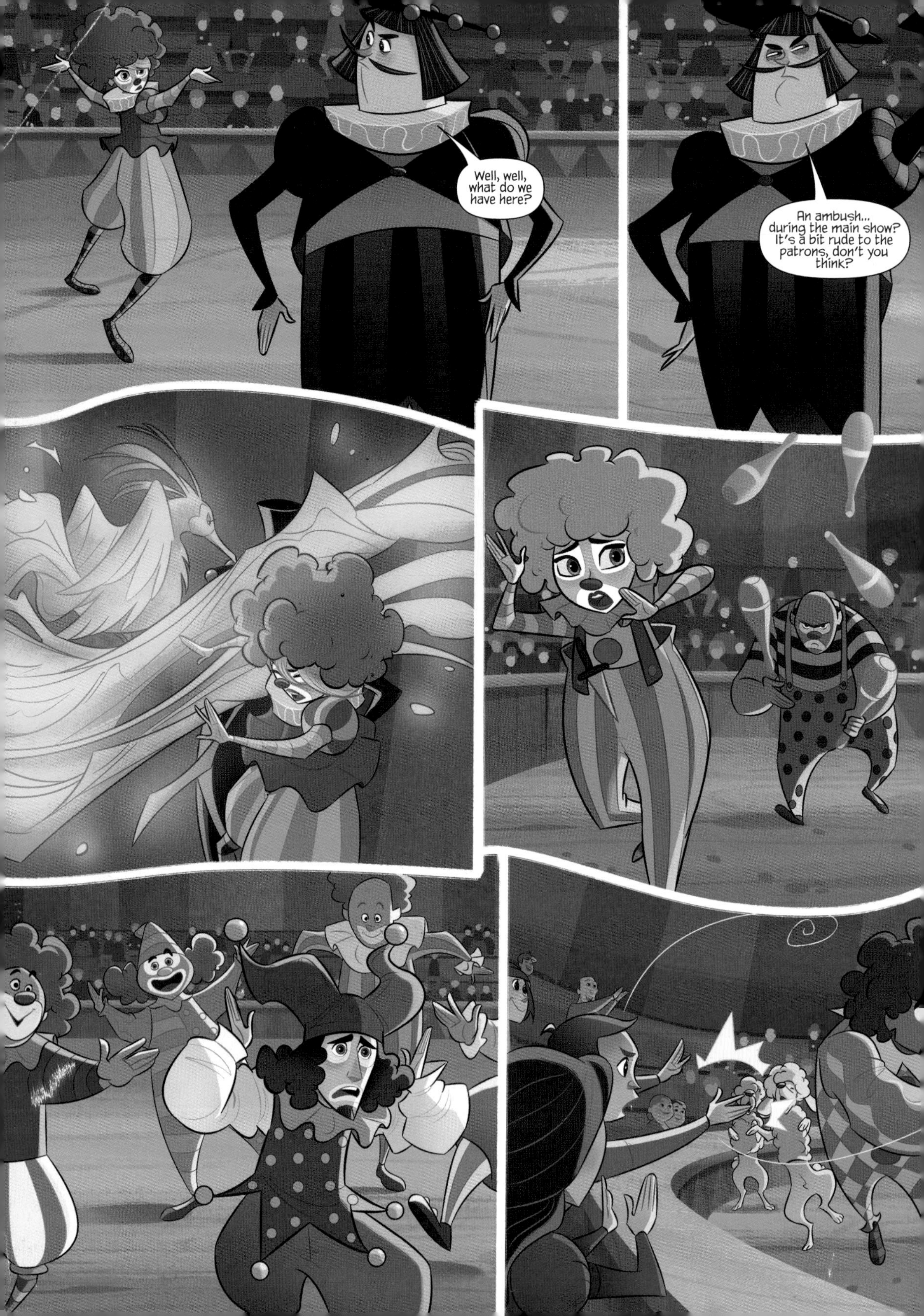
Well, well, what do we have here?
An ambush... during the main show? It's a bit rude to the patrons, don't you think?

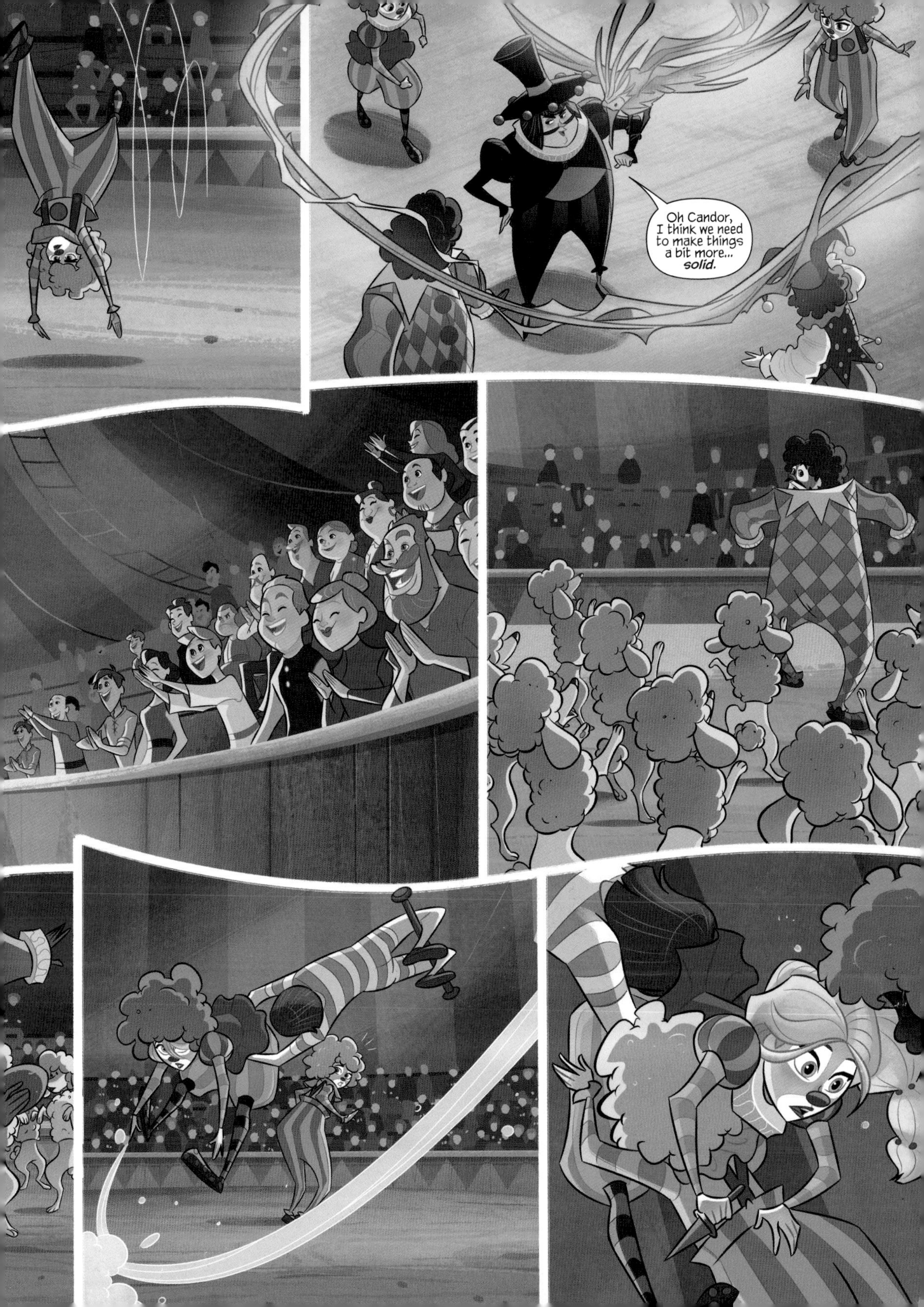
Oh Candor,
I think we need
to make things
a bit more...
solid.

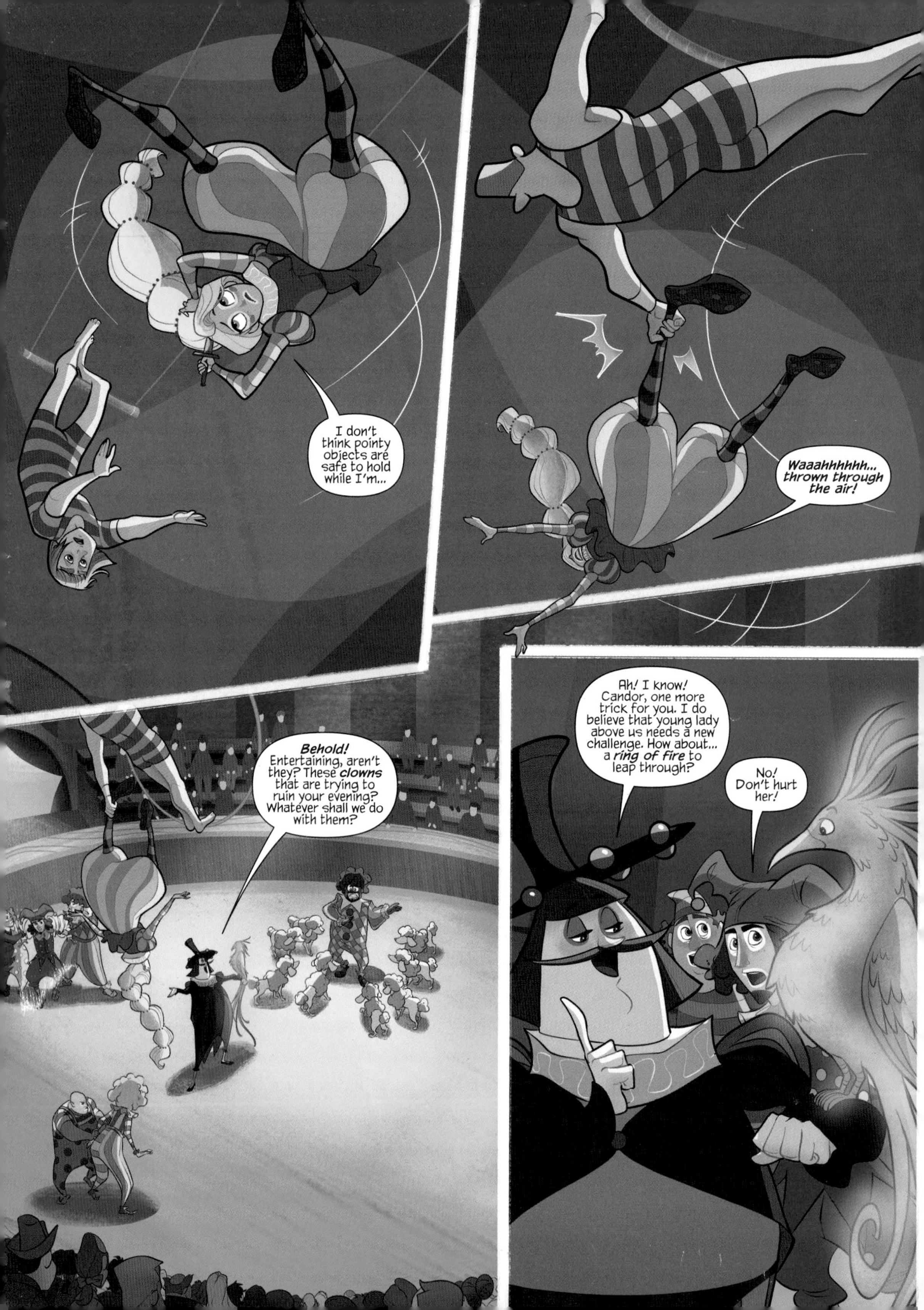
I don't think pointy objects are safe to hold while I'm...
Waaahhhhhh... thrown through the air!
Behold! Entertaining, aren't they? These clowns that are trying to ruin your evening? Whatever shall we do with them?
Ah! I know! Candor, one more trick for you. I do believe that young lady above us needs a new challenge. How about... a ring of fire to leap through?
No! Don't hurt her!

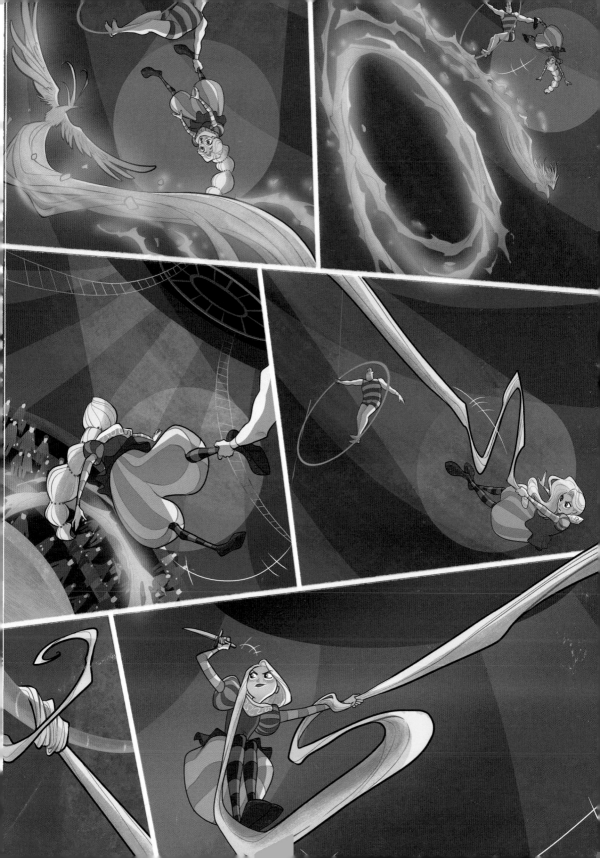

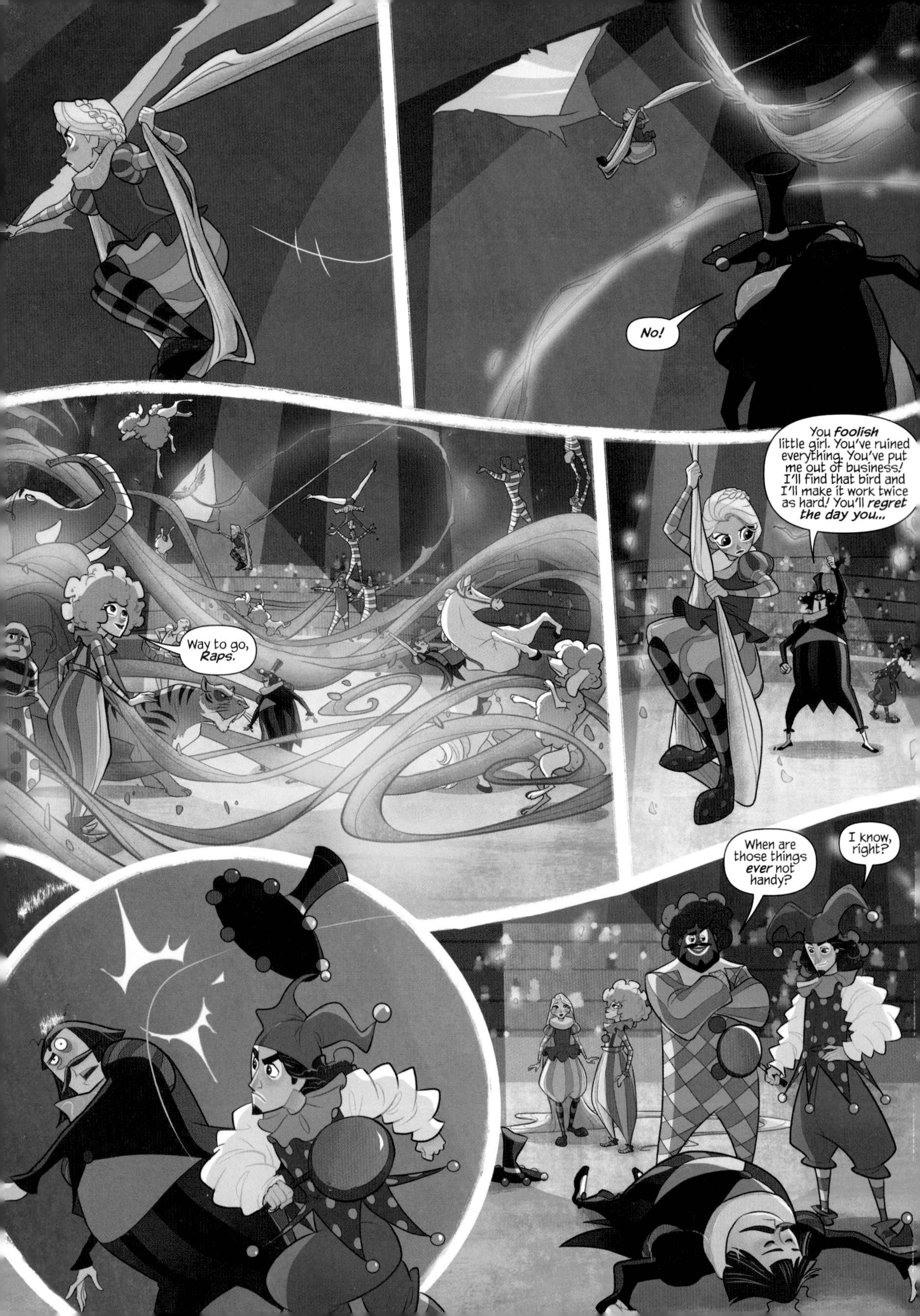
No!
Way to go, Raps.
You foolish little girl. You've ruined everything. You've put me out of business! I'll find that bird and I'll make it work twice as hard! You'll regret the day you...
When are those things ever not handy?
I know, right?

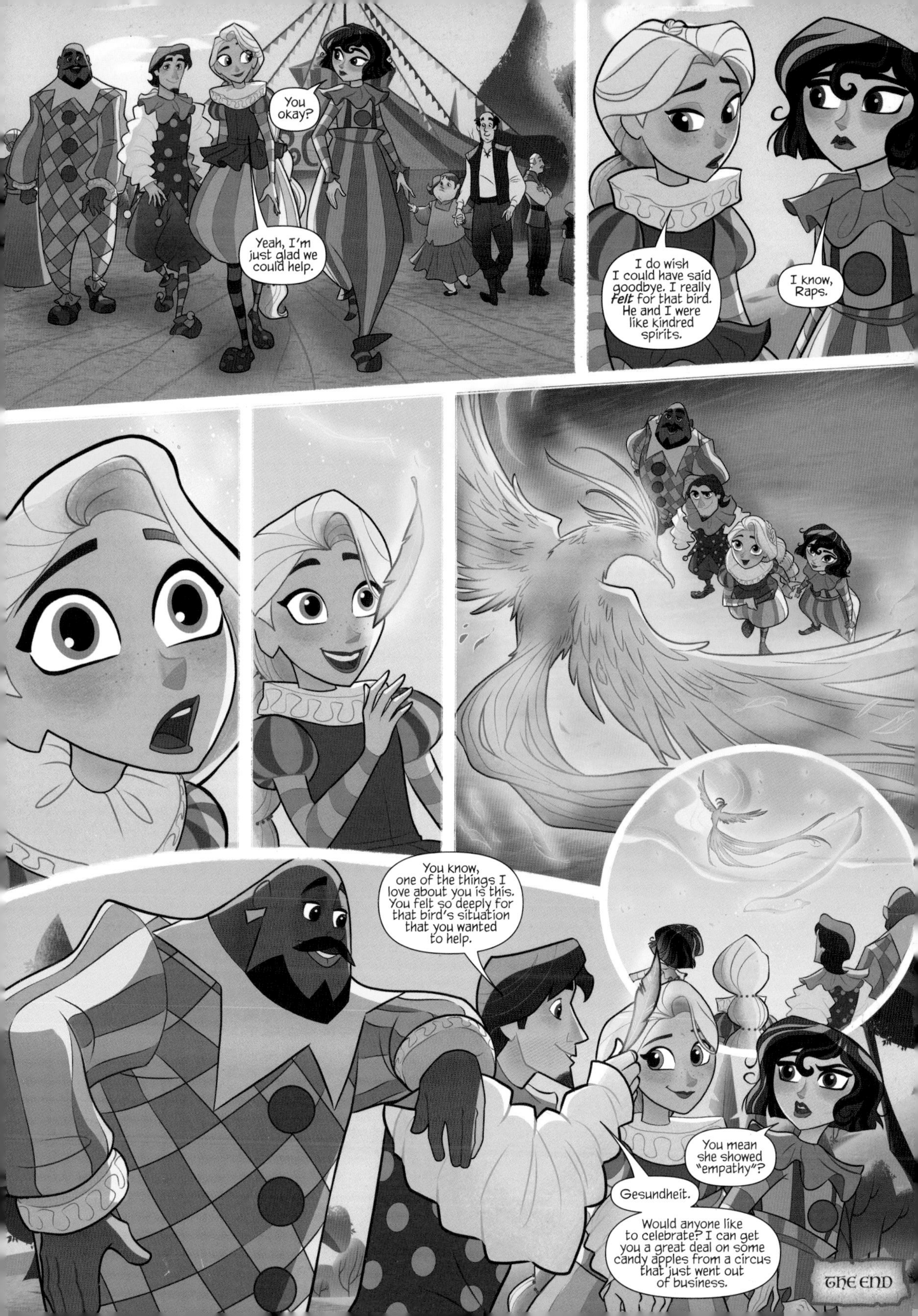
You okay?
Yeah, I'm just glad we could help.
I do wish I could have said goodbye. I really *felt* for that bird. He and I were like kindred spirits.
I know, Raps.
You know, one of the things I love about you is this. You felt so deeply for that bird's situation that you wanted to help.
You mean she showed "empathy"?
Gesundheit.
Would anyone like to celebrate? I can get you a great deal on some candy apples from a circus that just went out of business.
THE END

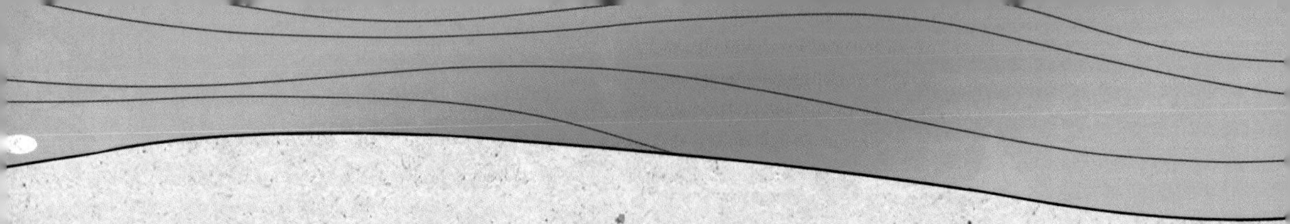

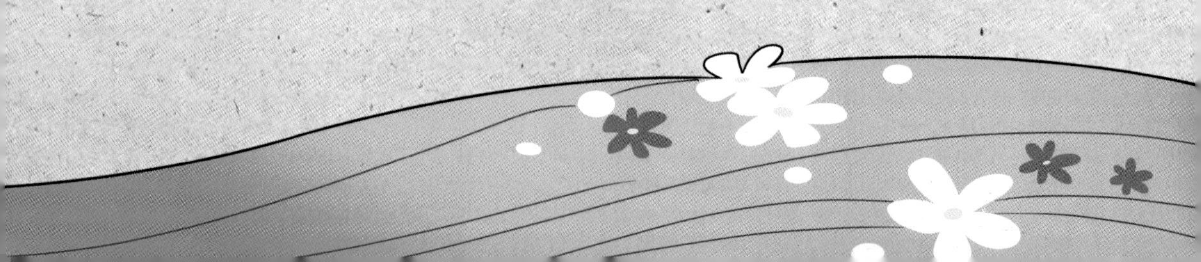

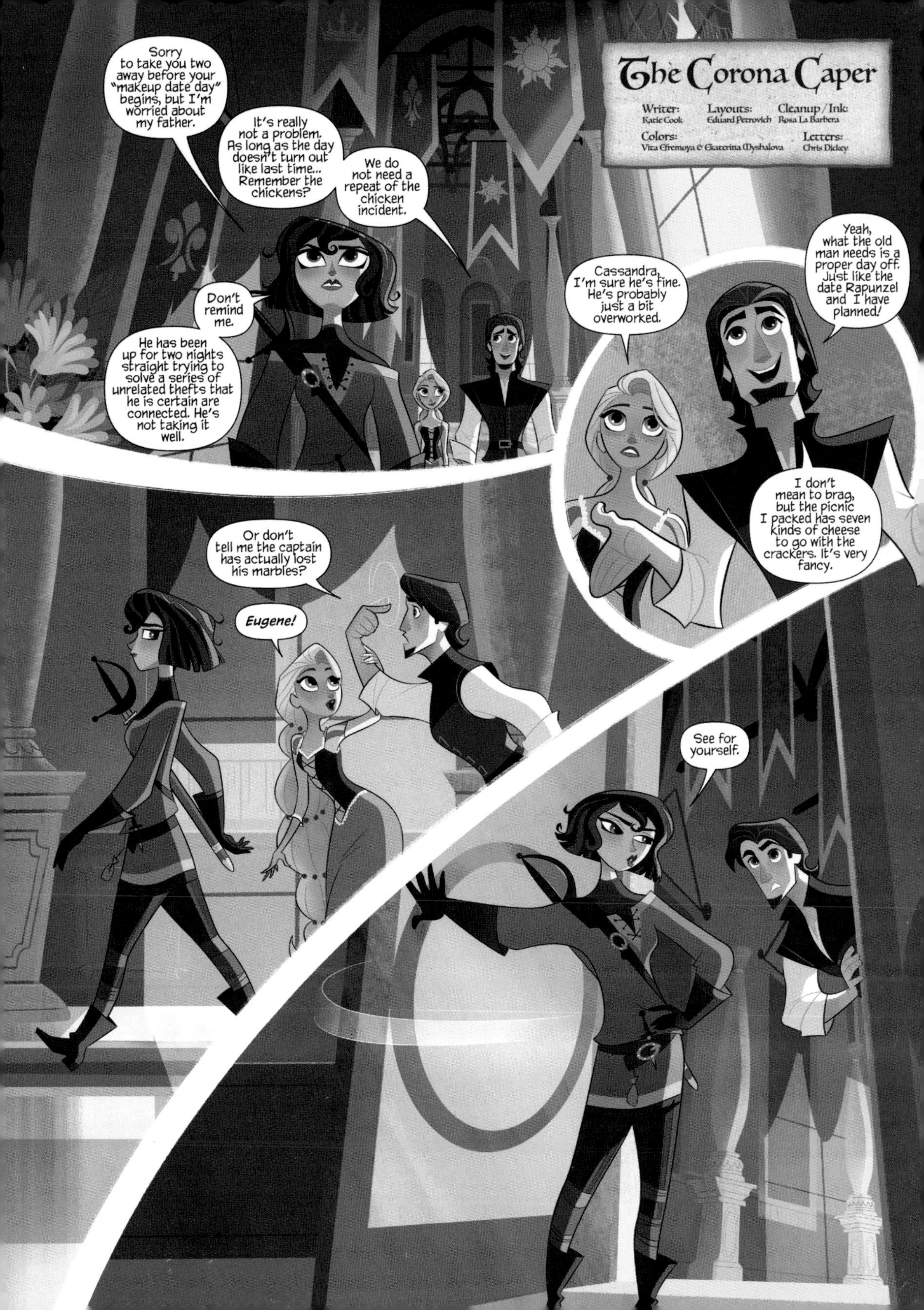
The Corona Caper
Writer: Katie Cook
Layouts: Eduard Petrovich
Cleanup/Ink: Rosa La Barbera
Colors: Vita Efremova & Ekaterina Myshalova
Letters: Chris Dickey
Sorry to take you two away before your "makeup date day" begins, but I'm worried about my father.
It's really not a problem. As long as the day doesn't turn out like last time... Remember the chickens?
We do not need a repeat of the chicken incident.
Don't remind me.
He has been up for two nights straight trying to solve a series of unrelated thefts that he is certain are connected. He's not taking it well.
Cassandra, I'm sure he's fine. He's probably just a bit overworked.
Yeah, what the old man needs is a proper day off. Just like the date Rapunzel and I have planned!
I don't mean to brag, but the picnic I packed has seven kinds of cheese to go with the crackers. It's very fancy.
Or don't tell me the captain has actually lost his marbles?
Eugene!
See for yourself.

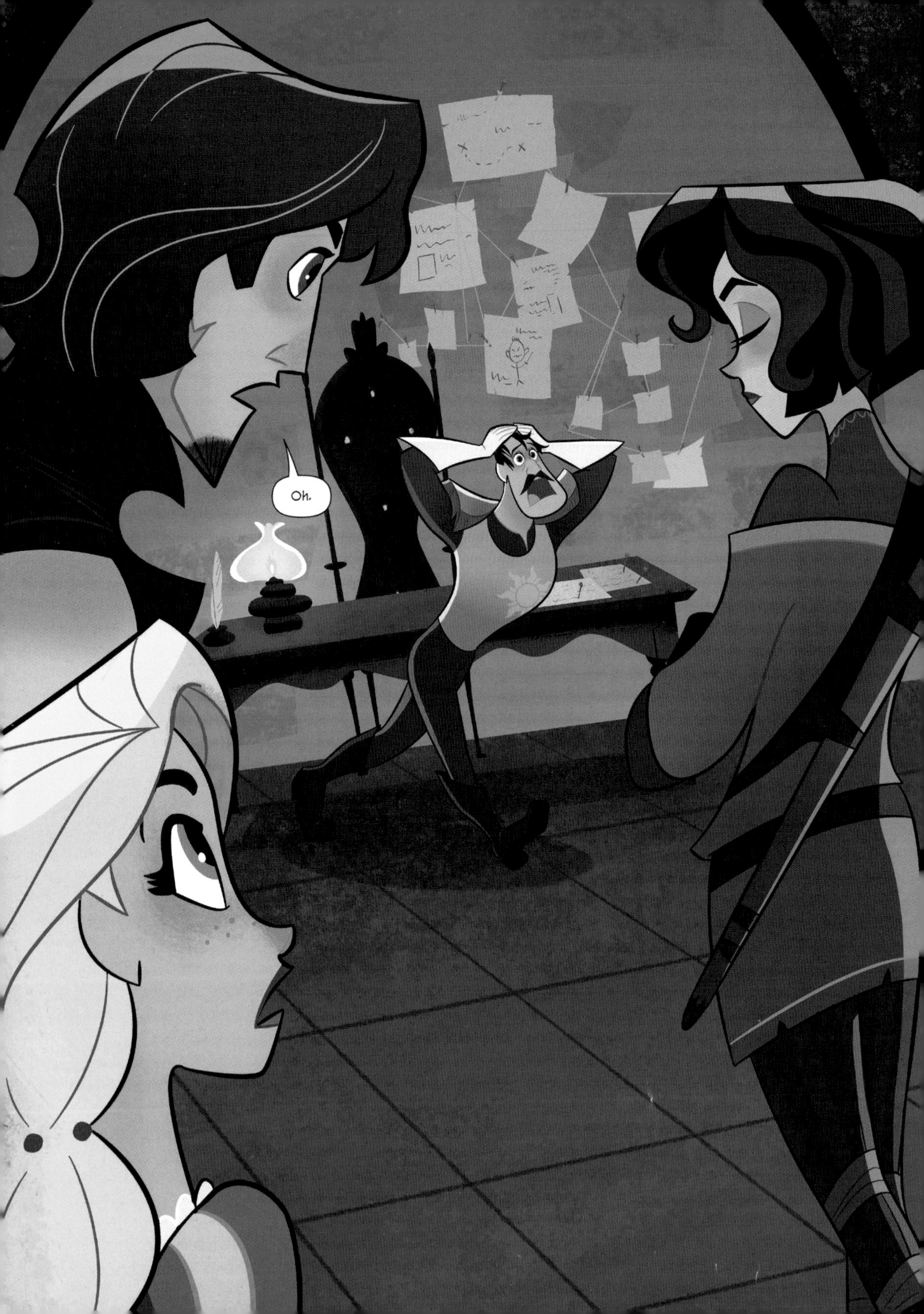
Oh.

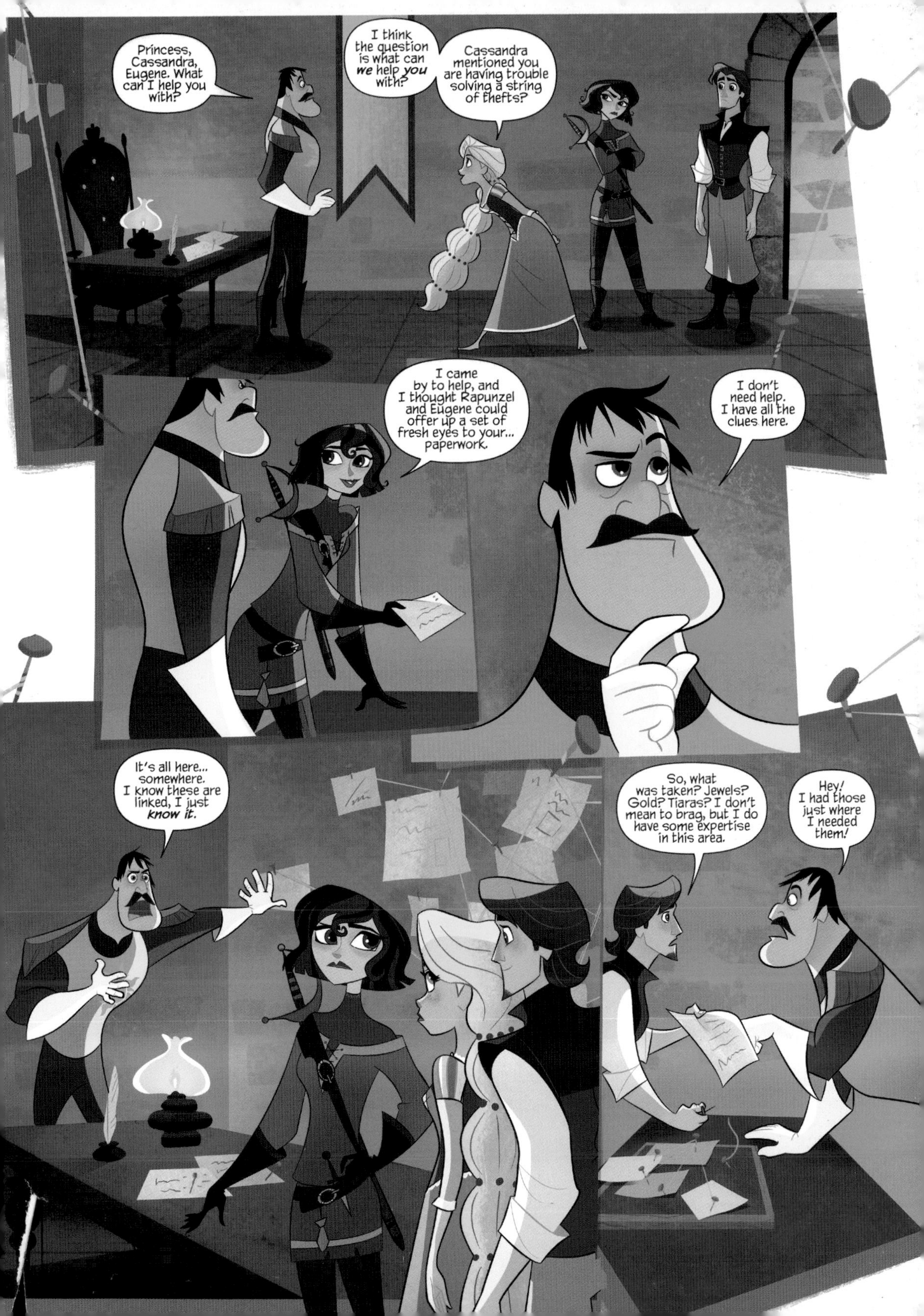
Princess, Cassandra, Eugene. What can I help you with?
I think the question is what can *we* help *you* with?
Cassandra mentioned you are having trouble solving a string of thefts?
I came by to help, and I thought Rapunzel and Eugene could offer up a set of fresh eyes to your... paperwork.
I don't need help. I have all the clues here.
It's all here... somewhere. I know these are linked, I just *know it.*
So, what was taken? Jewels? Gold? Tiaras? I don't mean to brag, but I do have some expertise in this area.
Hey! I had those just where I needed them!

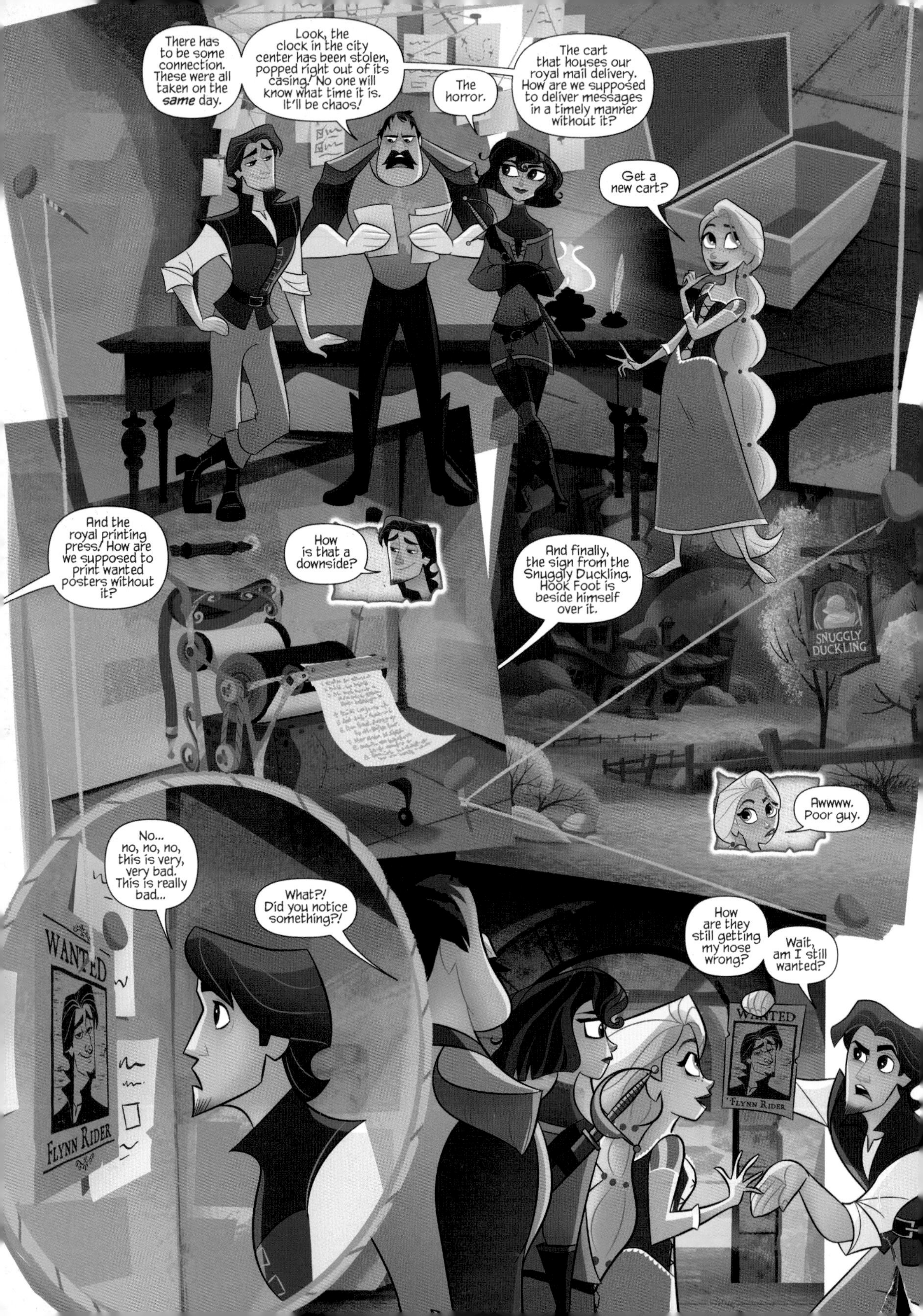
There has to be some connection. These were all taken on the *same* day.
Look, the clock in the city center has been stolen, popped right out of its casing! No one will know what time it is. It'll be chaos!
The horror.
The cart that houses our royal mail delivery. How are we supposed to deliver messages in a timely manner without it?
Get a new cart?
And the royal printing press! How are we supposed to print wanted posters without it?
How is that a downside?
And finally, the sign from the Snuggly Duckling. Hook Foot is beside himself over it.
SNUGGLY DUCKLING
Awwww. Poor guy.
WANTED
FLYNN RIDER
No... no, no, no, this is very, very bad. This is really bad...
What?! Did you notice something?!
How are they still getting my nose wrong?
Wait, am I still wanted?
WANTED
FLYNN RIDER

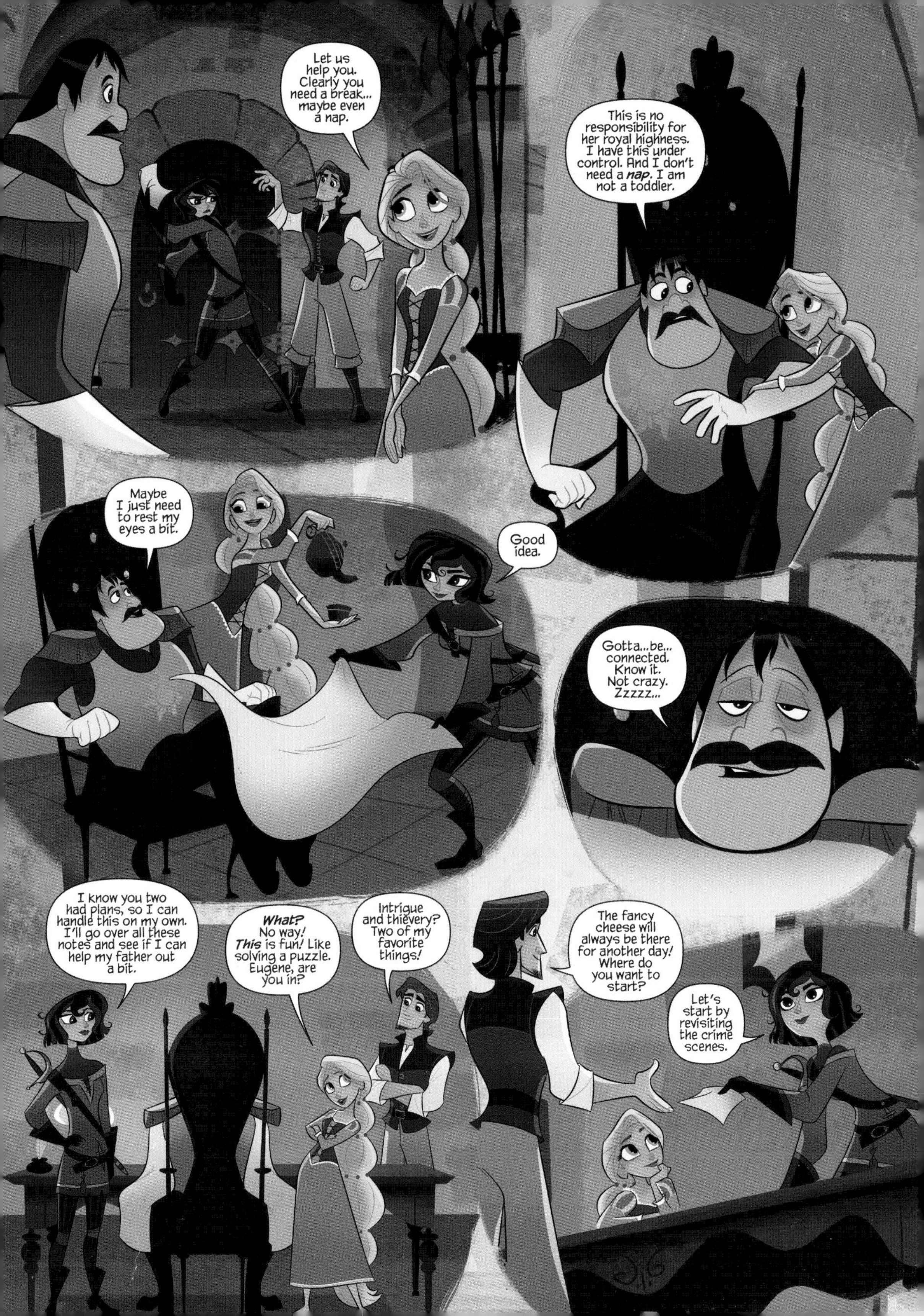
Let us help you. Clearly you need a break... maybe even a nap.
This is no responsibility for her royal highness. I have this under control. And I don't need a *nap*. I am not a toddler.
Maybe I just need to rest my eyes a bit.
Good idea.
Gotta...be... connected. Know it. Not crazy. Zzzzz...
I know you two had plans, so I can handle this on my own. I'll go over all these notes and see if I can help my father out a bit.
What? No way! *This* is fun! Like solving a puzzle. Eugene, are you in?
Intrigue and thievery? Two of my favorite things!
The fancy cheese will always be there for another day! Where do you want to start?
Let's start by revisiting the crime scenes.

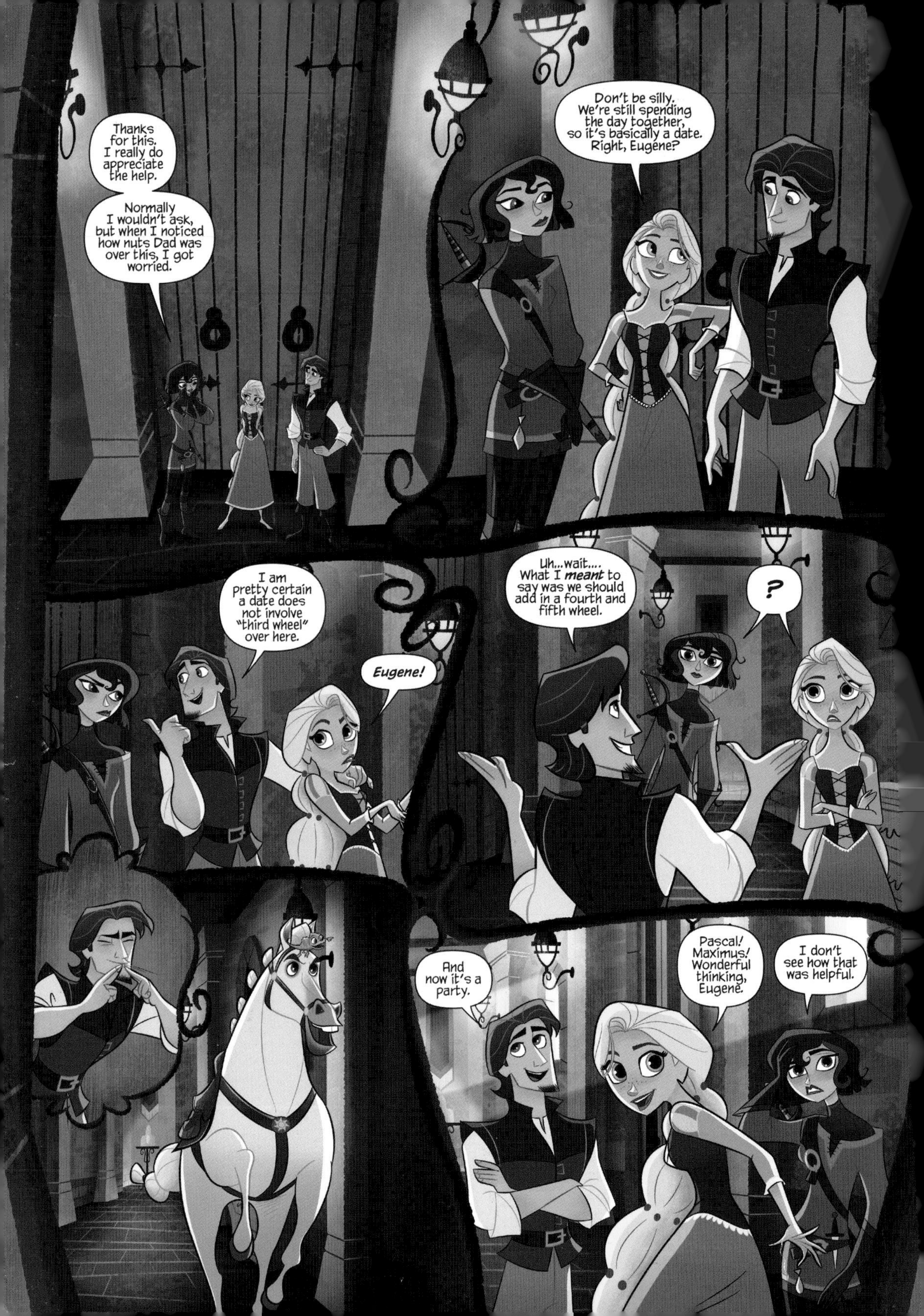
Thanks for this. I really do appreciate the help.
Normally I wouldn't ask, but when I noticed how nuts Dad was over this, I got worried.
Don't be silly. We're still spending the day together, so it's basically a date. Right, Eugene?
I am pretty certain a date does not involve "third wheel" over here.
Eugene!
Uh...wait.... What I meant to say was we should add in a fourth and fifth wheel.
?
And now it's a party.
Pascal! Maximus! Wonderful thinking, Eugene.
I don't see how that was helpful.

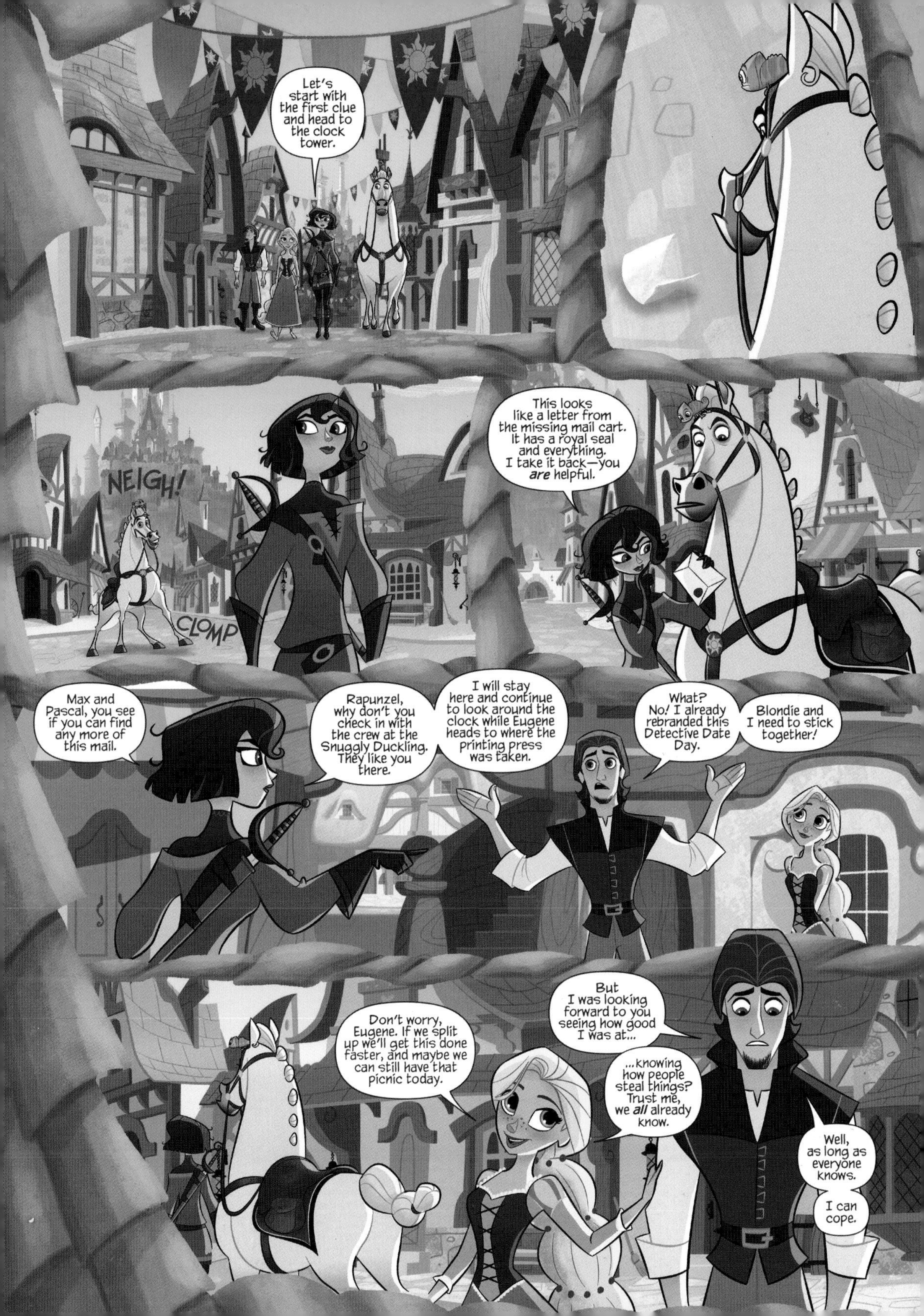

Let's start with the first clue and head to the clock tower.
NEIGH!
CLOMP
This looks like a letter from the missing mail cart. It has a royal seal and everything. I take it back—you *are* helpful.
Max and Pascal, you see if you can find any more of this mail.
Rapunzel, why don't you check in with the crew at the Snuggly Duckling. They like you there.
I will stay here and continue to look around the clock while Eugene heads to where the printing press was taken.
What? No! I already rebranded this Detective Date Day.
Blondie and I need to stick together!
Don't worry, Eugene. If we split up we'll get this done faster, and maybe we can still have that picnic today.
But I was looking forward to you seeing how good I was at...
...knowing how people steal things? Trust me, we *all* already know.
Well, as long as everyone knows.
I can cope.

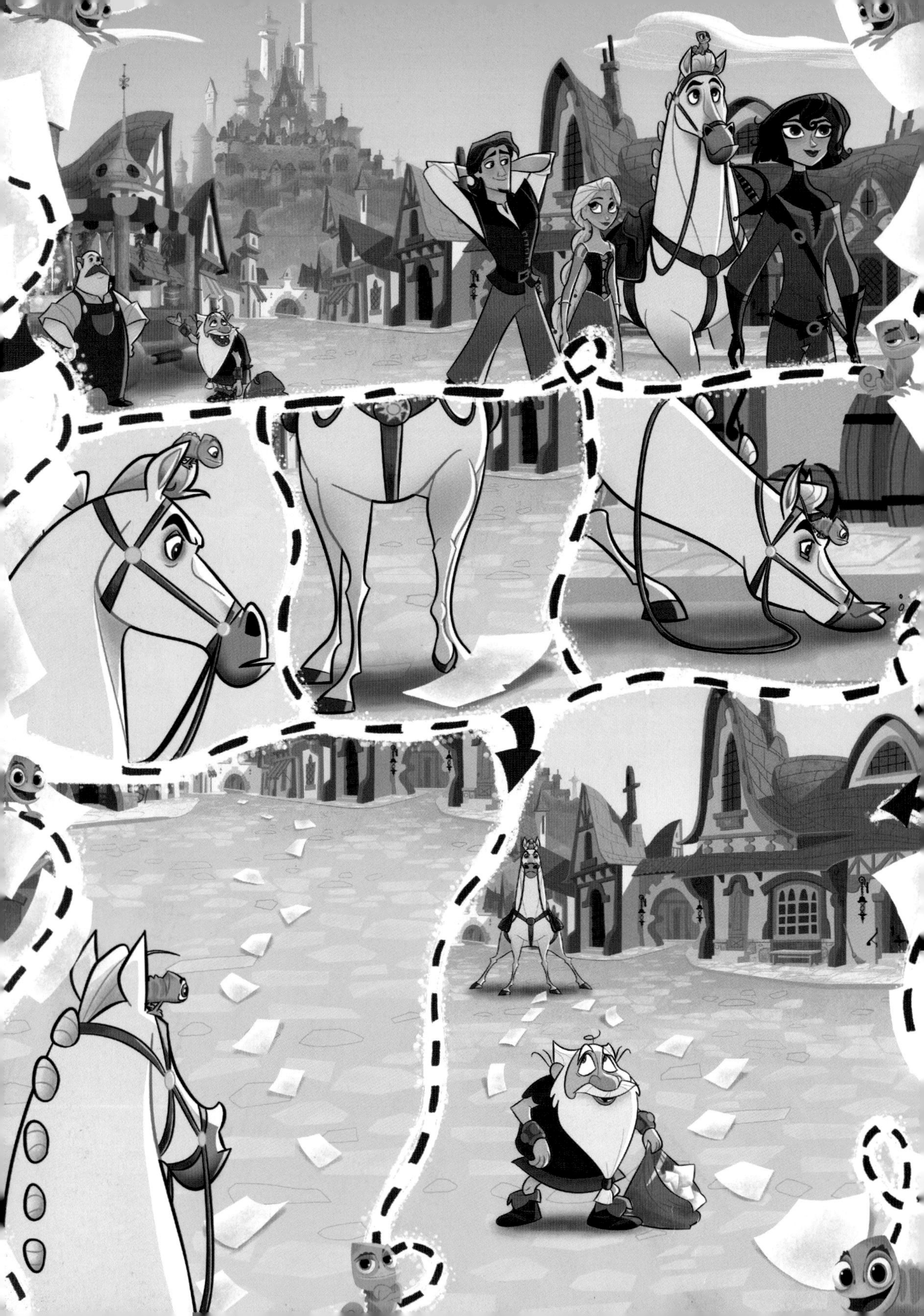

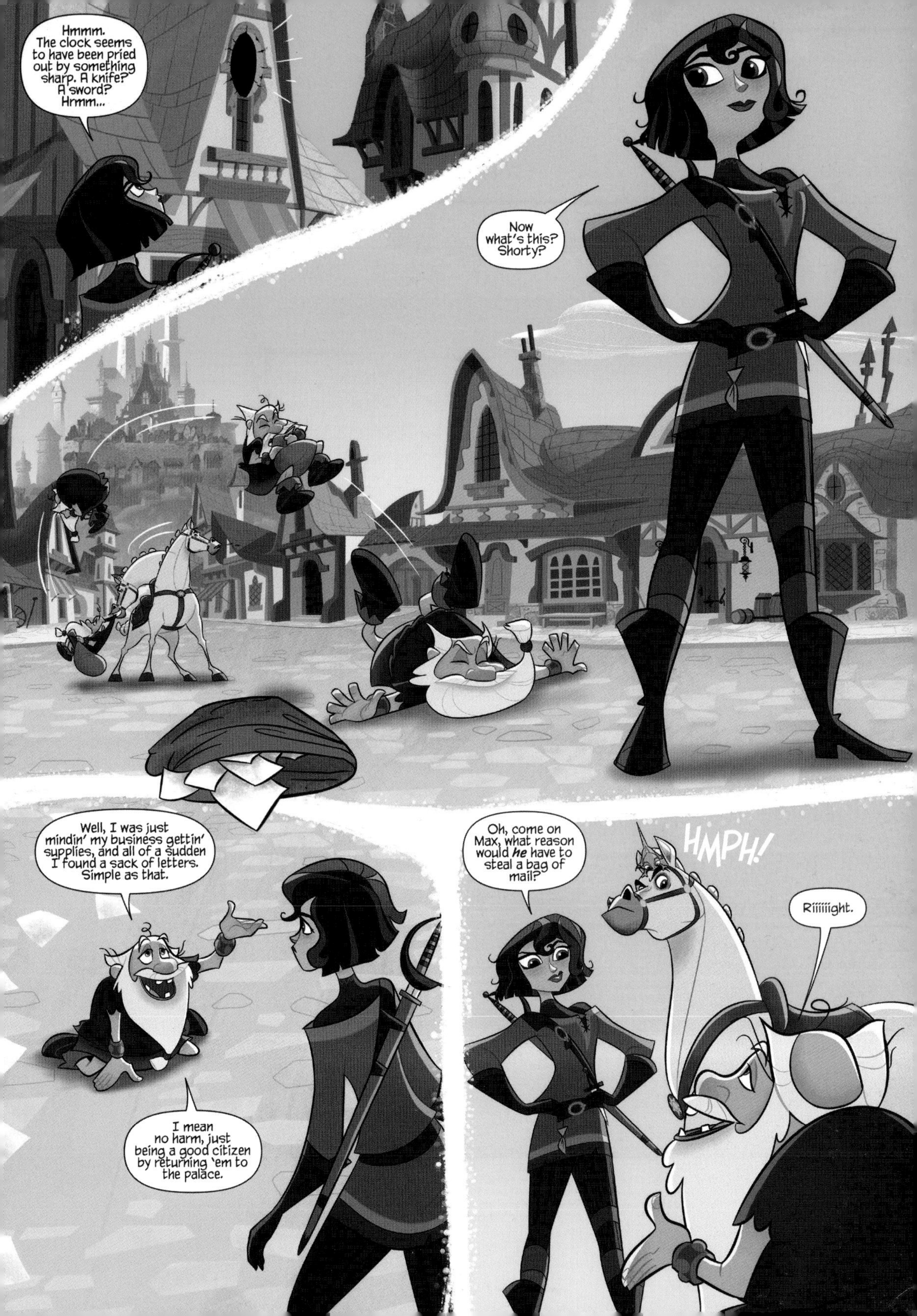
Hmmm. The clock seems to have been pried out by something sharp. A knife? A sword? Hrmm...
Now what's this? Shorty?
Well, I was just mindin' my business gettin' supplies, and all of a sudden I found a sack of letters. Simple as that.
I mean no harm, just being a good citizen by returning 'em to the palace.
Oh, come on Max, what reason would *he* have to steal a bag of mail?
HMPH!
Riiiiiight.

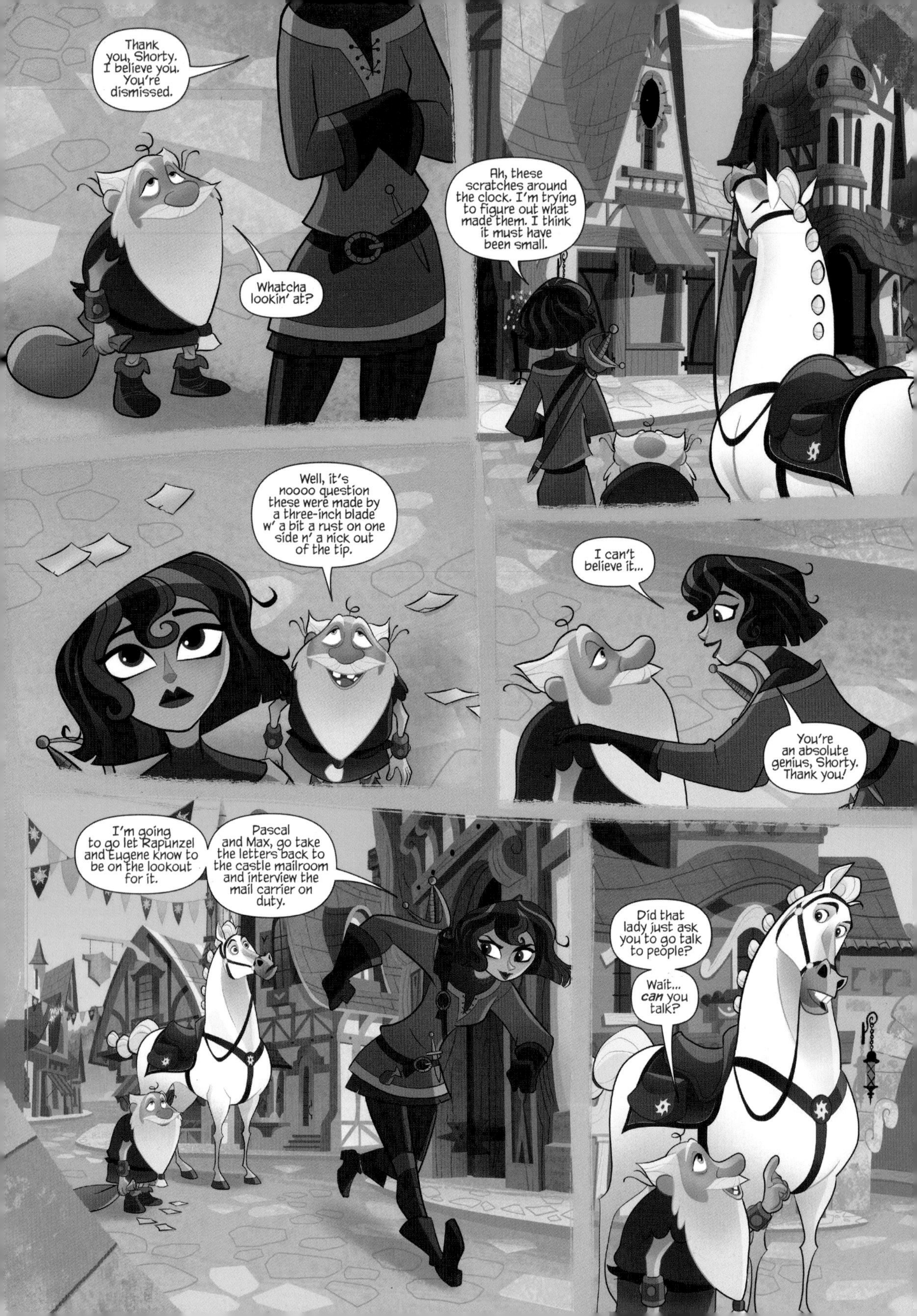

Thank you, Shorty. I believe you. You're dismissed.
Whatcha lookin' at?
Ah, these scratches around the clock. I'm trying to figure out what made them. I think it must have been small.
Well, it's noooo question these were made by a three-inch blade w' a bit a rust on one side n' a nick out of the tip.
I can't believe it...
You're an absolute genius, Shorty. Thank you!
I'm going to go let Rapunzel and Eugene know to be on the lookout for it.
Pascal and Max, go take the letters back to the castle mailroom and interview the mail carrier on duty.
Did that lady just ask you to go talk to people?
Wait... **can** you talk?

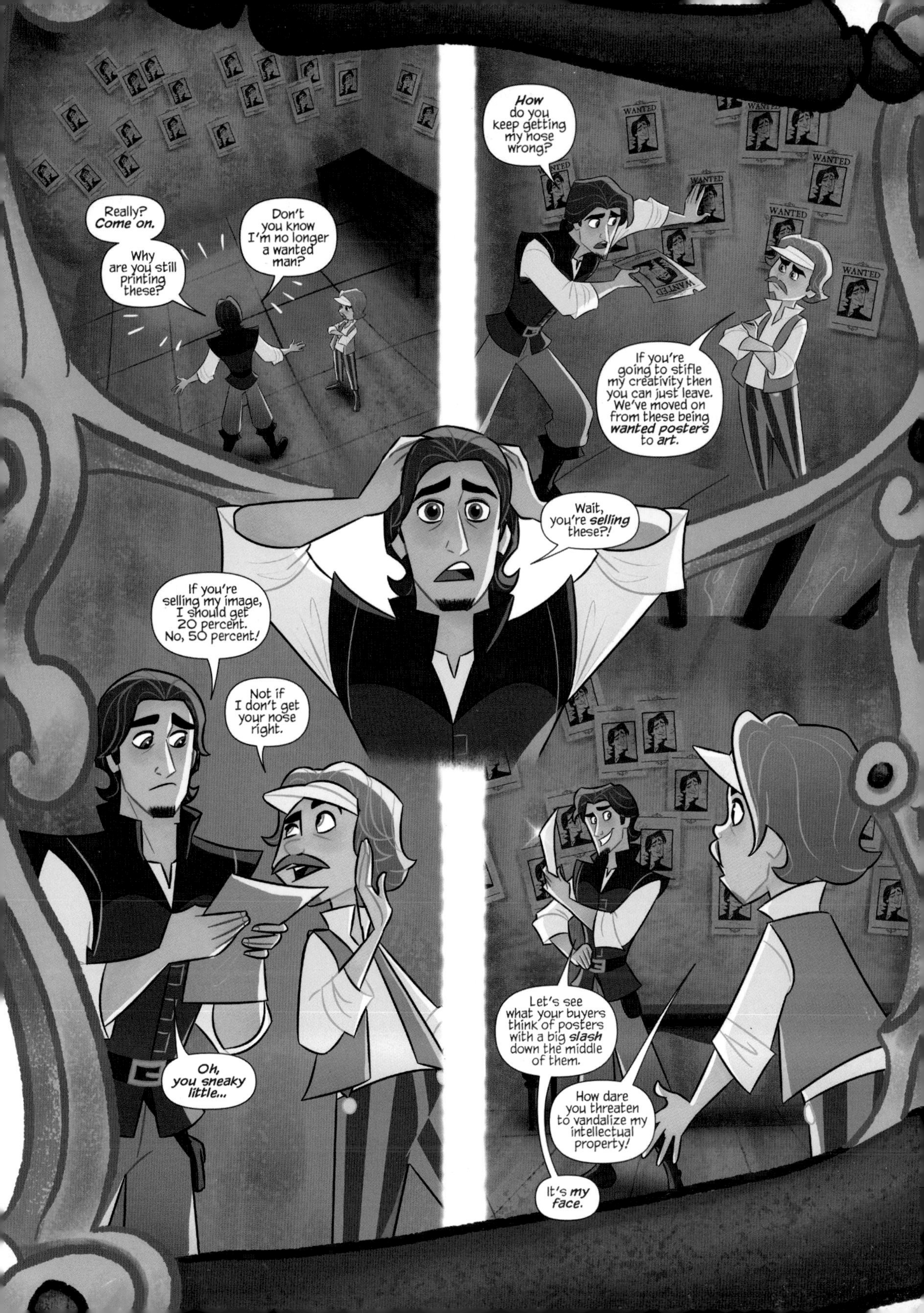

Really? *Come on.*
Why are you still printing these?
Don't you know I'm no longer a wanted man?
How do you keep getting my nose wrong?
If you're going to stifle my creativity then you can just leave. We've moved on from these being ***wanted posters*** to ***art***.
Wait, you're ***selling*** these?!
If you're selling my image, I should get 20 percent. No, 50 percent!
Not if I don't get your nose right.
Oh, you sneaky little...
Let's see what your buyers think of posters with a big ***slash*** down the middle of them.
How dare you threaten to vandalize my intellectual property!
It's ***my face***.

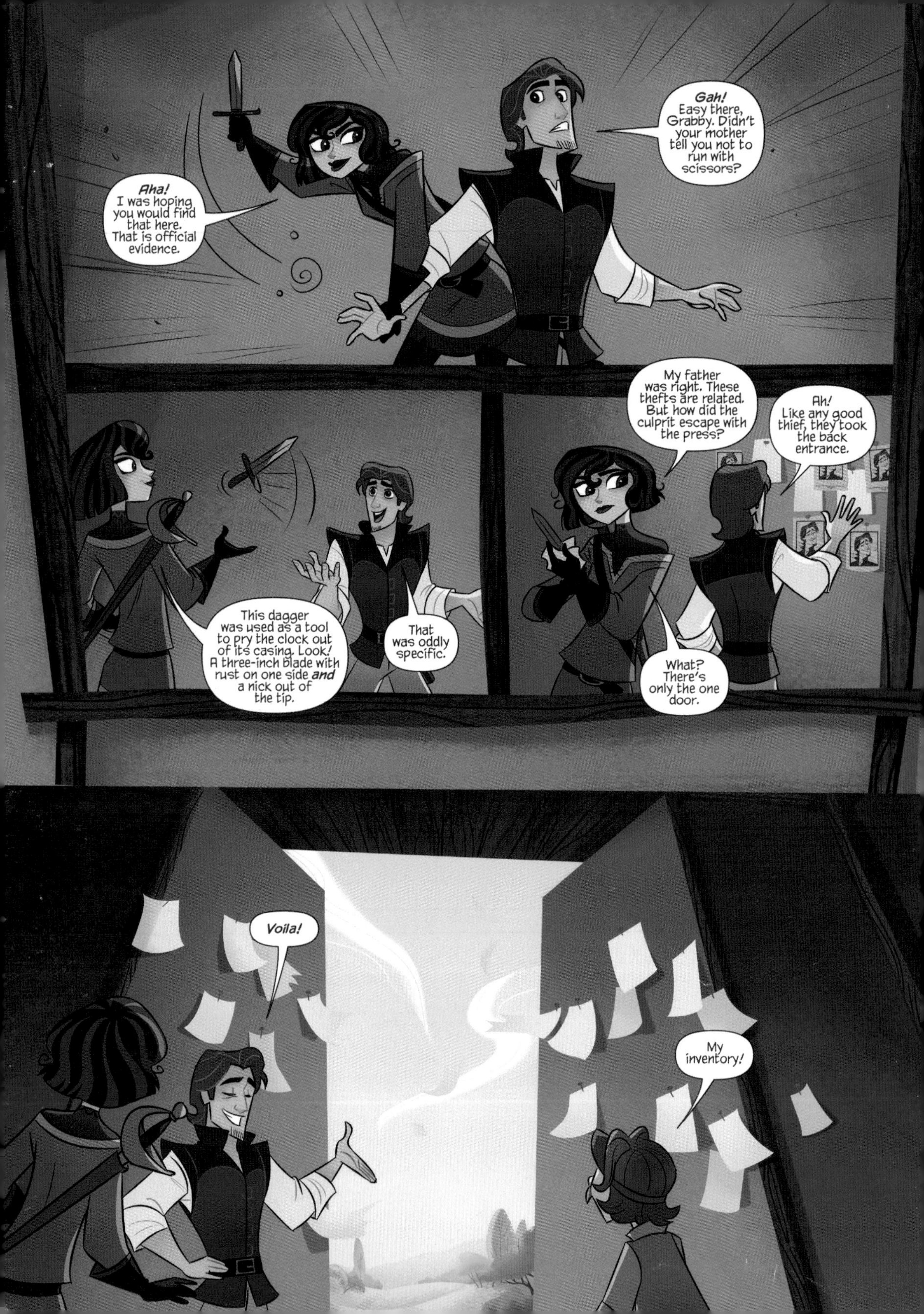
Gah! Easy there, Grabby. Didn't your mother tell you not to run with scissors?
Aha! I was hoping you would find that here. That is official evidence.
This dagger was used as a tool to pry the clock out of its casing. Look! A three-inch blade with rust on one side and a nick out of the tip.
That was oddly specific.
My father was right. These thefts are related. But how did the culprit escape with the press?
Ah! Like any good thief, they took the back entrance.
What? There's only the one door.
Voila!
My inventory!

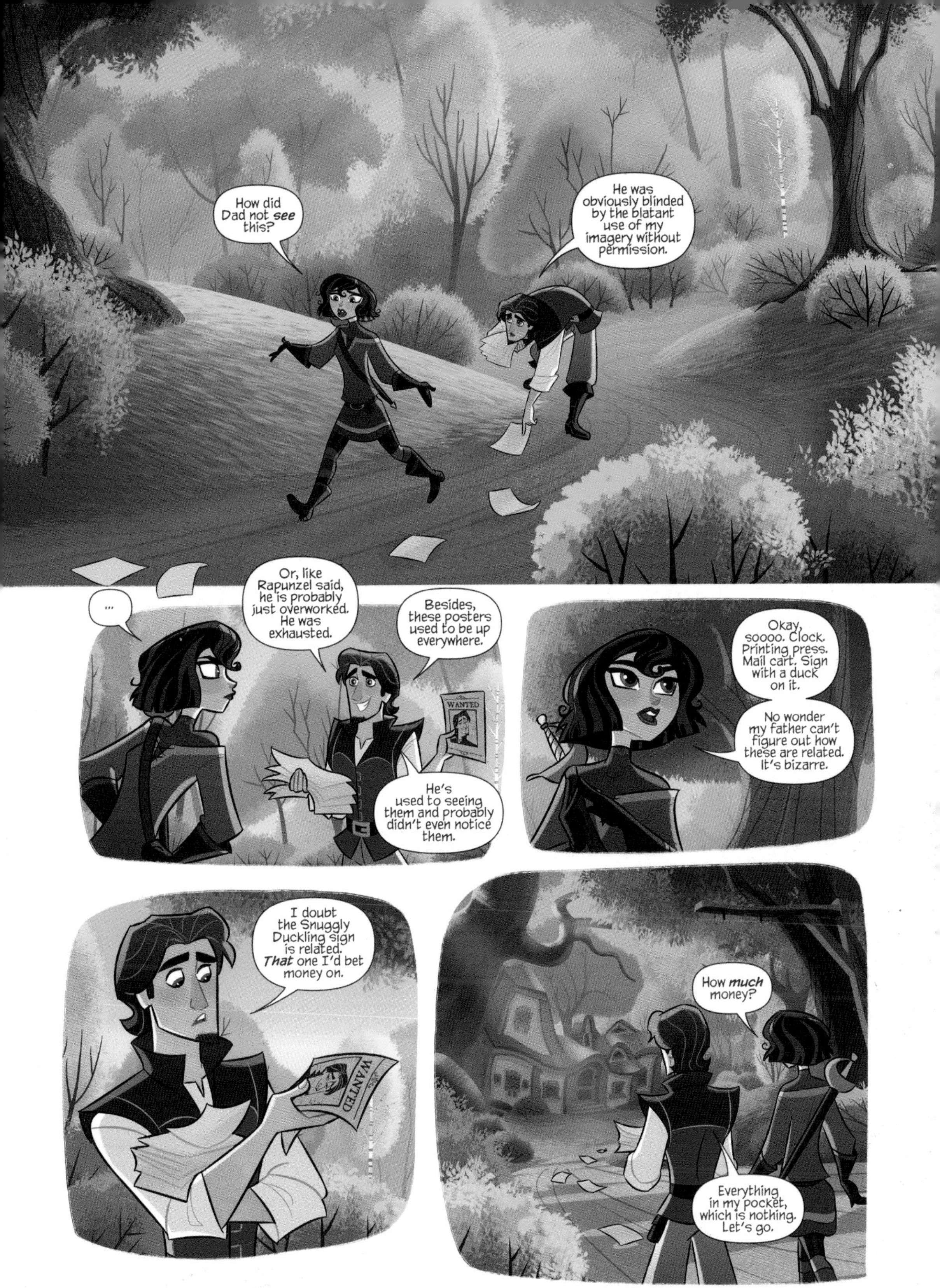

How did Dad not *see* this?
He was obviously blinded by the blatant use of my imagery without permission.
...
Or, like Rapunzel said, he is probably just overworked. He was exhausted.
Besides, these posters used to be up everywhere.
WANTED
He's used to seeing them and probably didn't even notice them.
Okay, soooo. Clock. Printing press. Mail cart. Sign with a duck on it.
No wonder my father can't figure out how these are related. It's bizarre.
I doubt the Snuggly Duckling sign is related. *That* one I'd bet money on.
WANTED
How *much* money?
Everything in my pocket, which is nothing. Let's go.

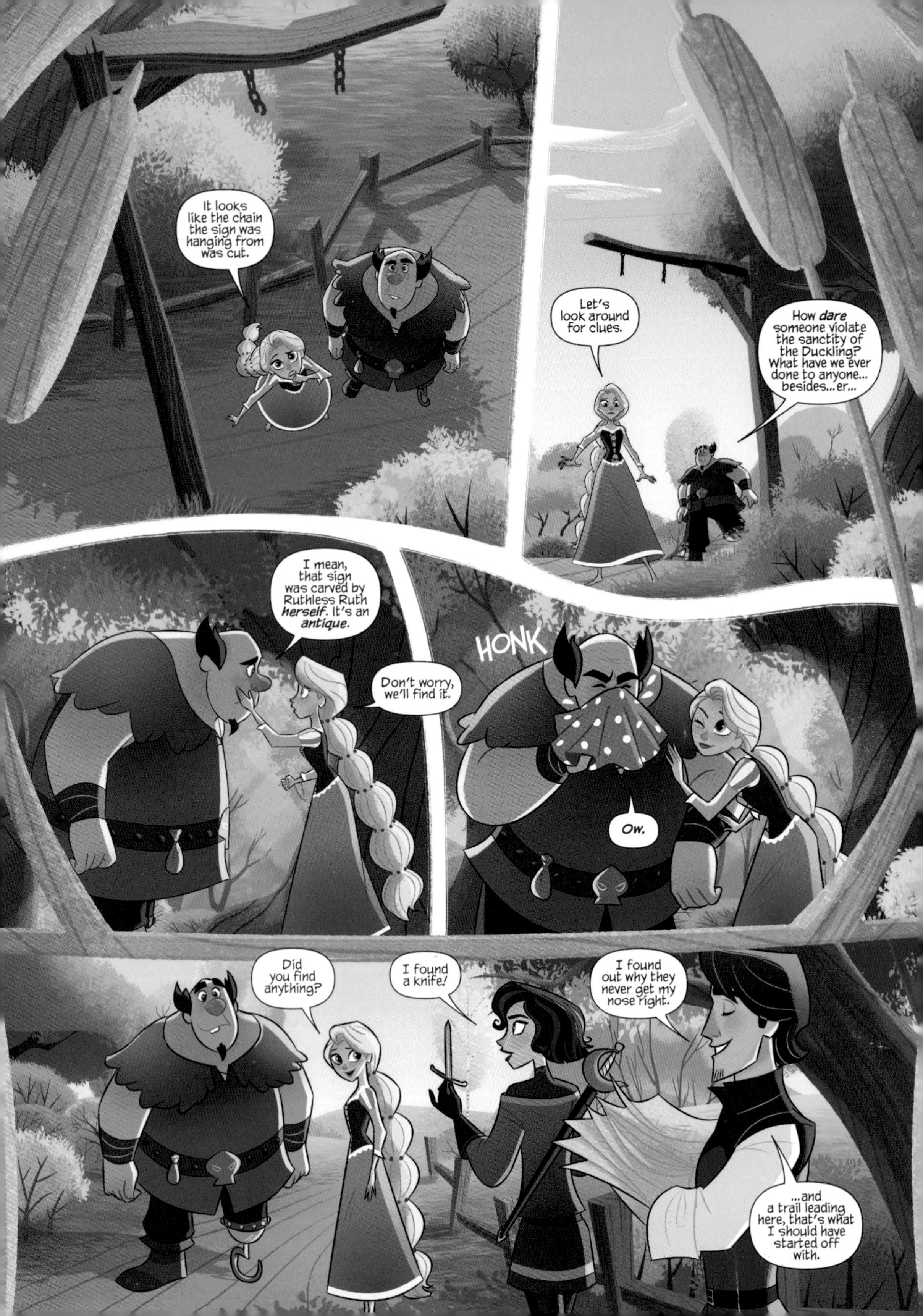
It looks like the chain the sign was hanging from was cut.
Let's look around for clues.
How *dare* someone violate the sanctity of the Duckling? What have we ever done to anyone... besides... er...
I mean, that sign was carved by Ruthless Ruth *herself*. It's an *antique*.
Don't worry, we'll find it.
HONK
Ow.
Did you find anything?
I found a knife!
I found out why they never get my nose right.
...and a trail leading here, that's what I should have started off with.

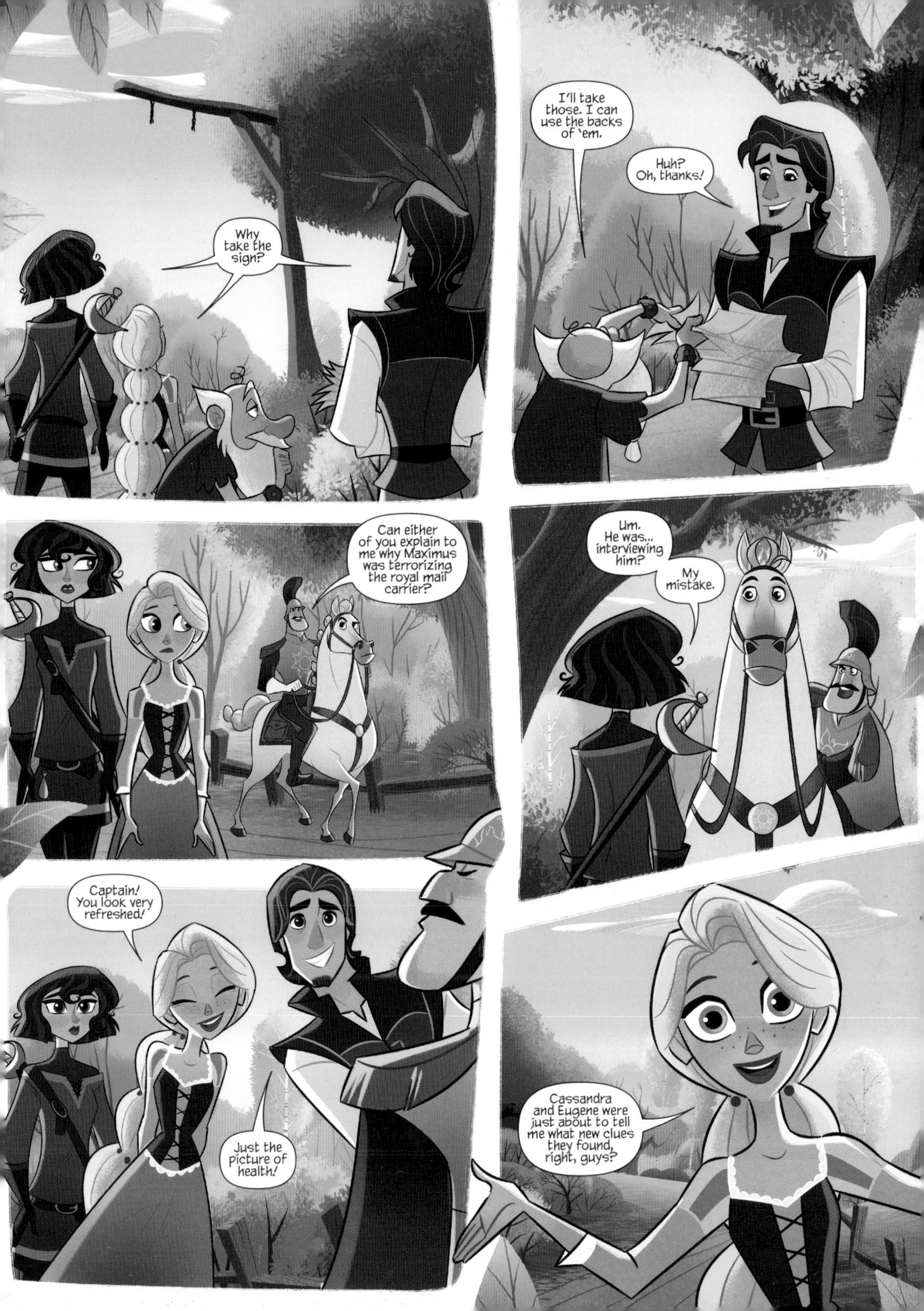
Why take the sign?
I'll take those. I can use the backs of 'em.
Huh? Oh, thanks!
Can either of you explain to me why Maximus was terrorizing the royal mail carrier?
Um. He was... interviewing him?
My mistake.
Captain! You look very refreshed!
Just the picture of health!
Cassandra and Eugene were just about to tell me what new clues they found, right, guys?

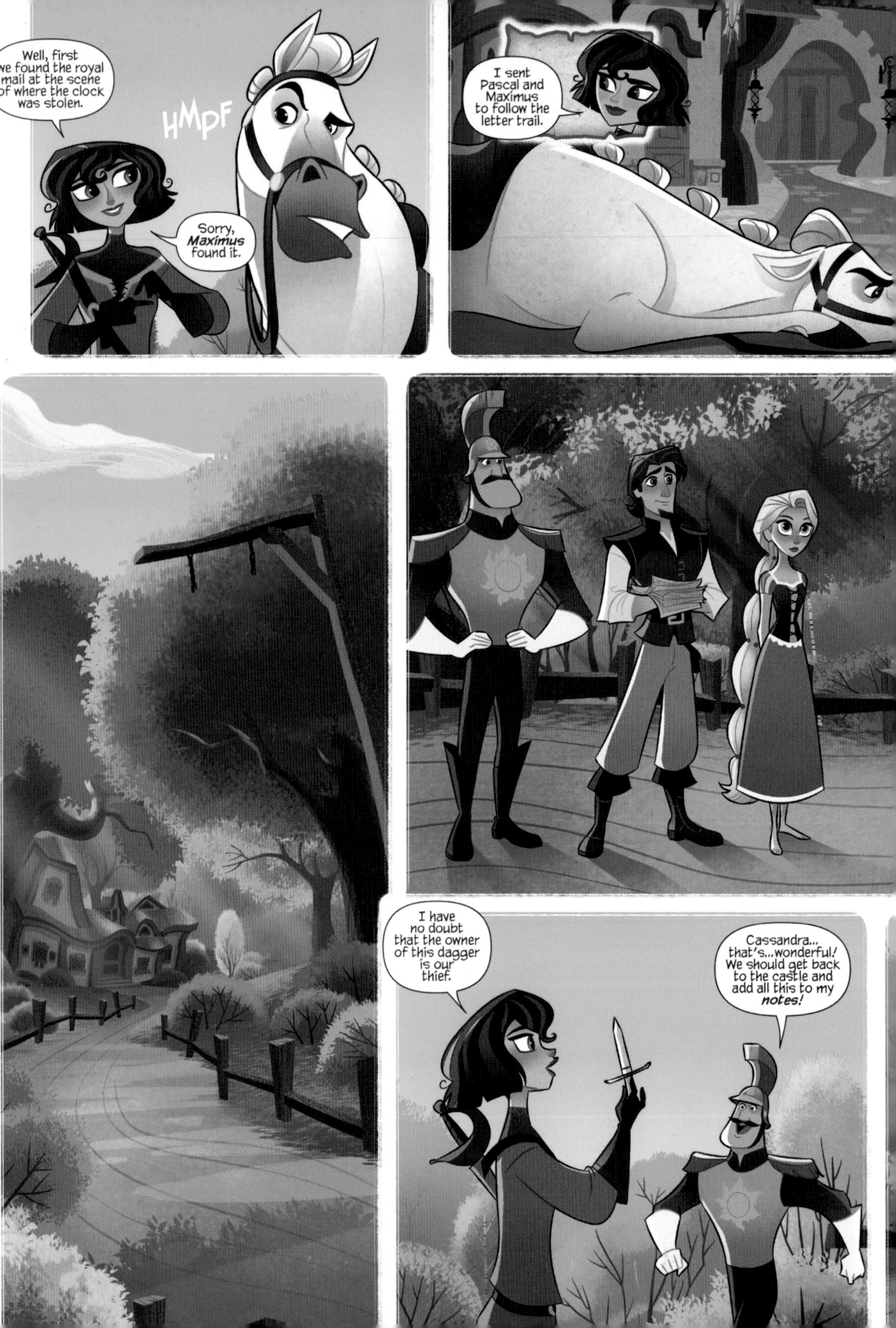

Well, first we found the royal mail at the scene of where the clock was stolen.
HMPF
Sorry, *Maximus* found it.
I sent Pascal and Maximus to follow the letter trail.
I have no doubt that the owner of this dagger is our thief.
Cassandra... that's...wonderful! We should get back to the castle and add all this to my *notes!*

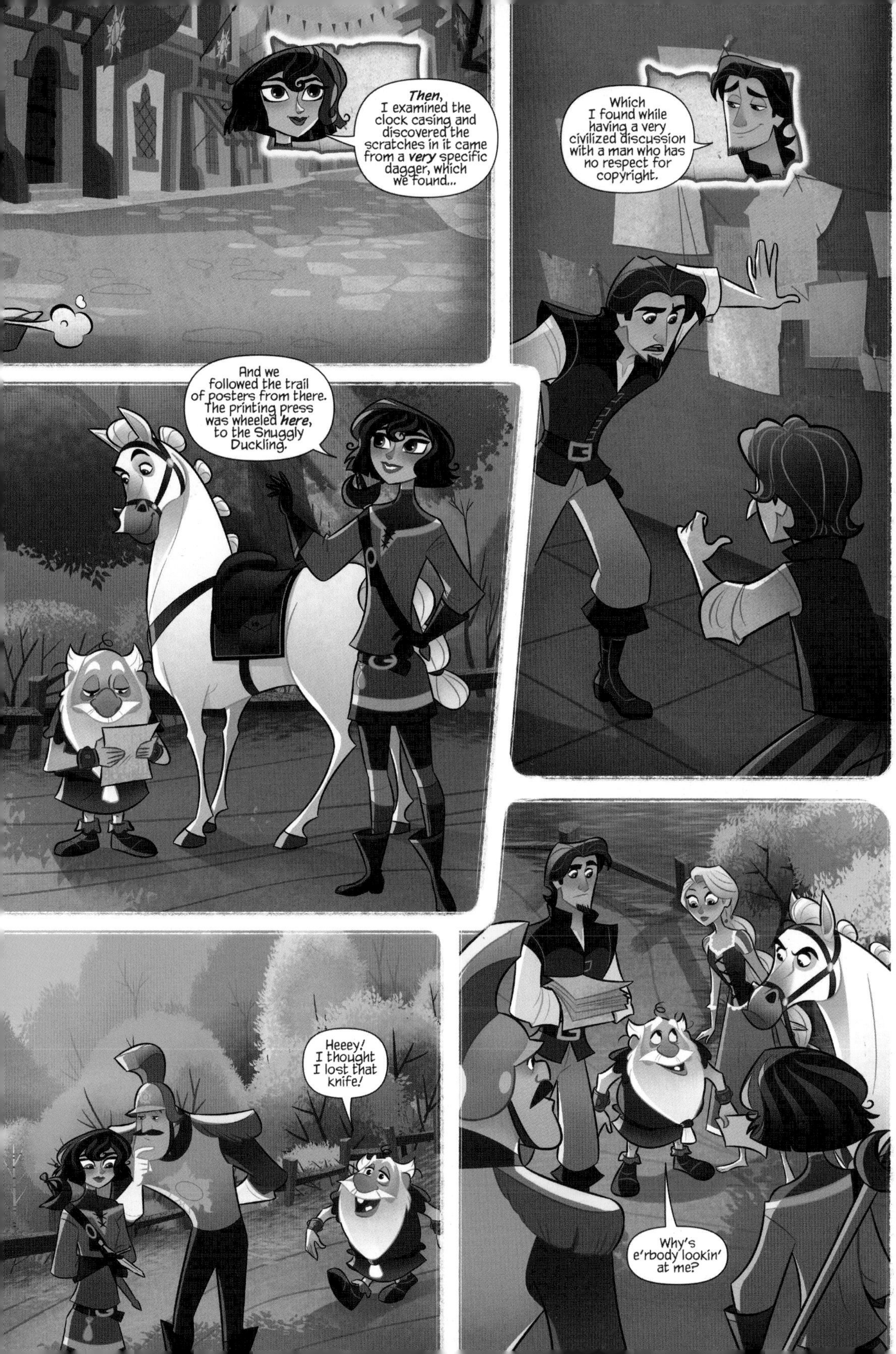

Then, I examined the clock casing and discovered the scratches in it came from a very specific dagger, which we found...
Which I found while having a very civilized discussion with a man who has no respect for copyright.
And we followed the trail of posters from there. The printing press was wheeled here, to the Snuggly Duckling.
Heeey! I thought I lost that knife!
Why's e'rbody lookin' at me?

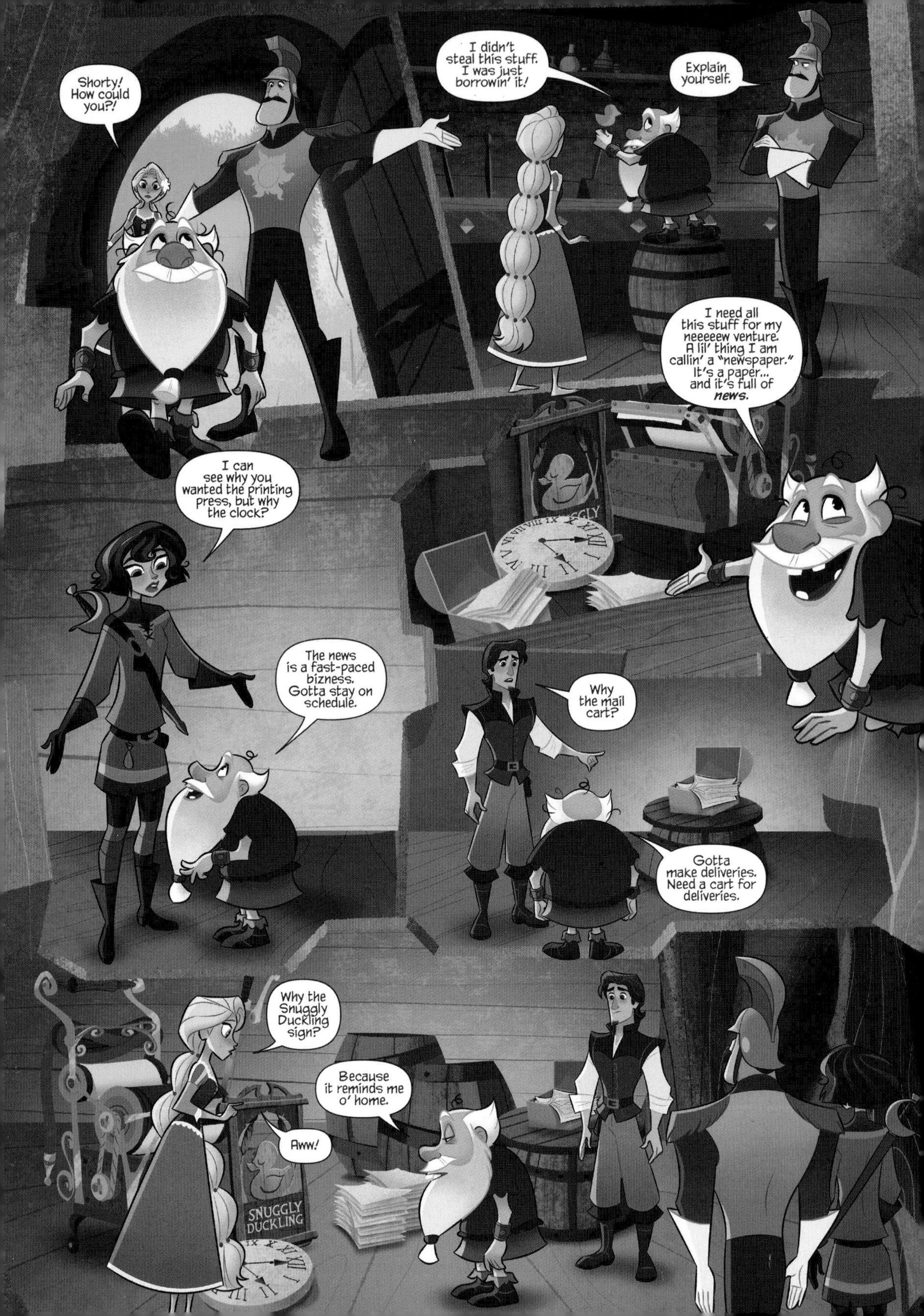
Shorty! How could you?!
I didn't steal this stuff. I was just borrowin' it!
Explain yourself.
I need all this stuff for my neeeeew venture. A lil' thing I am callin' a "newspaper." It's a paper... and it's full of ***news.***
I can see why you wanted the printing press, but why the clock?
The news is a fast-paced bizness. Gotta stay on schedule.
Why the mail cart?
Gotta make deliveries. Need a cart for deliveries.
Why the Snuggly Duckling sign?
Because it reminds me o' home.
Aww!
SNUGGLY DUCKLING

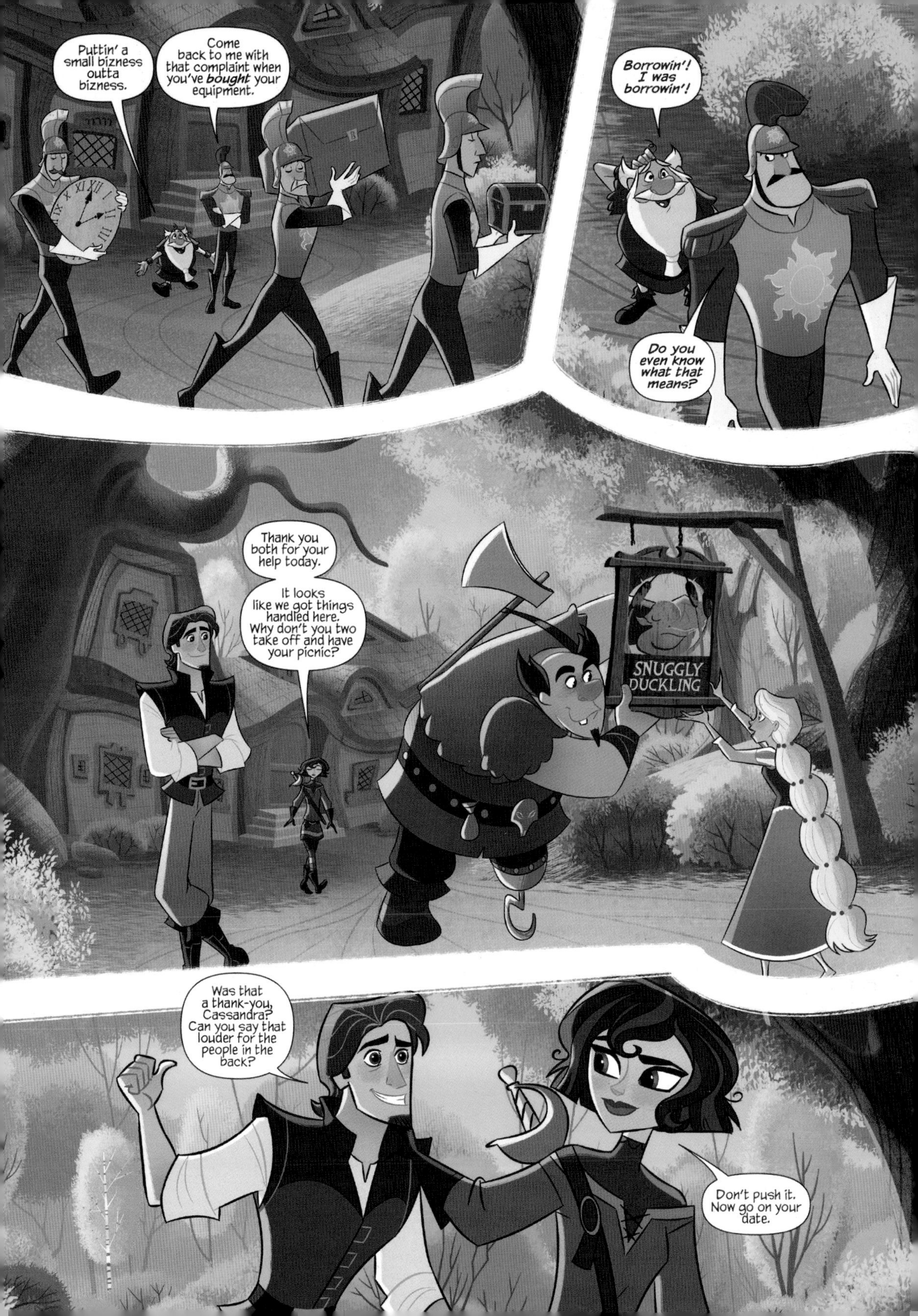

Puttin' a small bizness outta bizness.
Come back to me with that complaint when you've *bought* your equipment.
Borrowin'! I was borrowin'!
Do you even know what that means?
Thank you both for your help today.
It looks like we got things handled here. Why don't you two take off and have your picnic?
SNUGGLY DUCKLING
Was that a thank-you, Cassandra? Can you say that louder for the people in the back?
Don't push it. Now go on your date.

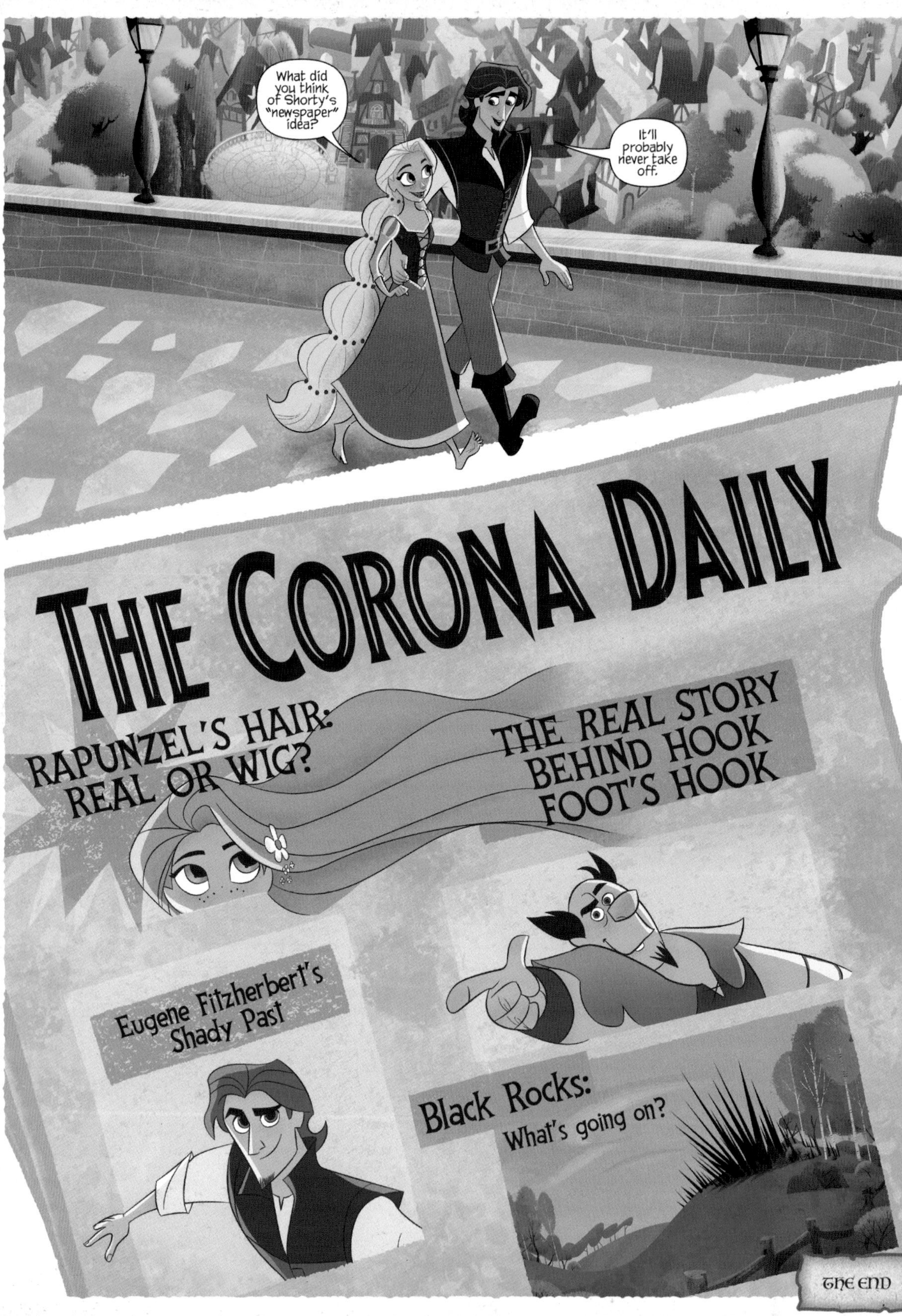
What did you think of Shorty's "newspaper" idea?
It'll probably never take off.
THE CORONA DAILY
RAPUNZEL'S HAIR: REAL OR WIG?
THE REAL STORY BEHIND HOOK FOOT'S HOOK
Eugene Fitzherbert's Shady Past
Black Rocks:
What's going on?
THE END

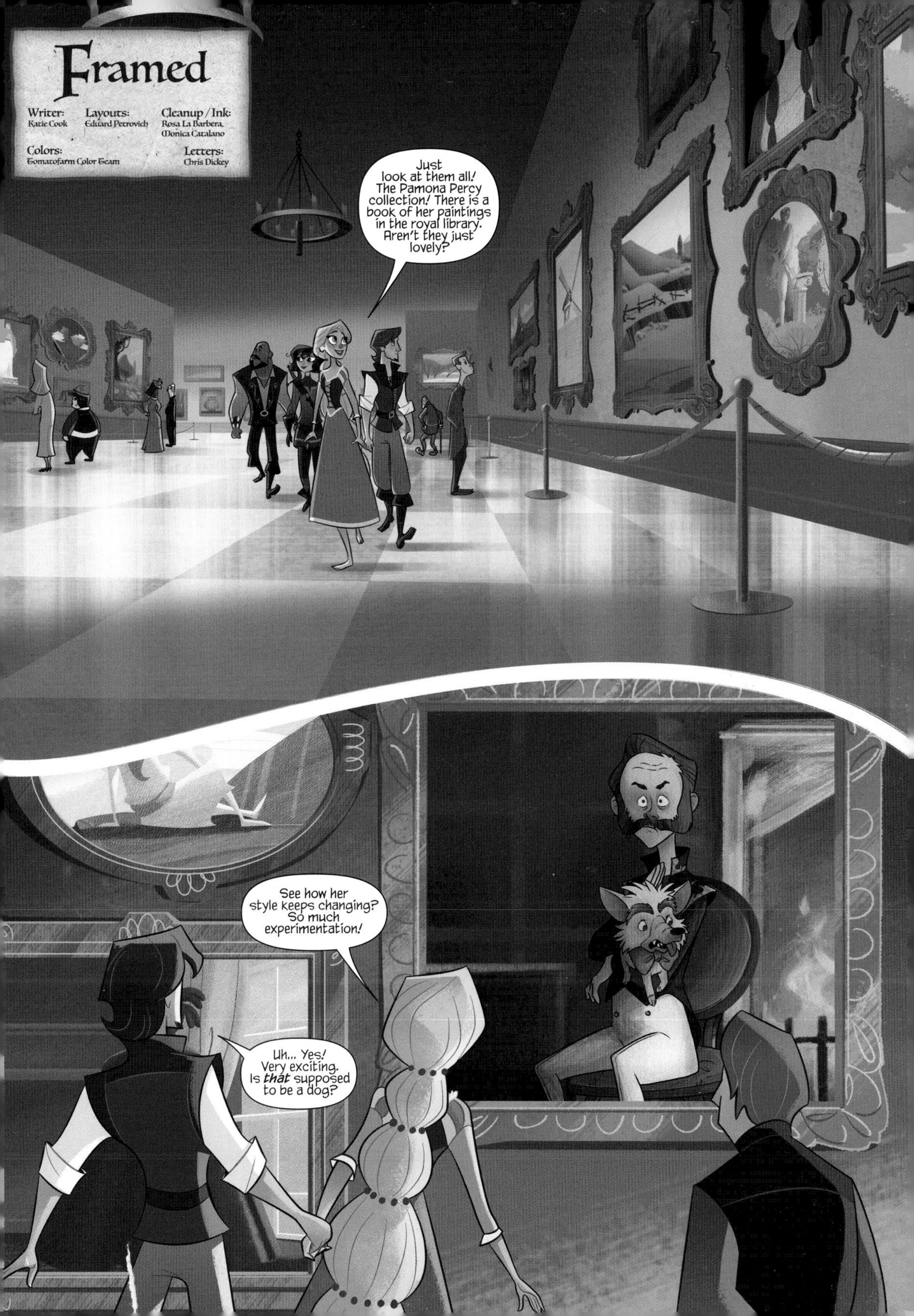
Framed
Writer: Katie Cook
Layouts: Eduard Petrovich
Cleanup / Ink: Rosa La Barbera, Monica Catalano
Colors: Tomatofarm Color Team
Letters: Chris Dickey
Just look at them all! The Pamona Percy collection! There is a book of her paintings in the royal library. Aren't they just lovely?
See how her style keeps changing? So much experimentation!
Uh... Yes! Very exciting. Is ***that*** supposed to be a dog?

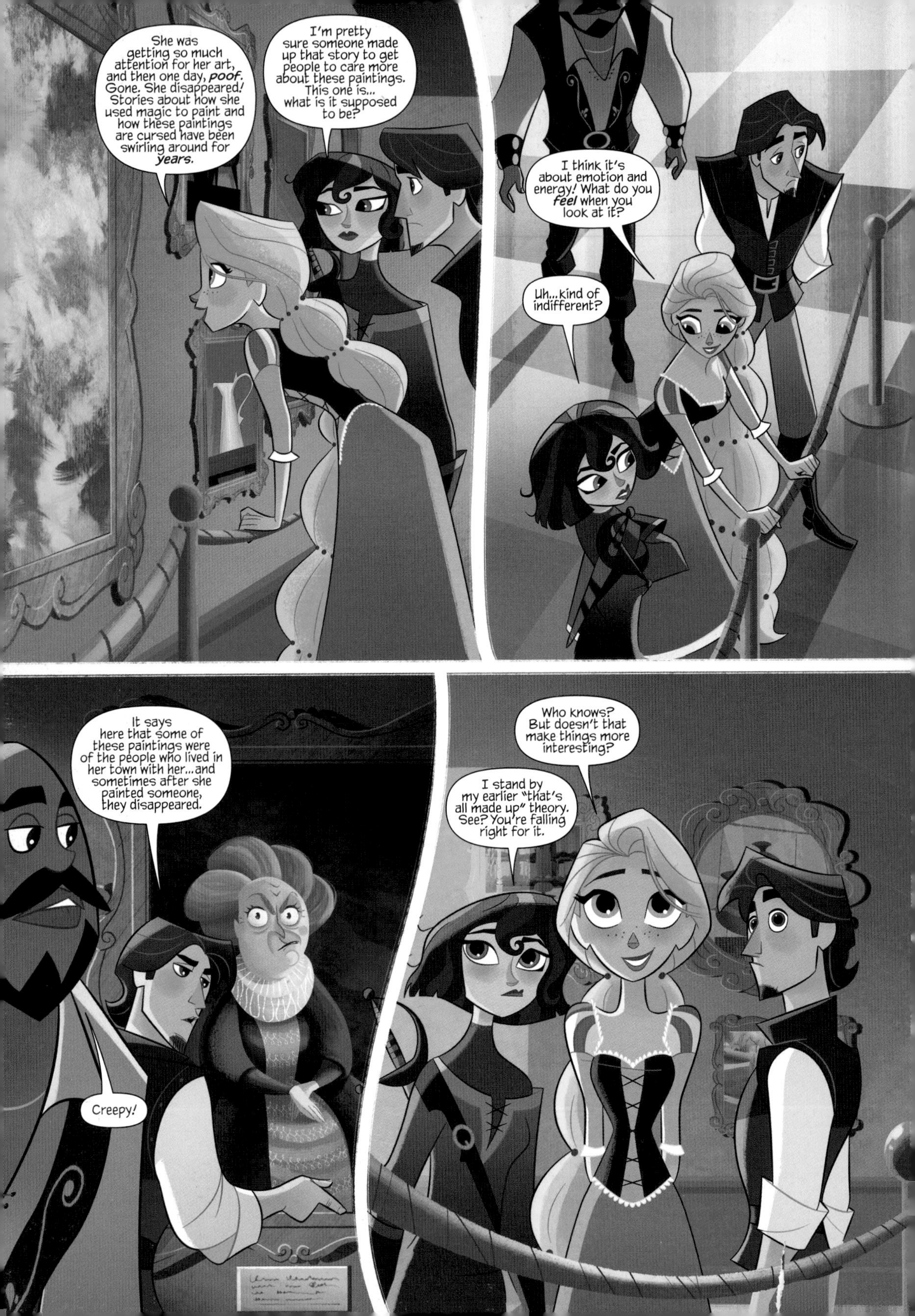

She was getting so much attention for her art, and then one day, ***poof***. Gone. She disappeared! Stories about how she used magic to paint and how these paintings are cursed have been swirling around for ***years***.
I'm pretty sure someone made up that story to get people to care more about these paintings. This one is... what is it supposed to be?
I think it's about emotion and energy! What do you ***feel*** when you look at it?
Uh...kind of indifferent?
It says here that some of these paintings were of the people who lived in her town with her...and sometimes after she painted someone, they disappeared.
Creepy!
Who knows? But doesn't that make things more interesting?
I stand by my earlier "that's all made up" theory. See? You're falling right for it.

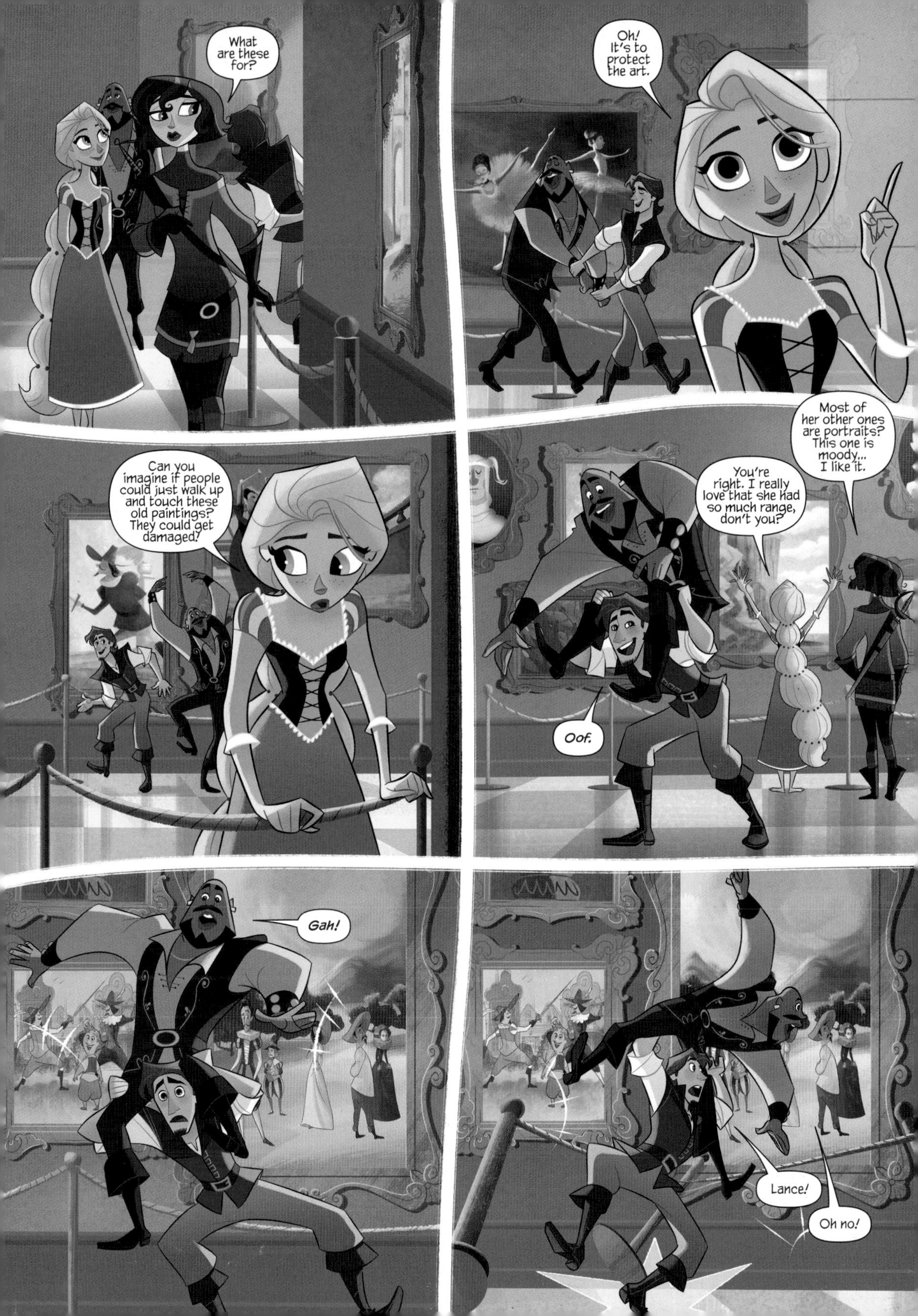
What are these for?
Oh! It's to protect the art.
Can you imagine if people could just walk up and touch these old paintings? They could get damaged.
Most of her other ones are portraits? This one is moody... I like it.
You're right. I really love that she had so much range, don't you?
Oof.
Gah!
Lance!
Oh no!

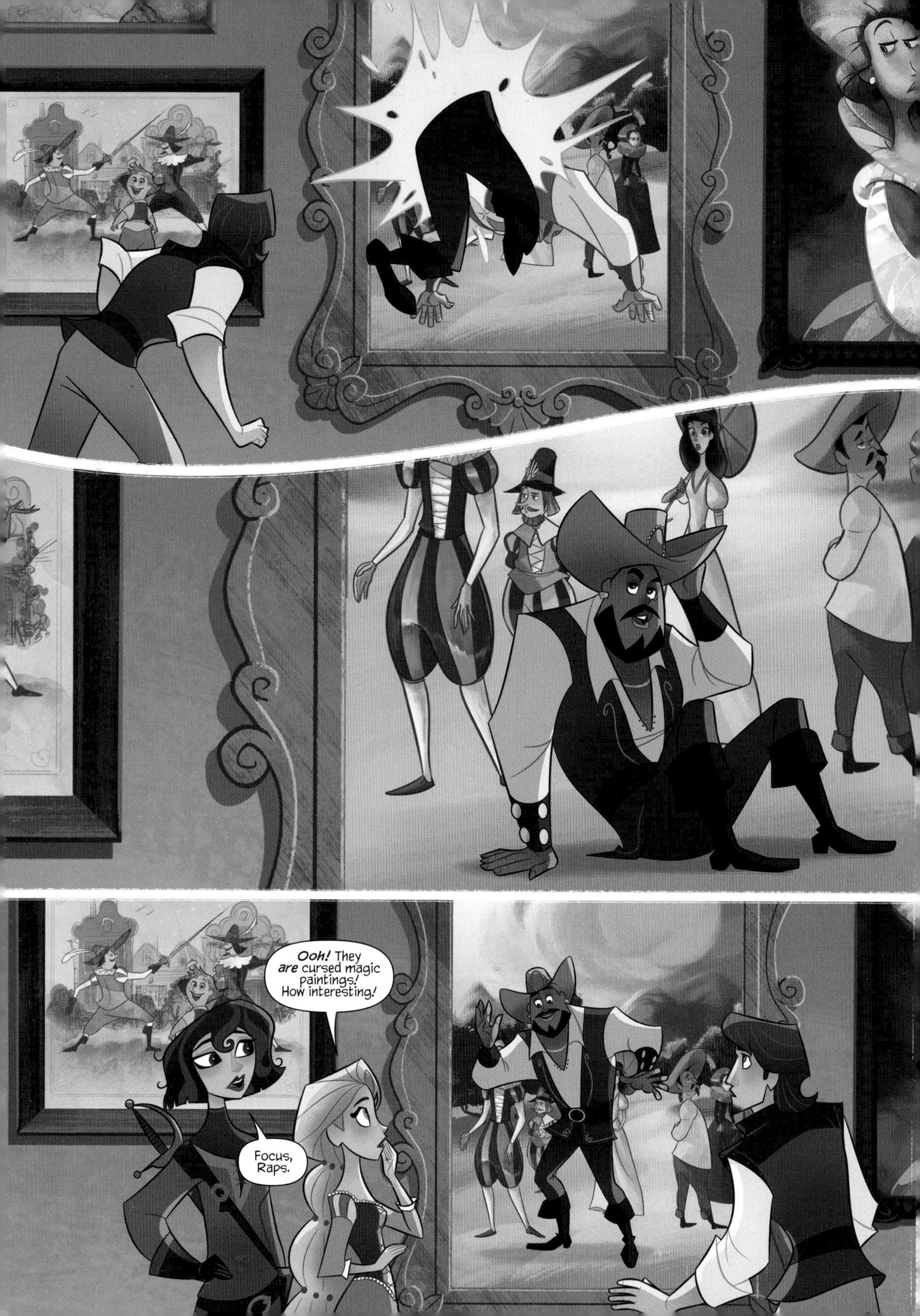
Ooh! They *are* cursed magic paintings! How interesting!
Focus, Raps.

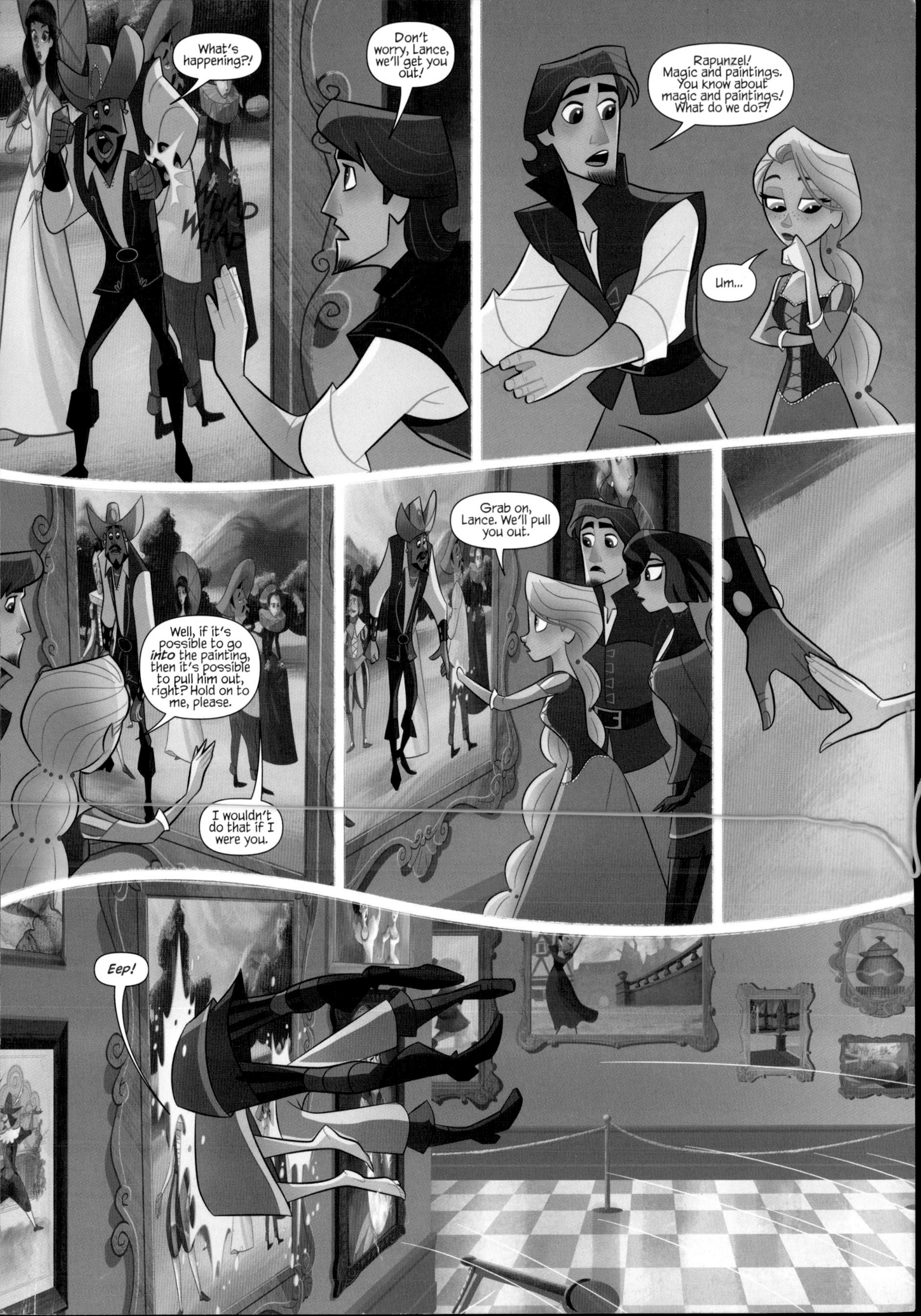
What's happening?!
WHAP WHAP
Don't worry, Lance, we'll get you out!
Rapunzel! Magic and paintings. You know about magic and paintings! What do we do?!
Um...
Well, if it's possible to go *into* the painting, then it's possible to pull him out, right? Hold on to me, please.
I wouldn't do that if I were you.
Grab on, Lance. We'll pull you out.
Eep!

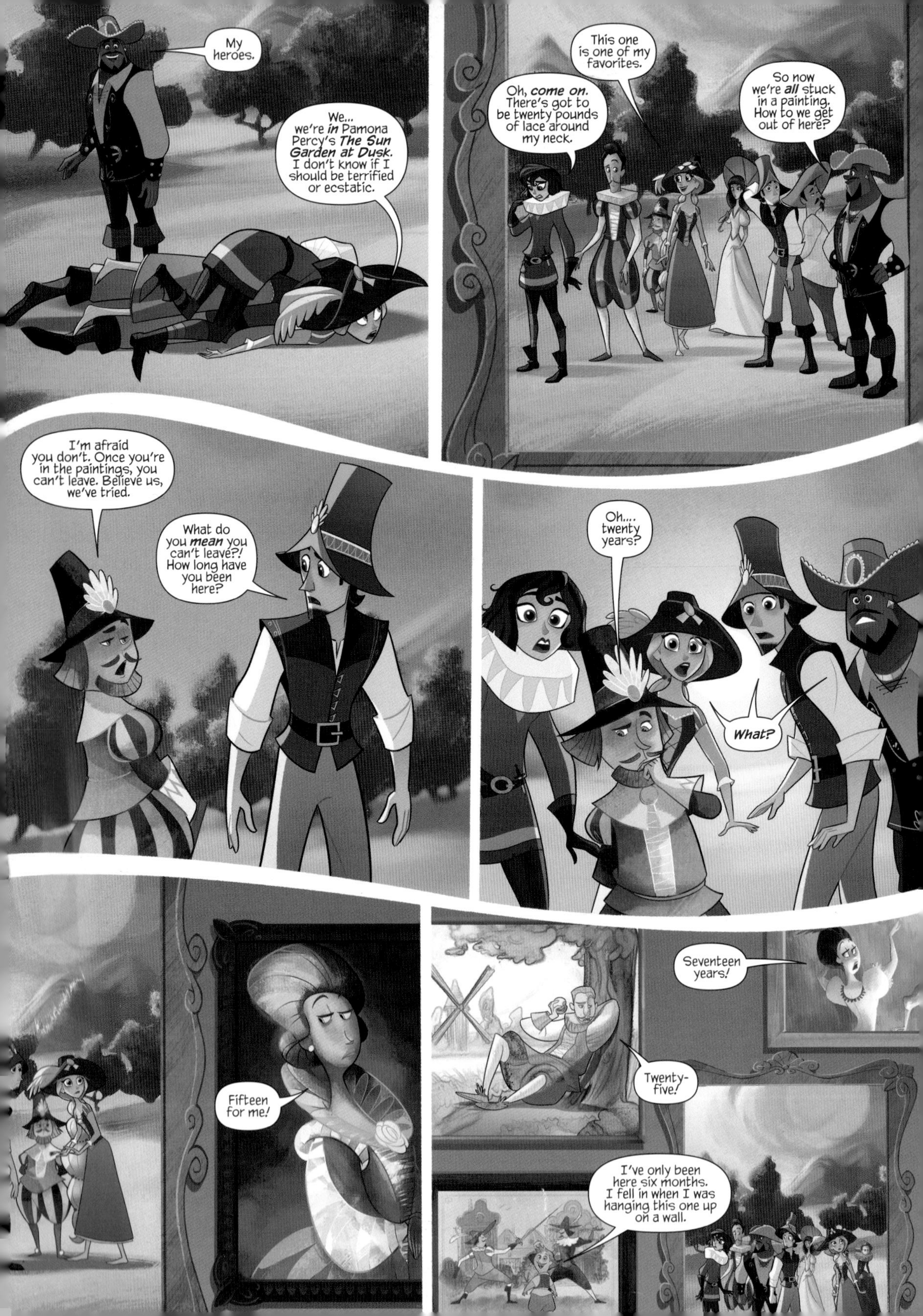
My heroes.
We... we're *in* Pamona Percy's ***The Sun Garden at Dusk***. I don't know if I should be terrified or ecstatic.
This one is one of my favorites.
Oh, ***come on***. There's got to be twenty pounds of lace around my neck.
So now we're ***all*** stuck in a painting. How to we get out of here?
I'm afraid you don't. Once you're in the paintings, you can't leave. Believe us, we've tried.
What do you ***mean*** you can't leave?! How long have you been here?
Oh.... twenty years?
What?
Fifteen for me!
Seventeen years!
Twenty-five!
I've only been here six months. I fell in when I was hanging this one up on a wall.

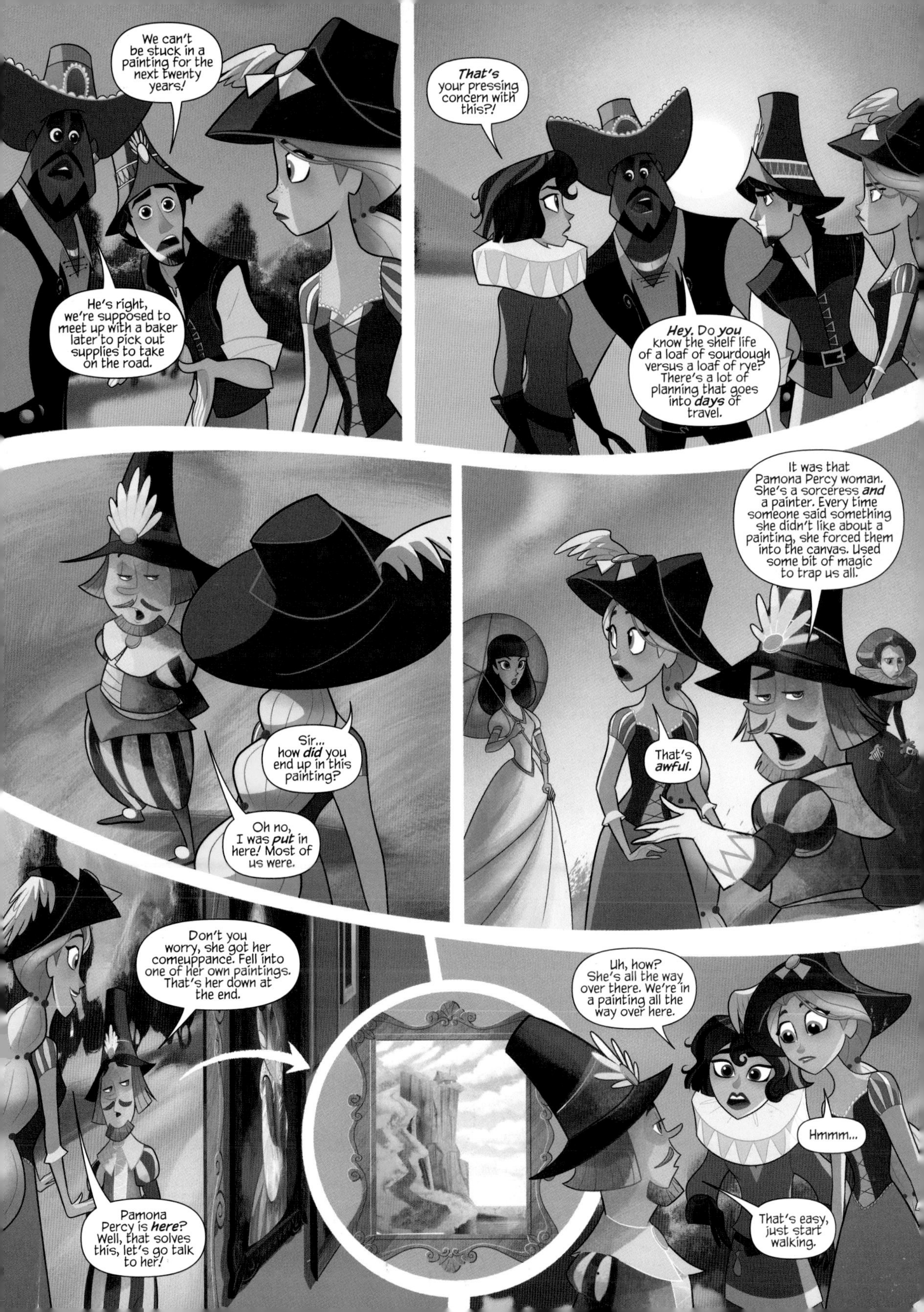
We can't be stuck in a painting for the next twenty years!
He's right, we're supposed to meet up with a baker later to pick out supplies to take on the road.
That's your pressing concern with this?!
Hey. Do you know the shelf life of a loaf of sourdough versus a loaf of rye? There's a lot of planning that goes into days of travel.
Sir... how did you end up in this painting?
Oh no, I was put in here! Most of us were.
It was that Pamona Percy woman. She's a sorceress and a painter. Every time someone said something she didn't like about a painting, she forced them into the canvas. Used some bit of magic to trap us all.
That's awful.
Don't you worry, she got her comeuppance. Fell into one of her own paintings. That's her down at the end.
Pamona Percy is here? Well, that solves this, let's go talk to her!
Uh, how? She's all the way over there. We're in a painting all the way over here.
Hmmm...
That's easy, just start walking.

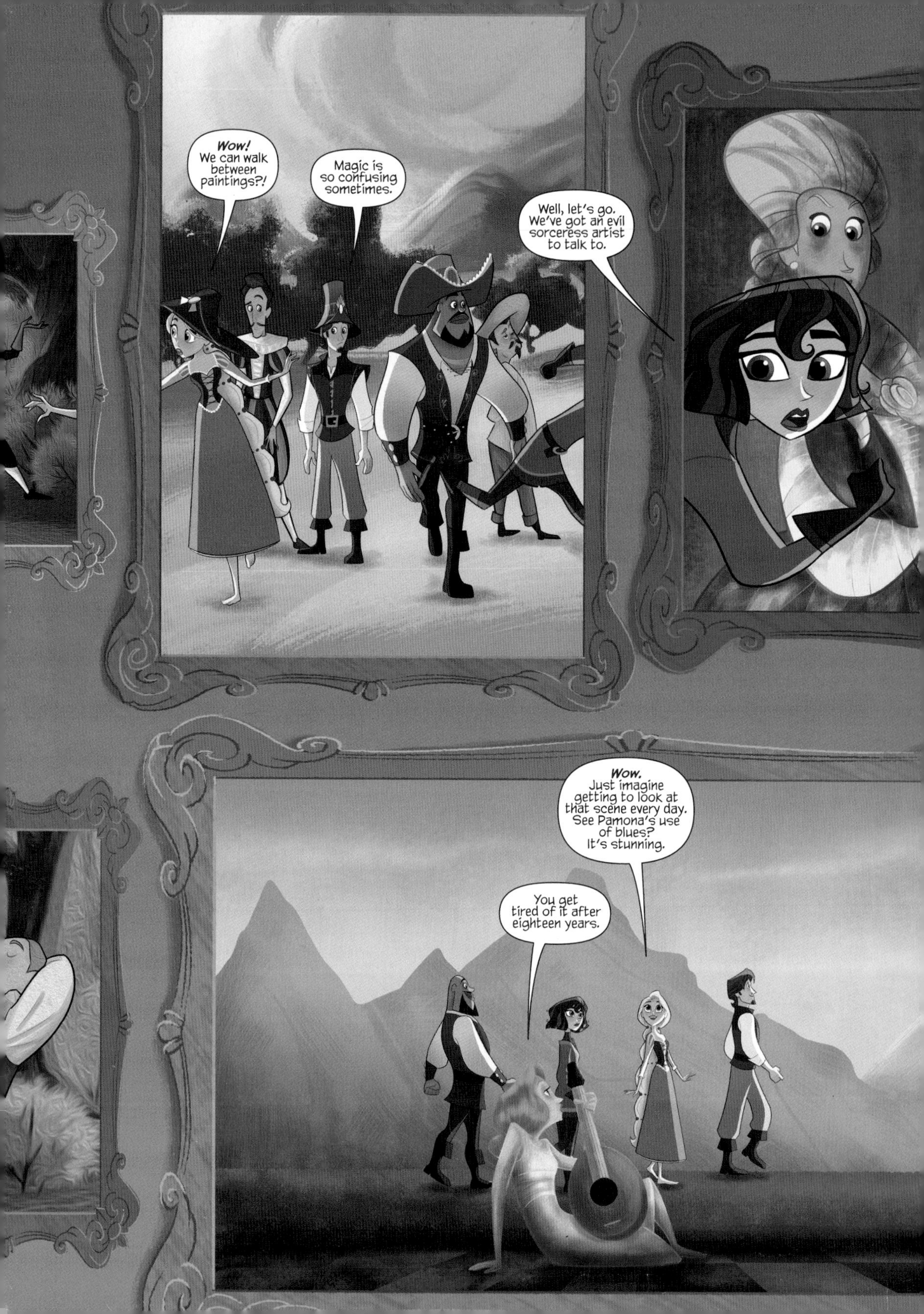
Wow! We can walk between paintings?!
Magic is so confusing sometimes.
Well, let's go. We've got an evil sorceress artist to talk to.
Wow. Just imagine getting to look at that scene every day. See Pamona's use of blues? It's stunning.
You get tired of it after eighteen years.

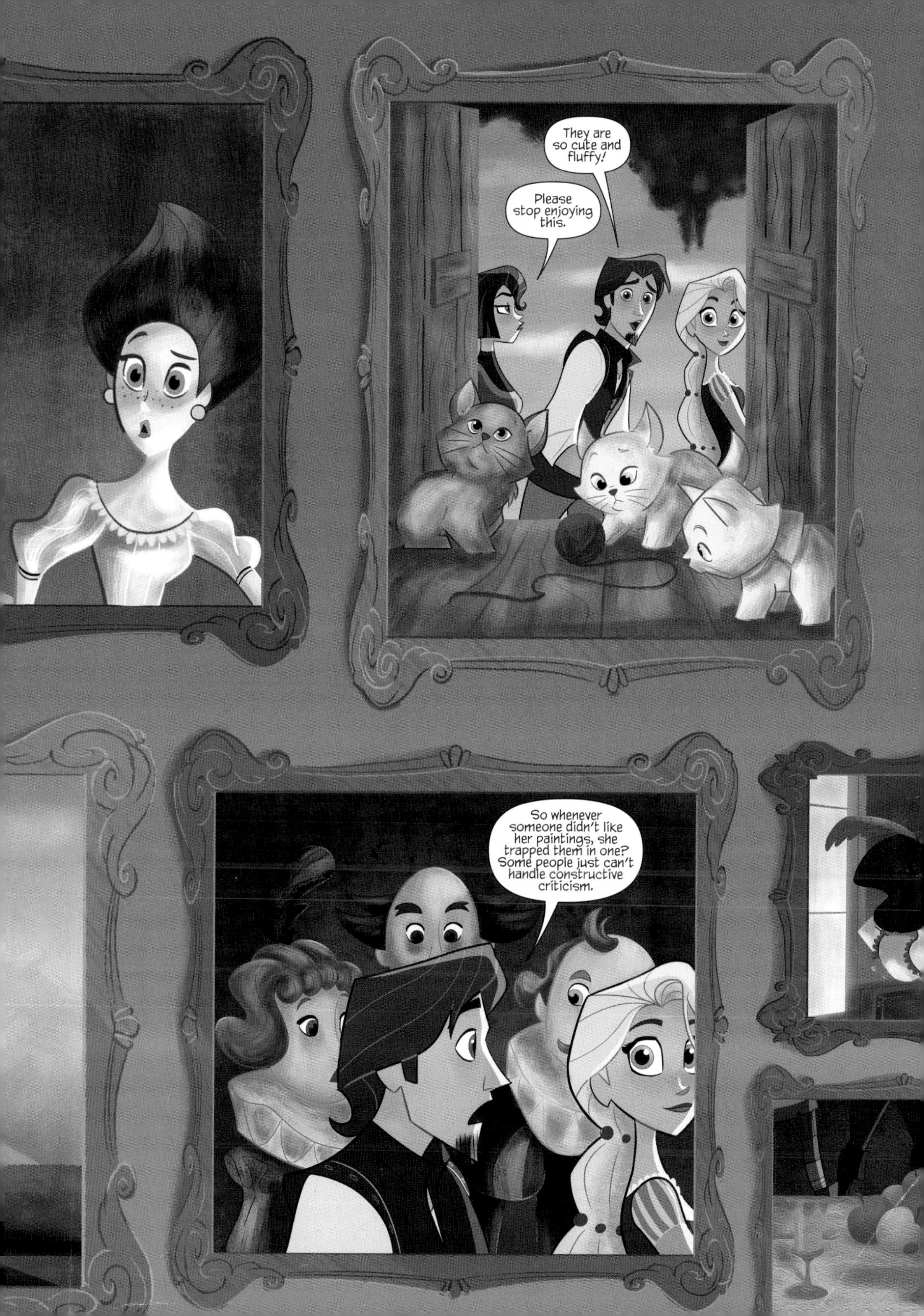
They are so cute and fluffy!
Please stop enjoying this.
So whenever someone didn't like her paintings, she trapped them in one? Some people just can't handle constructive criticism.

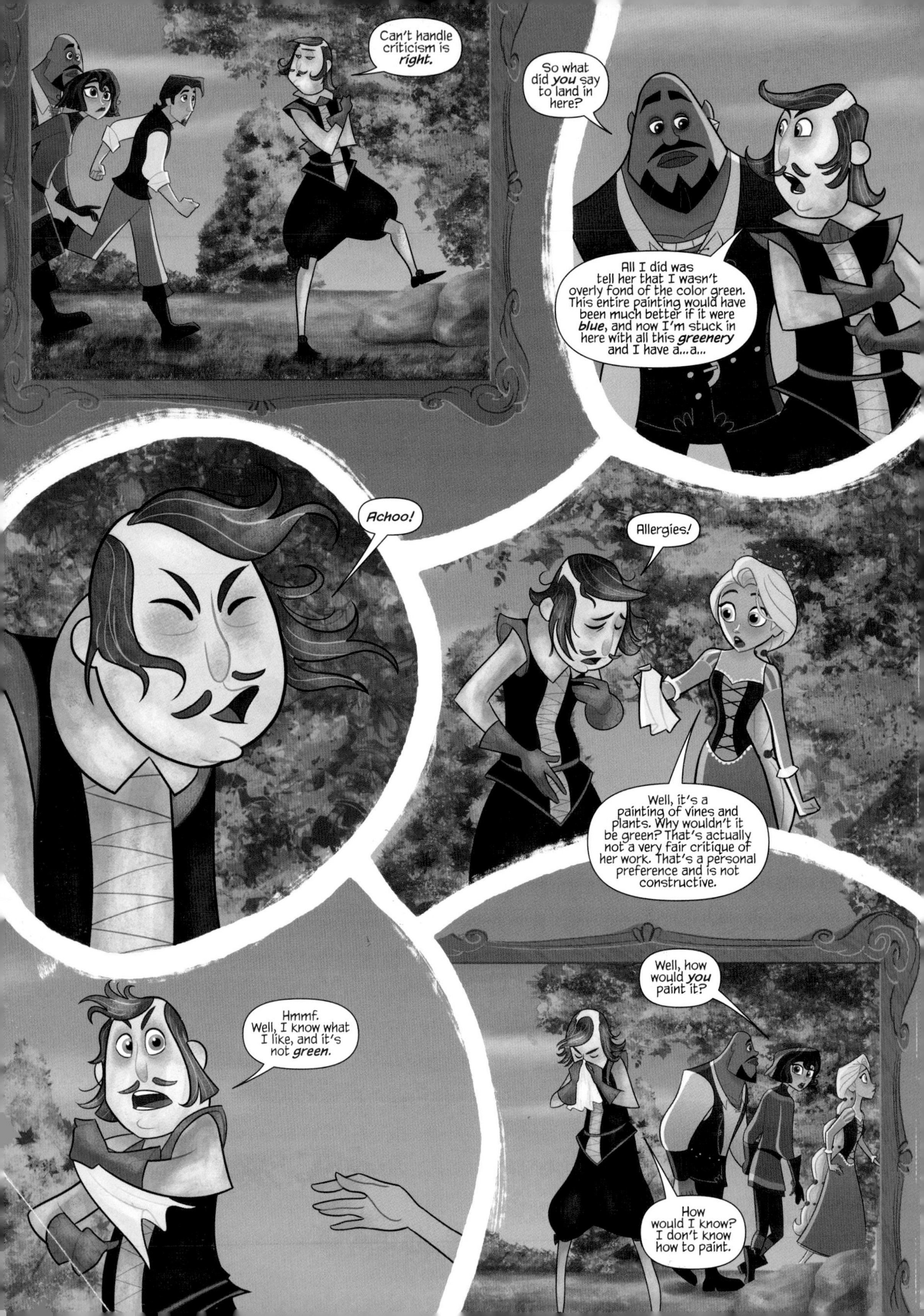
Can't handle criticism is *right.*
So what did *you* say to land in here?
All I did was tell her that I wasn't overly fond of the color green. This entire painting would have been much better if it were *blue*, and now I'm stuck in here with all this *greenery* and I have a...a...
Achoo!
Allergies!
Well, it's a painting of vines and plants. Why wouldn't it be green? That's actually not a very fair critique of her work. That's a personal preference and is not constructive.
Hmmf. Well, I know what I like, and it's not *green*.
Well, how would *you* paint it?
How would I know? I don't know how to paint.

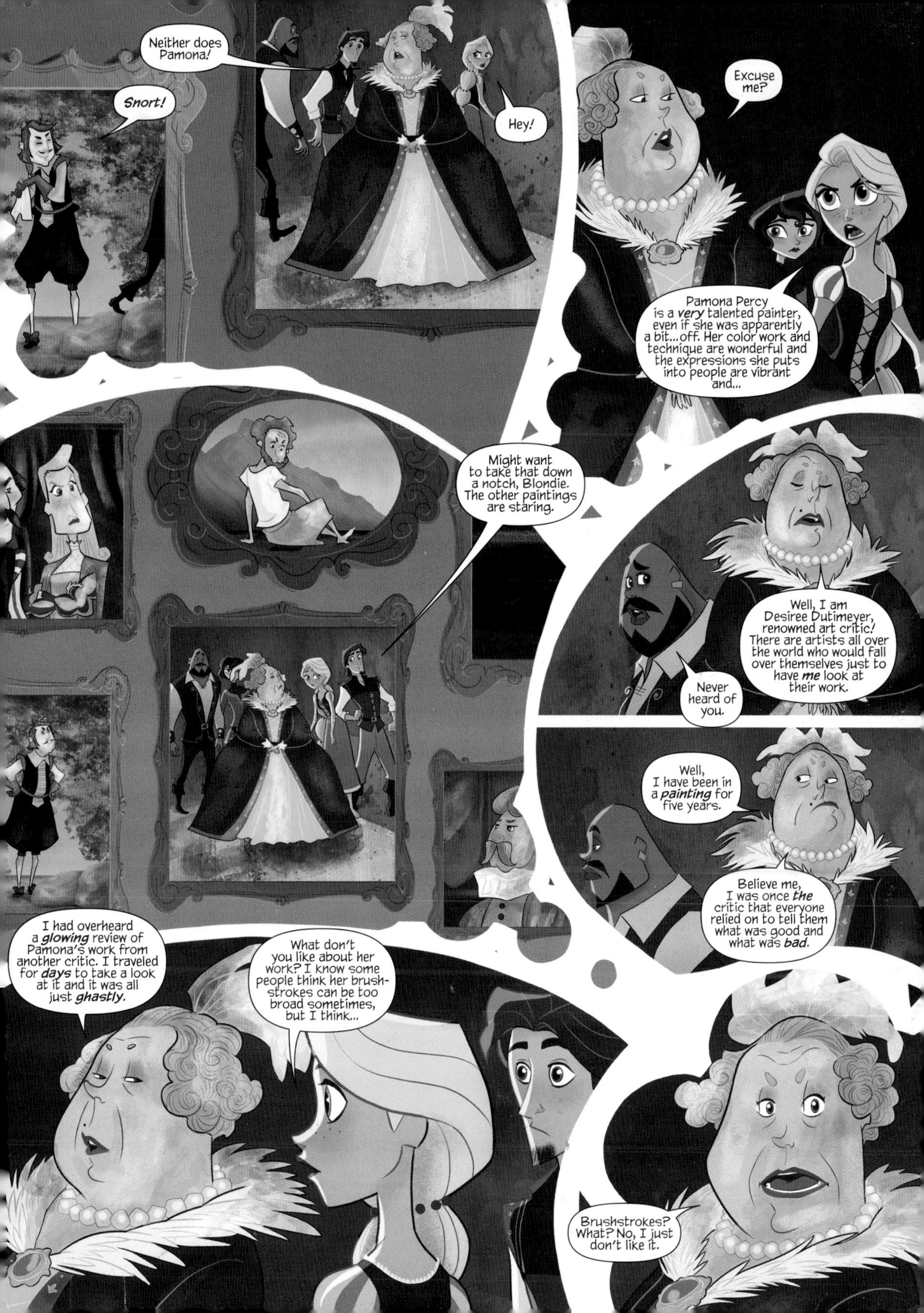
Neither does Pamona!
Snort!
Hey!
Excuse me?
Pamona Percy is a *very* talented painter, even if she was apparently a bit...off. Her color work and technique are wonderful and the expressions she puts into people are vibrant and...
Might want to take that down a notch, Blondie. The other paintings are staring.
Well, I am Desiree Dutimeyer, renowned art critic! There are artists all over the world who would fall over themselves just to have *me* look at their work.
Never heard of you.
Well, I have been in a *painting* for five years.
Believe me, I was once *the* critic that everyone relied on to tell them what was good and what was *bad*.
I had overheard a *glowing* review of Pamona's work from another critic. I traveled for *days* to take a look at it and it was all just *ghastly*.
What don't you like about her work? I know some people think her brush-strokes can be too broad sometimes, but I think...
Brushstrokes? What? No, I just don't like it.

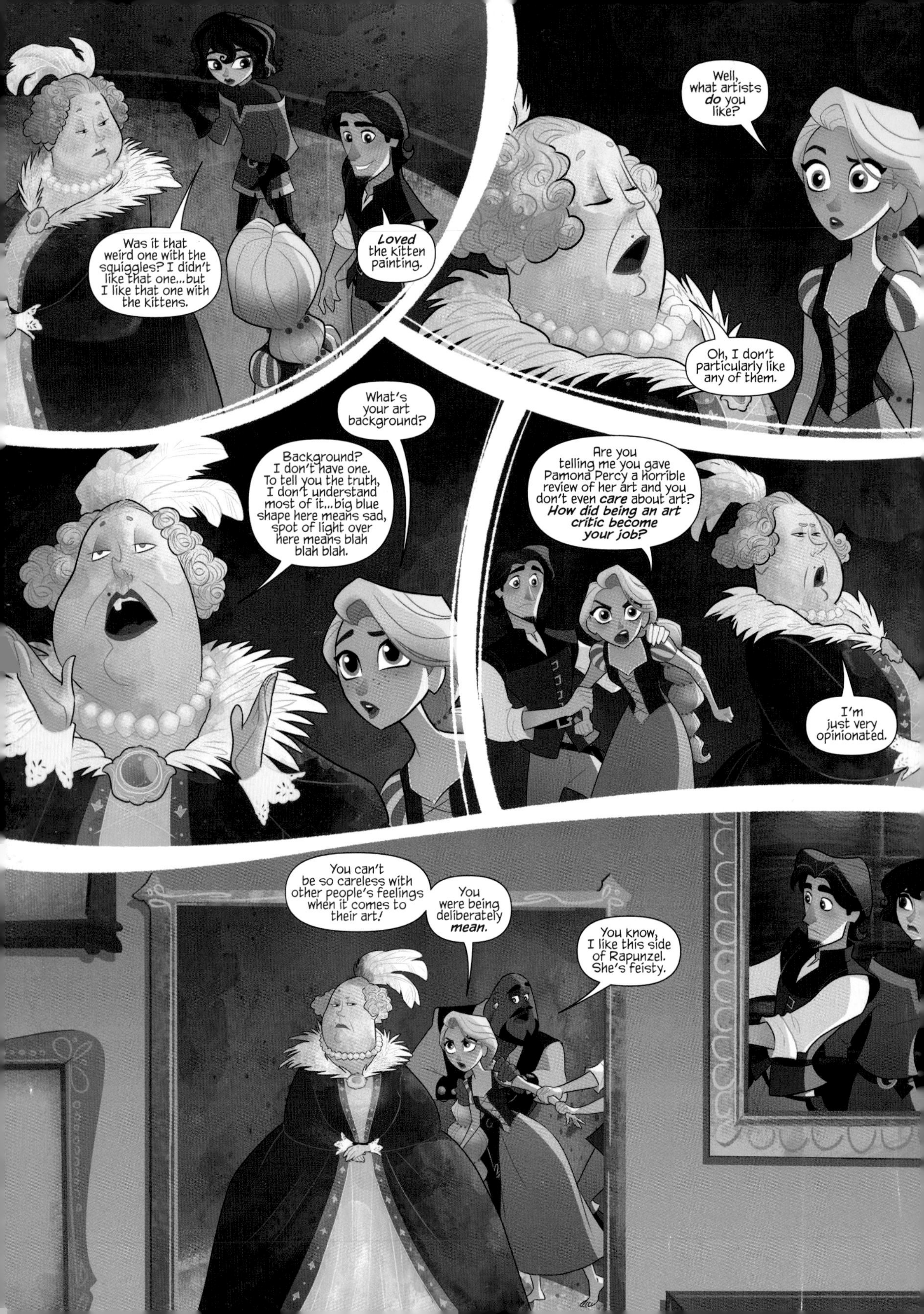
Was it that weird one with the squiggles? I didn't like that one...but I like that one with the kittens.
Loved the kitten painting.
Well, what artists ***do*** you like?
Oh, I don't particularly like any of them.
What's your art background?
Background? I don't have one. To tell you the truth, I don't understand most of it...big blue shape here means sad, spot of light over here means blah blah blah.
Are you telling me you gave Pamona Percy a horrible review of her art and you don't even ***care*** about art? ***How did being an art critic become your job?***
I'm just very opinionated.
You can't be so careless with other people's feelings when it comes to their art!
You were being deliberately ***mean.***
You know, I like this side of Rapunzel. She's feisty.

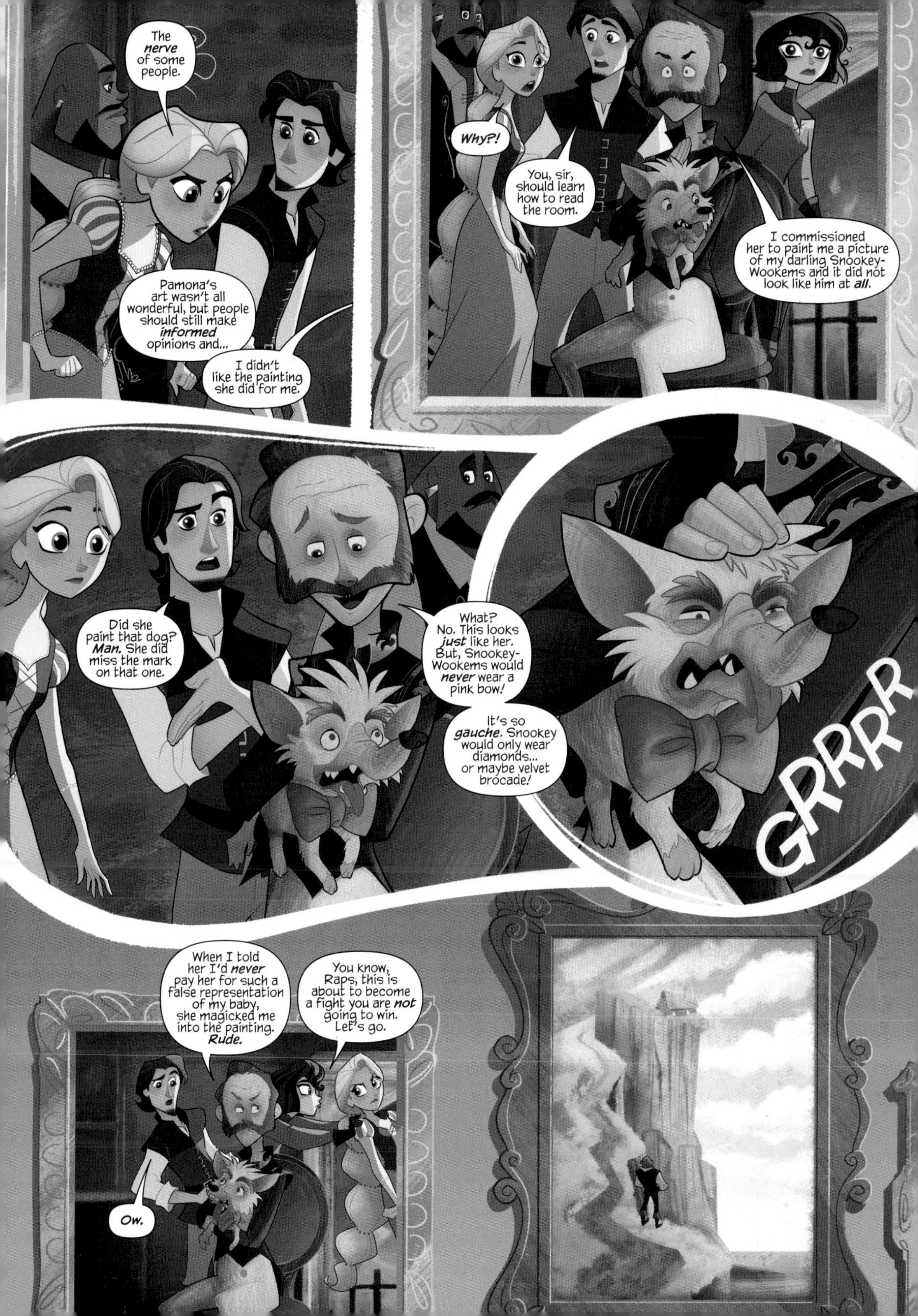
The nerve of some people.
Pamona's art wasn't all wonderful, but people should still make informed opinions and...
I didn't like the painting she did for me.
Why?!
You, sir, should learn how to read the room.
I commissioned her to paint me a picture of my darling Snookey-Wookems and it did not look like him at all.
Did she paint that dog? Man. She did miss the mark on that one.
What? No. This looks just like her. But, Snookey-Wookems would never wear a pink bow!
It's so gauche. Snookey would only wear diamonds... or maybe velvet brocade!
GRRRR
When I told her I'd never pay her for such a false representation of my baby, she magicked me into the painting. Rude.
You know, Raps, this is about to become a fight you are not going to win. Let's go.
Ow.

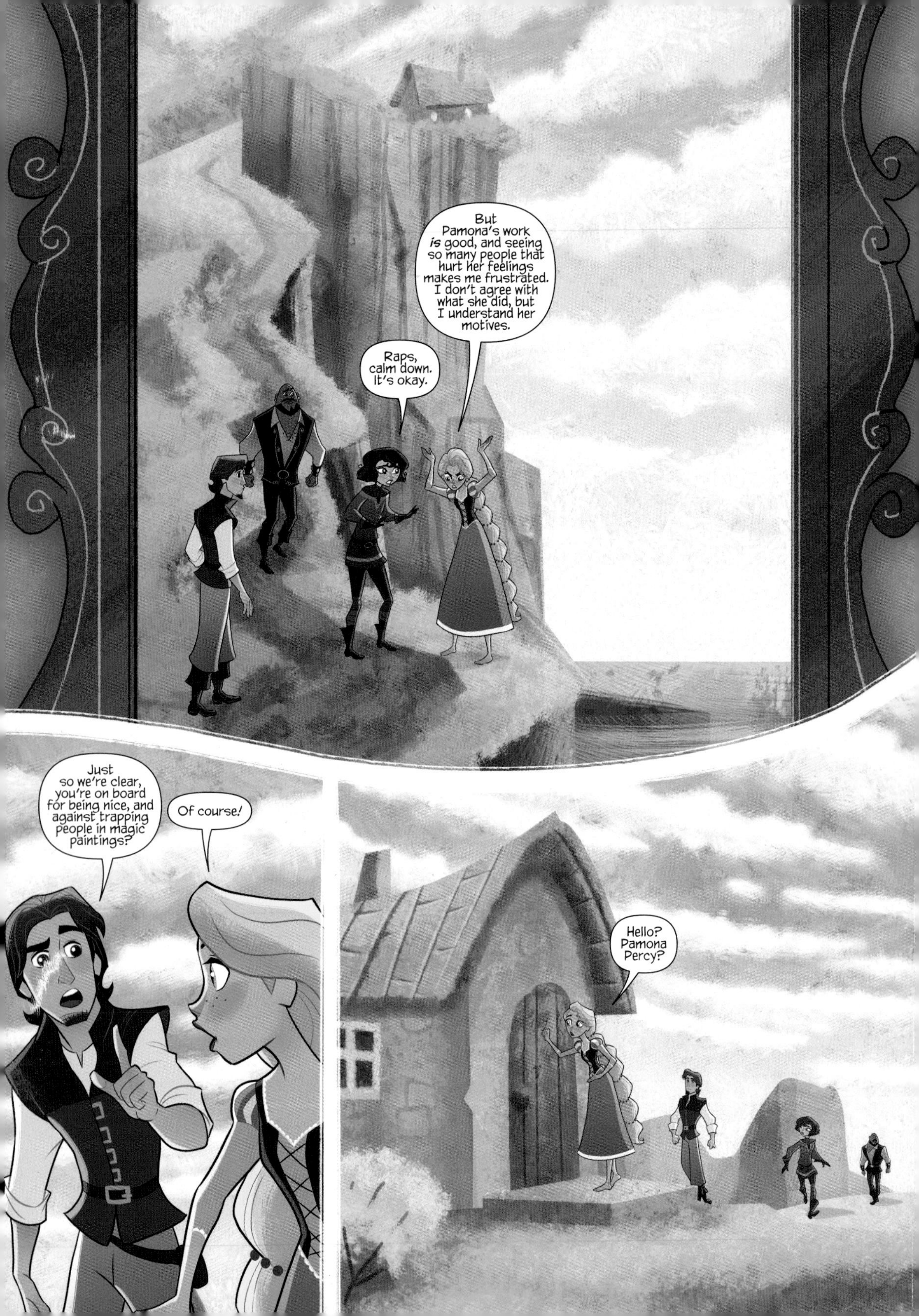
But Pamona's work *is* good, and seeing so many people that hurt her feelings makes me frustrated. I don't agree with what she did, but I understand her motives.
Raps, calm down. It's okay.
Just so we're clear, you're on board for being nice, and against trapping people in magic paintings?
Of course!
Hello? Pamona Percy?

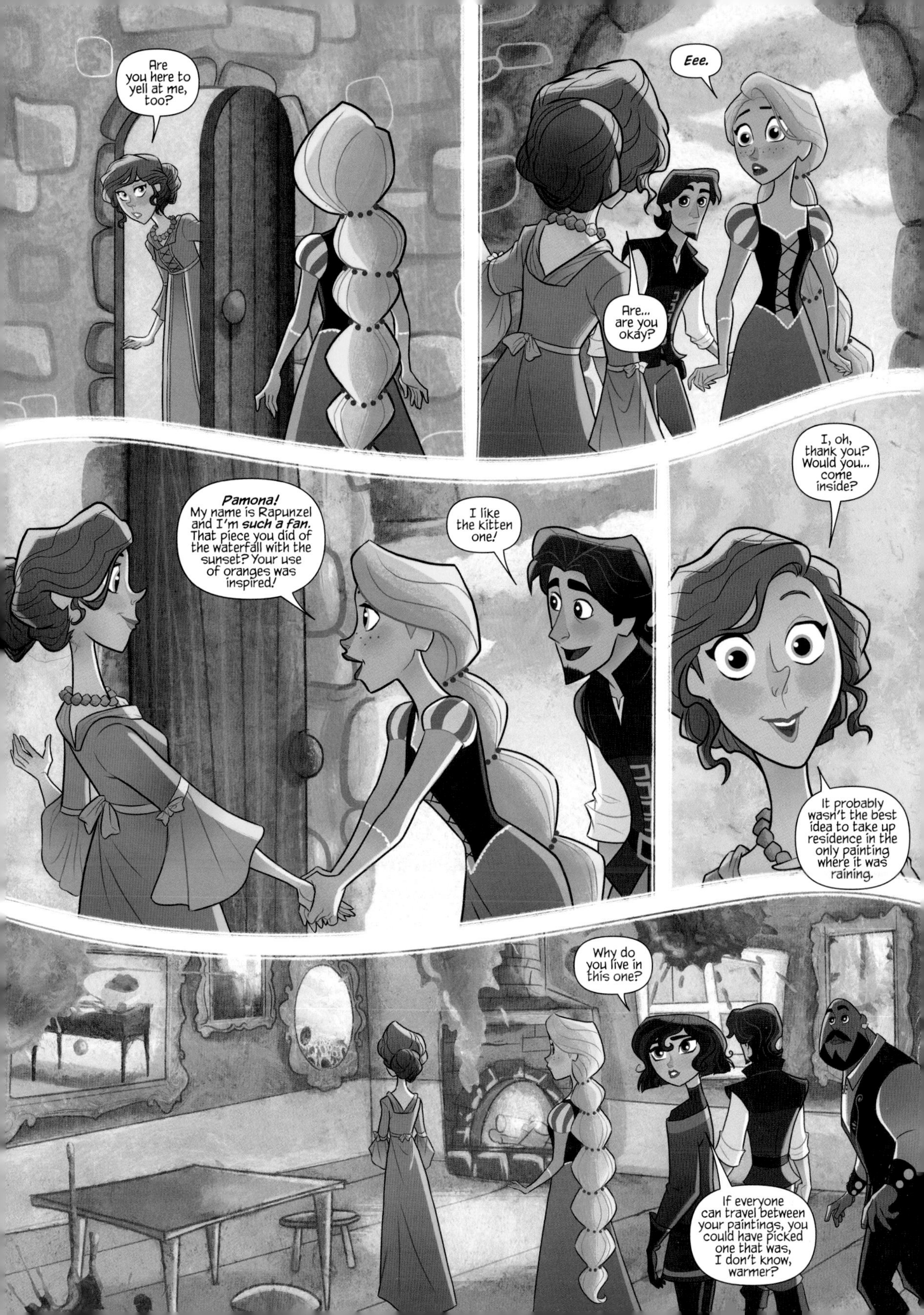
Are you here to yell at me, too?
Eee.
Are... are you okay?
Pamona! My name is Rapunzel and I'm such a fan. That piece you did of the waterfall with the sunset? Your use of oranges was inspired!
I like the kitten one!
I, oh, thank you? Would you... come inside?
It probably wasn't the best idea to take up residence in the only painting where it was raining.
Why do you live in this one?
If everyone can travel between your paintings, you could have picked one that was, I don't know, warmer?

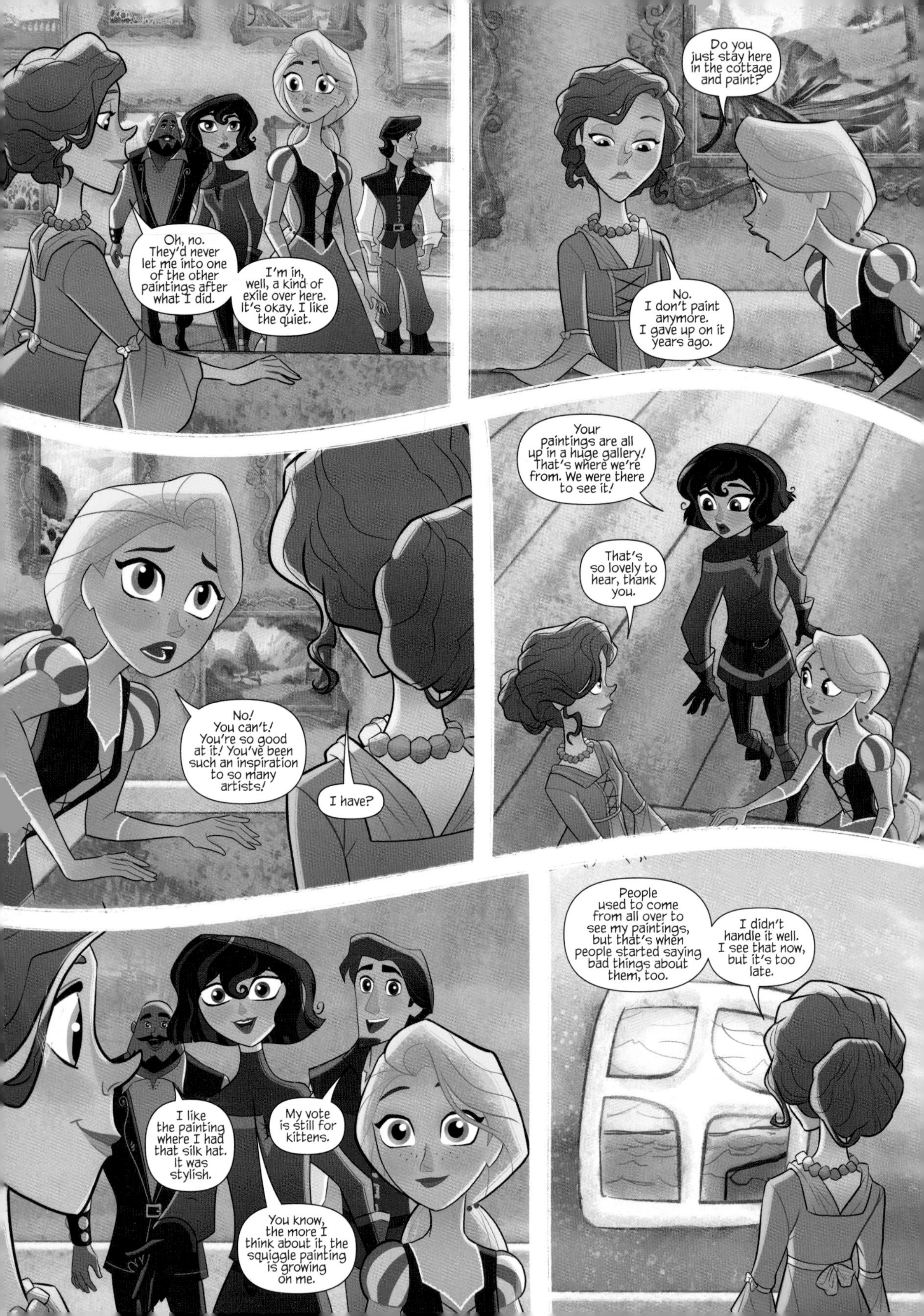

Oh, no. They'd never let me into one of the other paintings after what I did.
I'm in, well, a kind of exile over here. It's okay. I like the quiet.
Do you just stay here in the cottage and paint?
No. I don't paint anymore. I gave up on it years ago.
No! You can't! You're so good at it! You've been such an inspiration to so many artists!
I have?
Your paintings are all up in a huge gallery! That's where we're from. We were there to see it!
That's so lovely to hear, thank you.
I like the painting where I had that silk hat. It was stylish.
My vote is still for kittens.
You know, the more I think about it, the squiggle painting is growing on me.
People used to come from all over to see my paintings, but that's when people started saying bad things about them, too.
I didn't handle it well. I see that now, but it's too late.

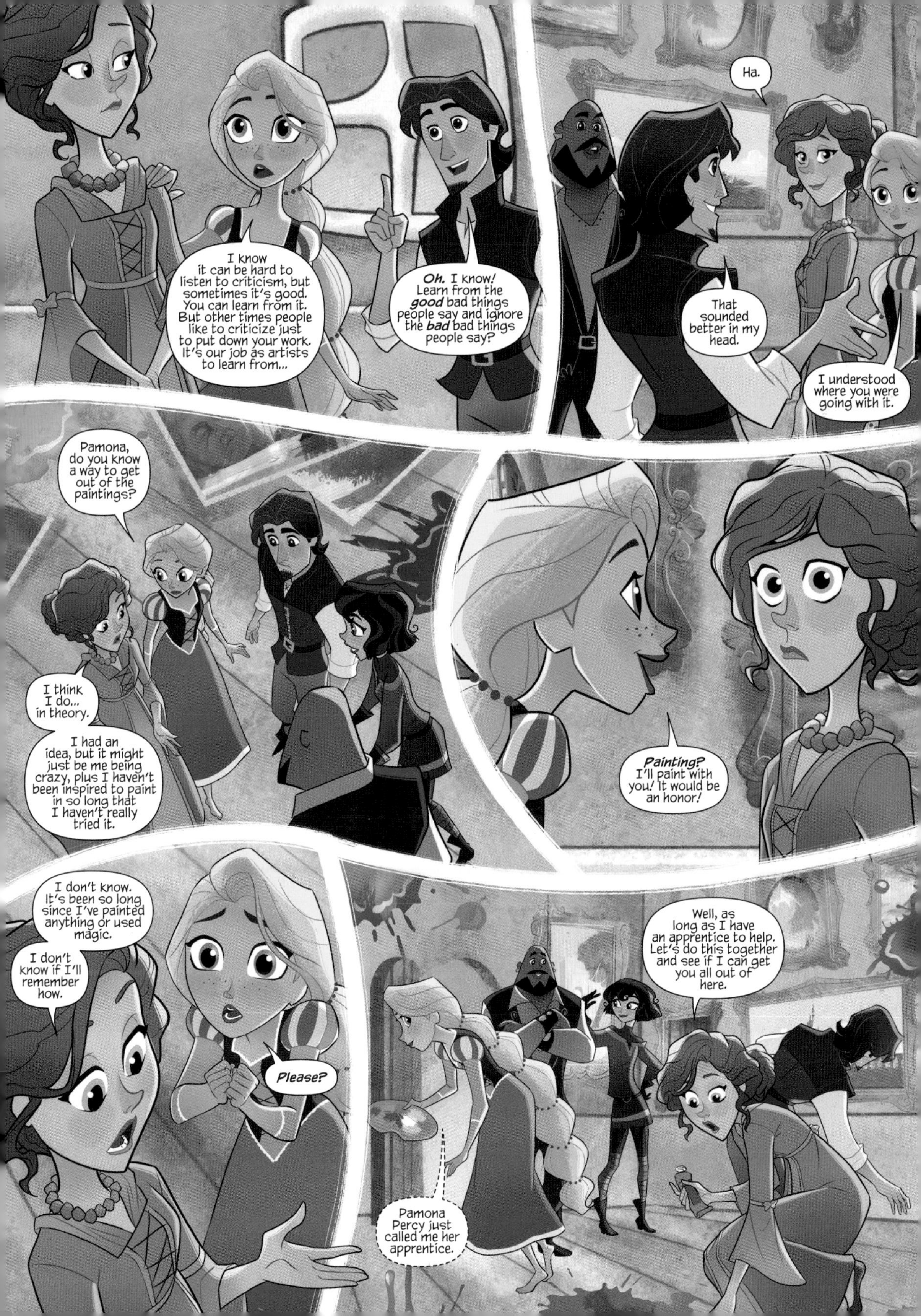
I know it can be hard to listen to criticism, but sometimes it's good. You can learn from it. But other times people like to criticize just to put down your work. It's our job as artists to learn from...
Oh. I know! Learn from the good bad things people say and ignore the bad bad things people say?
Ha.
That sounded better in my head.
I understood where you were going with it.
Pamona, do you know a way to get out of the paintings?
I think I do... in theory.
I had an idea, but it might just be me being crazy, plus I haven't been inspired to paint in so long that I haven't really tried it.
Painting? I'll paint with you! It would be an honor!
I don't know. It's been so long since I've painted anything or used magic.
I don't know if I'll remember how.
Please?
Well, as long as I have an apprentice to help. Let's do this together and see if I can get you all out of here.
Pamona Percy just called me her apprentice.

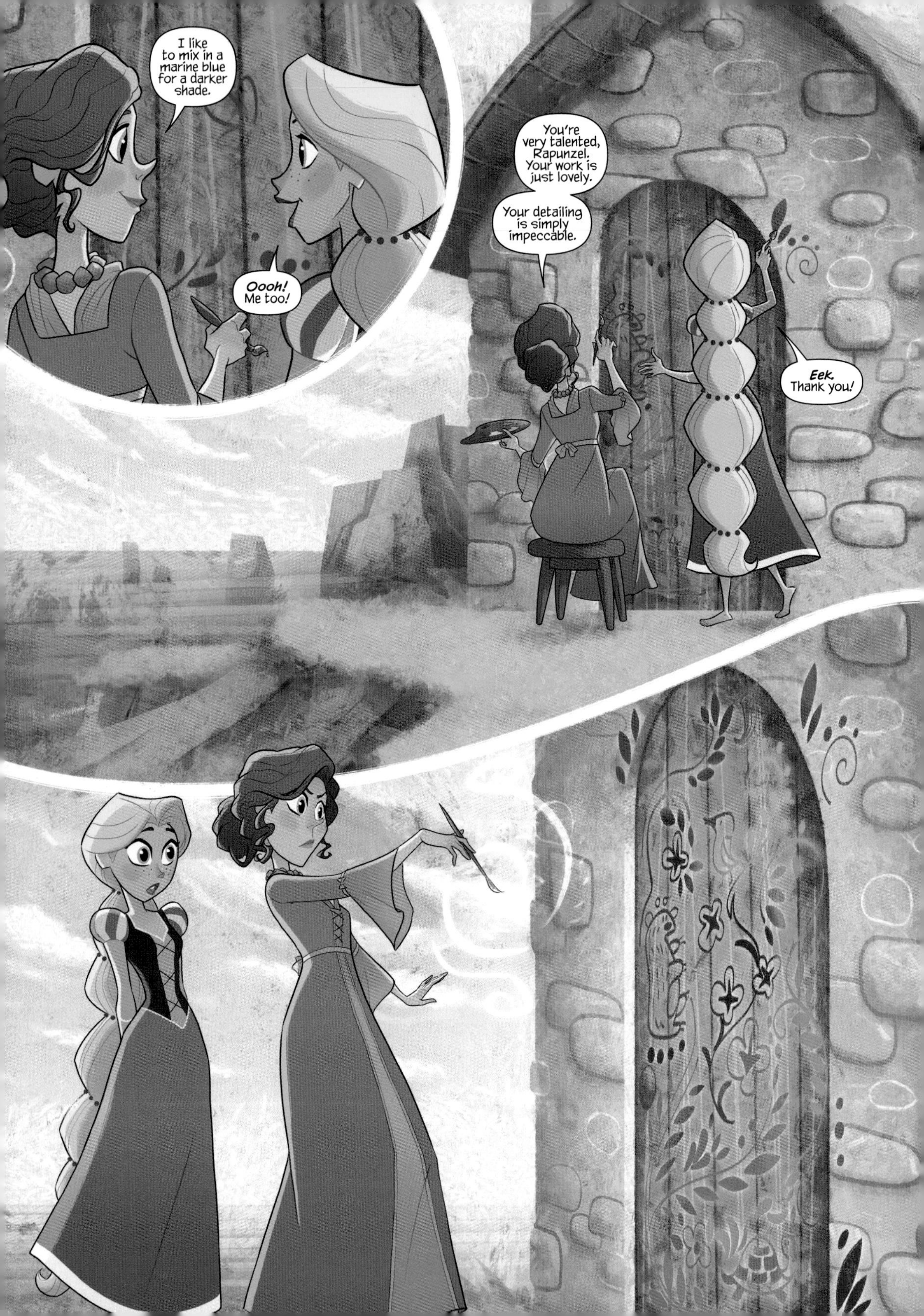

I like to mix in a marine blue for a darker shade.
Oooh! Me too!
You're very talented, Rapunzel. Your work is just lovely.
Your detailing is simply impeccable.
Eek. Thank you!

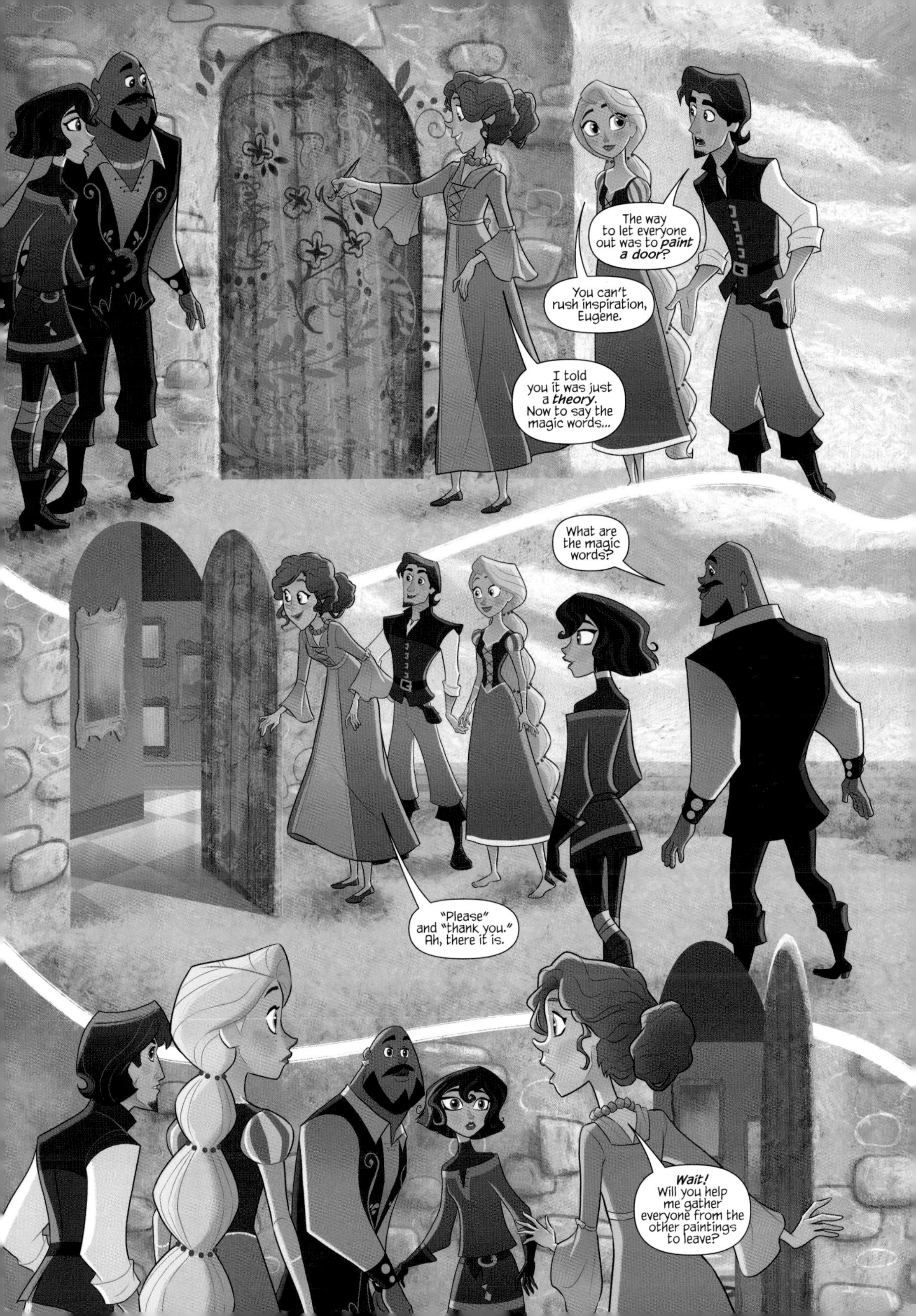
The way to let everyone out was to *paint a door*?
You can't rush inspiration, Eugene.
I told you it was just a *theory*. Now to say the magic words...
What are the magic words?
"Please" and "thank you." Ah, there it is.
Wait! Will you help me gather everyone from the other paintings to leave?

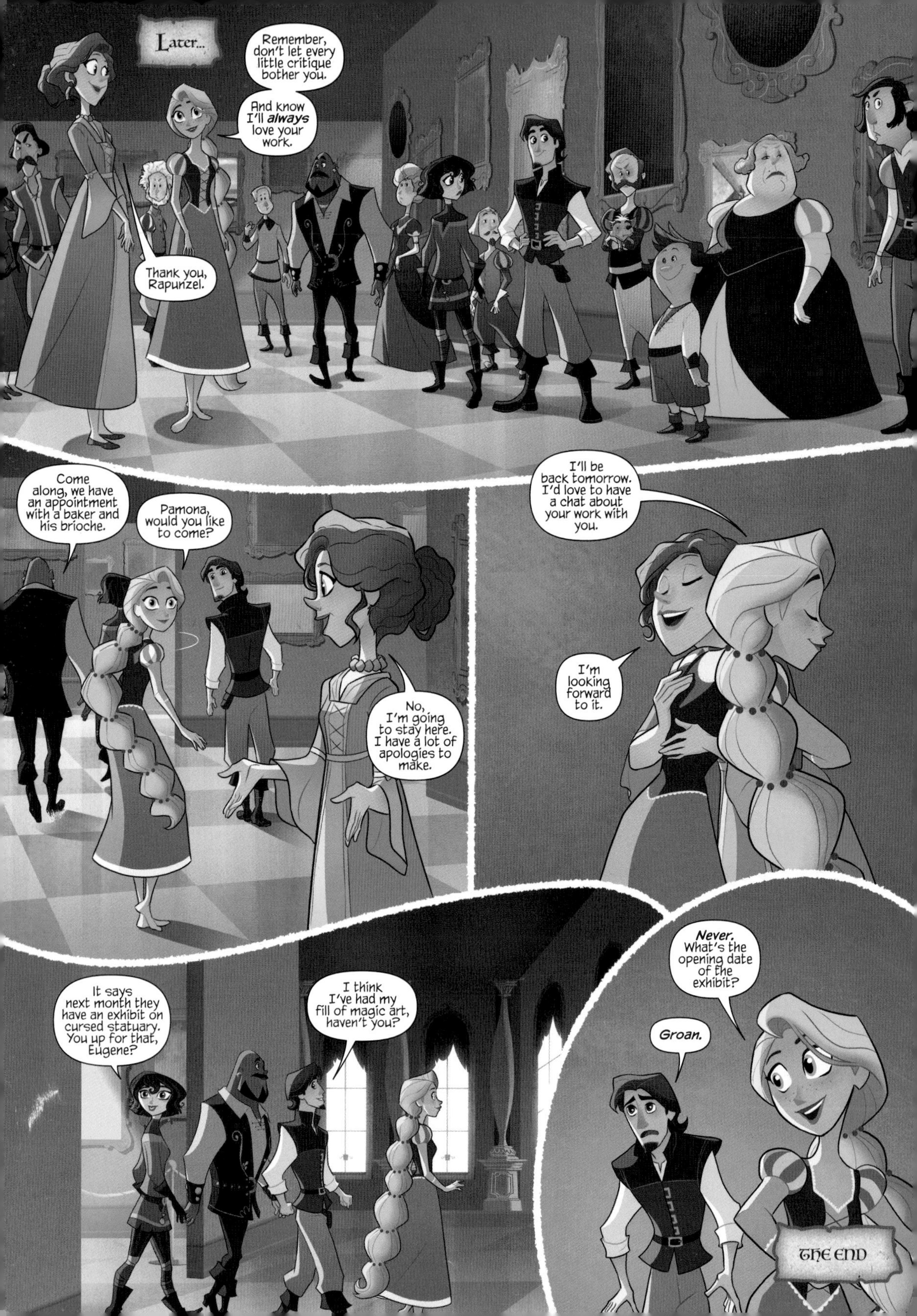
Later...
Remember, don't let every little critique bother you.
And know I'll *always* love your work.
Thank you, Rapunzel.
Come along, we have an appointment with a baker and his brioche.
Pamona, would you like to come?
No, I'm going to stay here. I have a lot of apologies to make.
I'll be back tomorrow. I'd love to have a chat about your work with you.
I'm looking forward to it.
It says next month they have an exhibit on cursed statuary. You up for that, Eugene?
I think I've had my fill of magic art, haven't you?
Never. What's the opening date of the exhibit?
Groan.
THE END

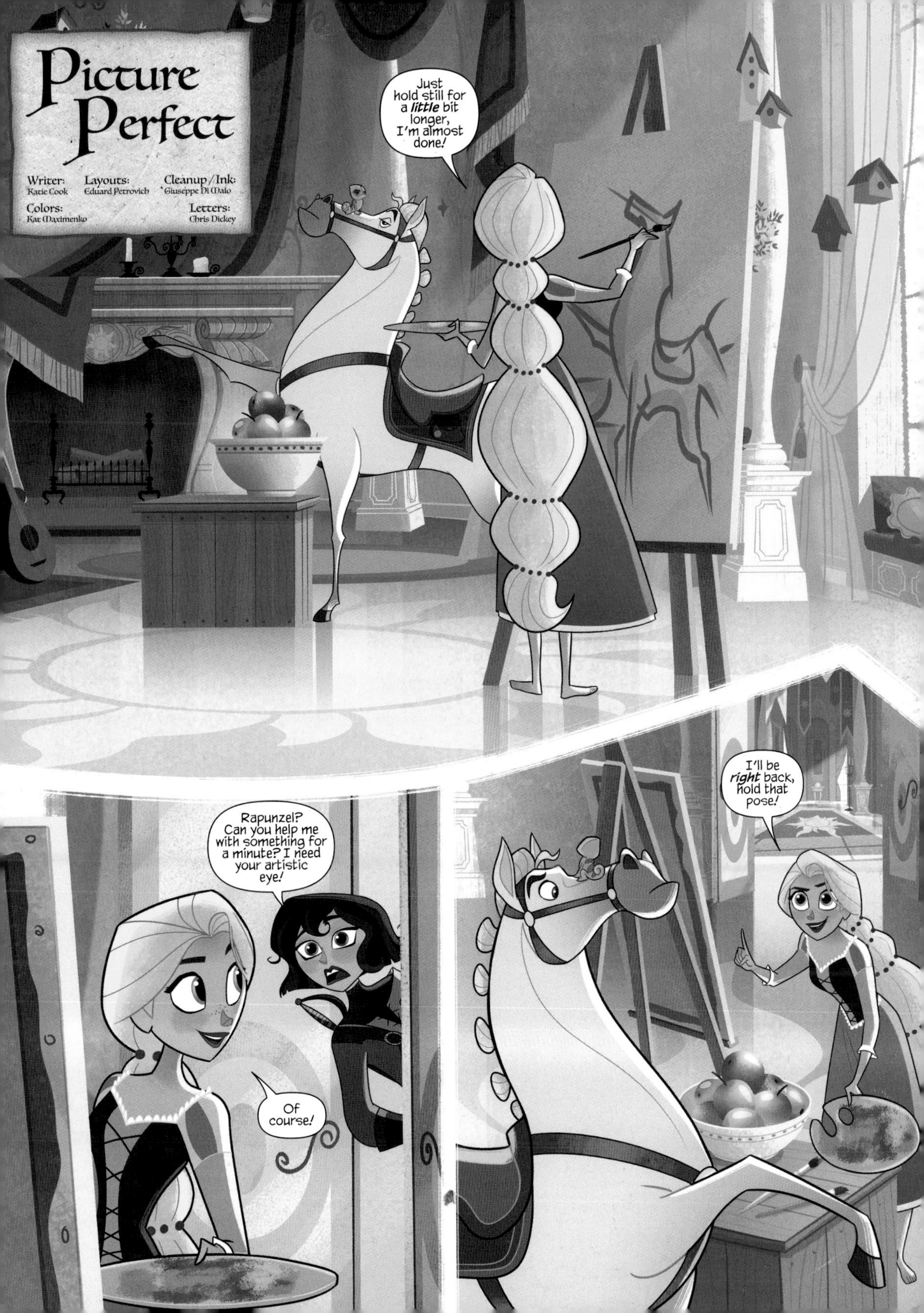
Picture Perfect
Writer: Katie Cook
Layouts: Eduard Petrovich
Cleanup/Ink: Giuseppe Di Maio
Colors: Kat Maximenko
Letters: Chris Dickey
Just hold still for a *little* bit longer, I'm almost done!
Rapunzel? Can you help me with something for a minute? I need your artistic eye!
Of course!
I'll be *right* back, hold that pose!

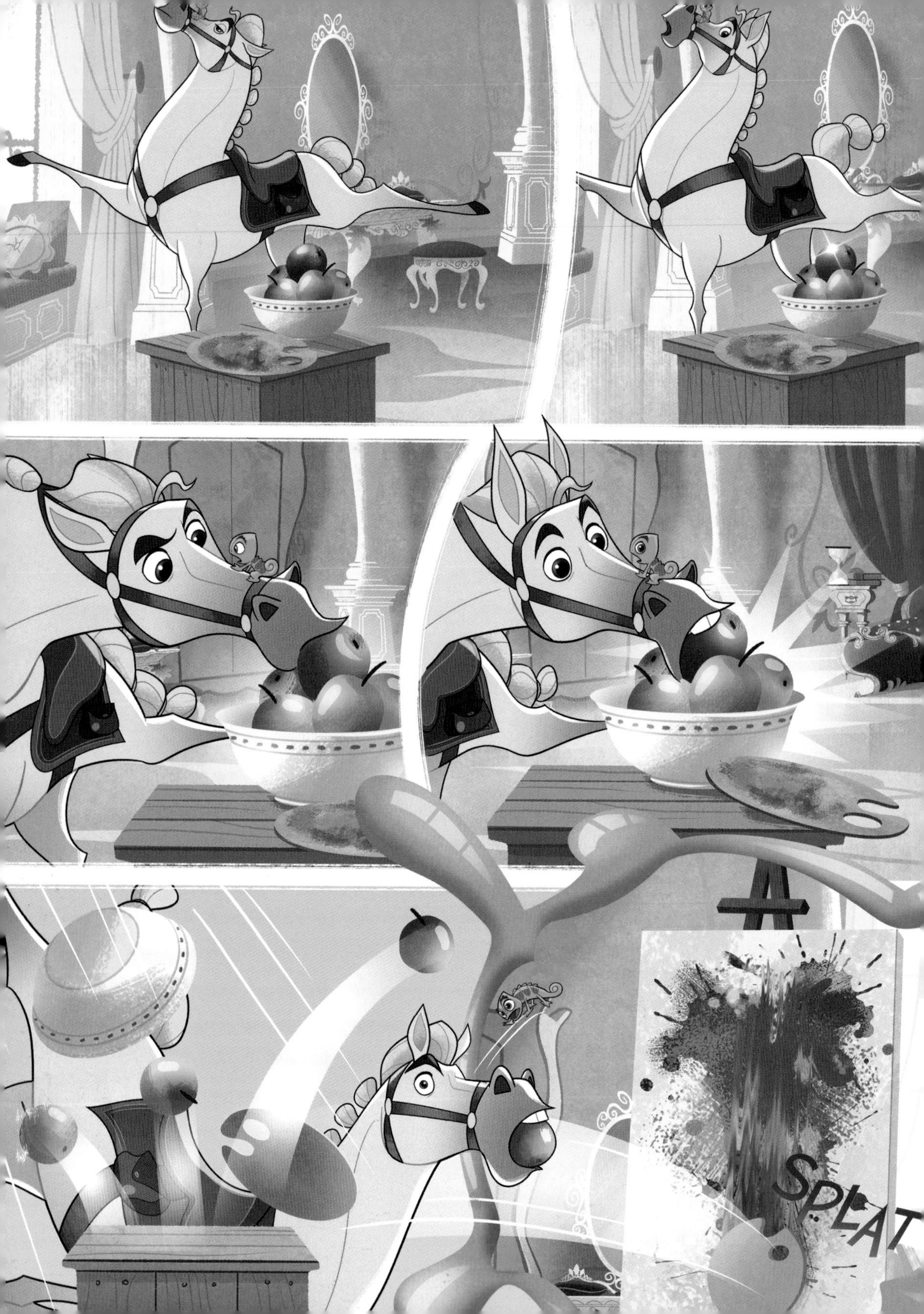
SPLAT

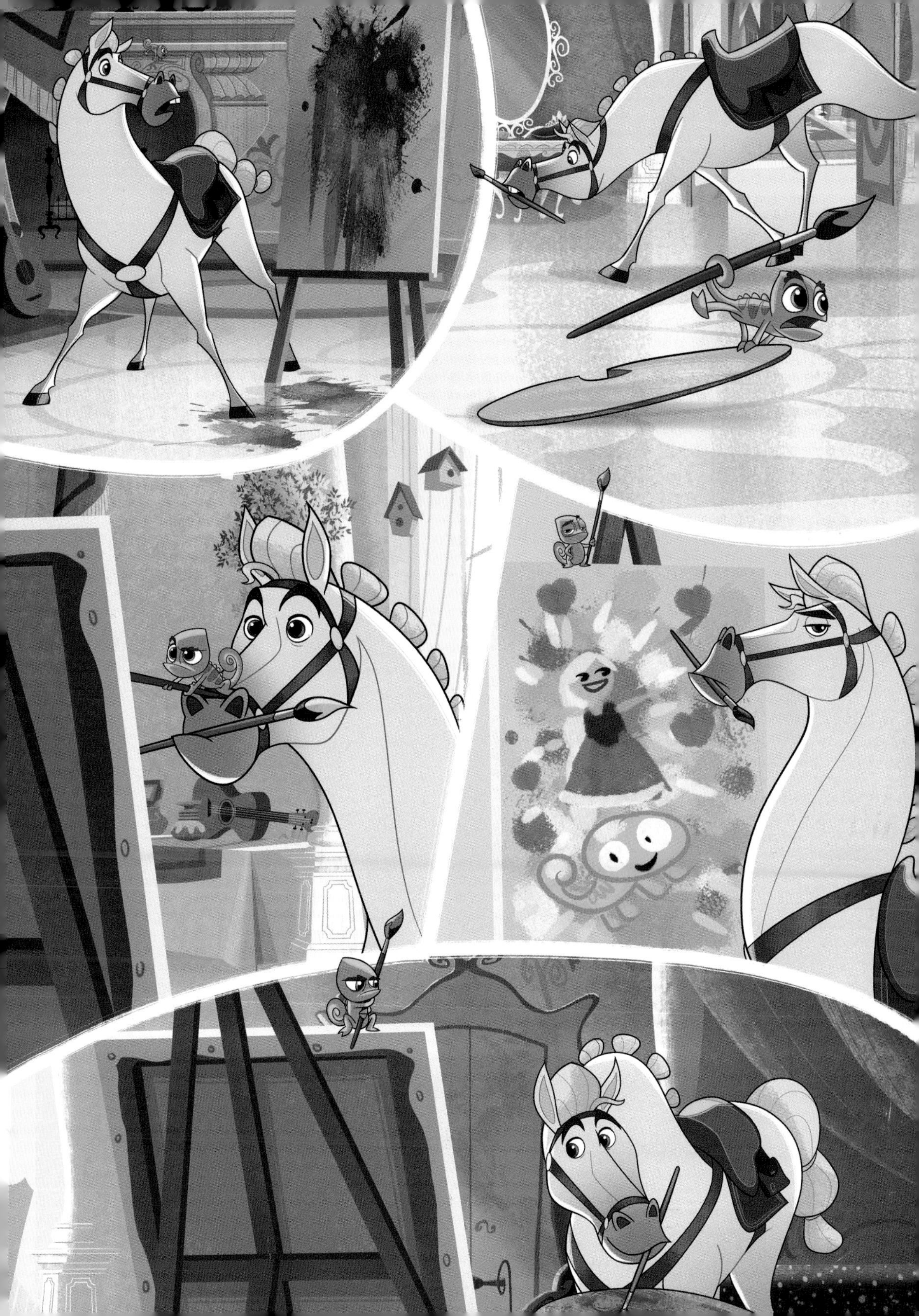

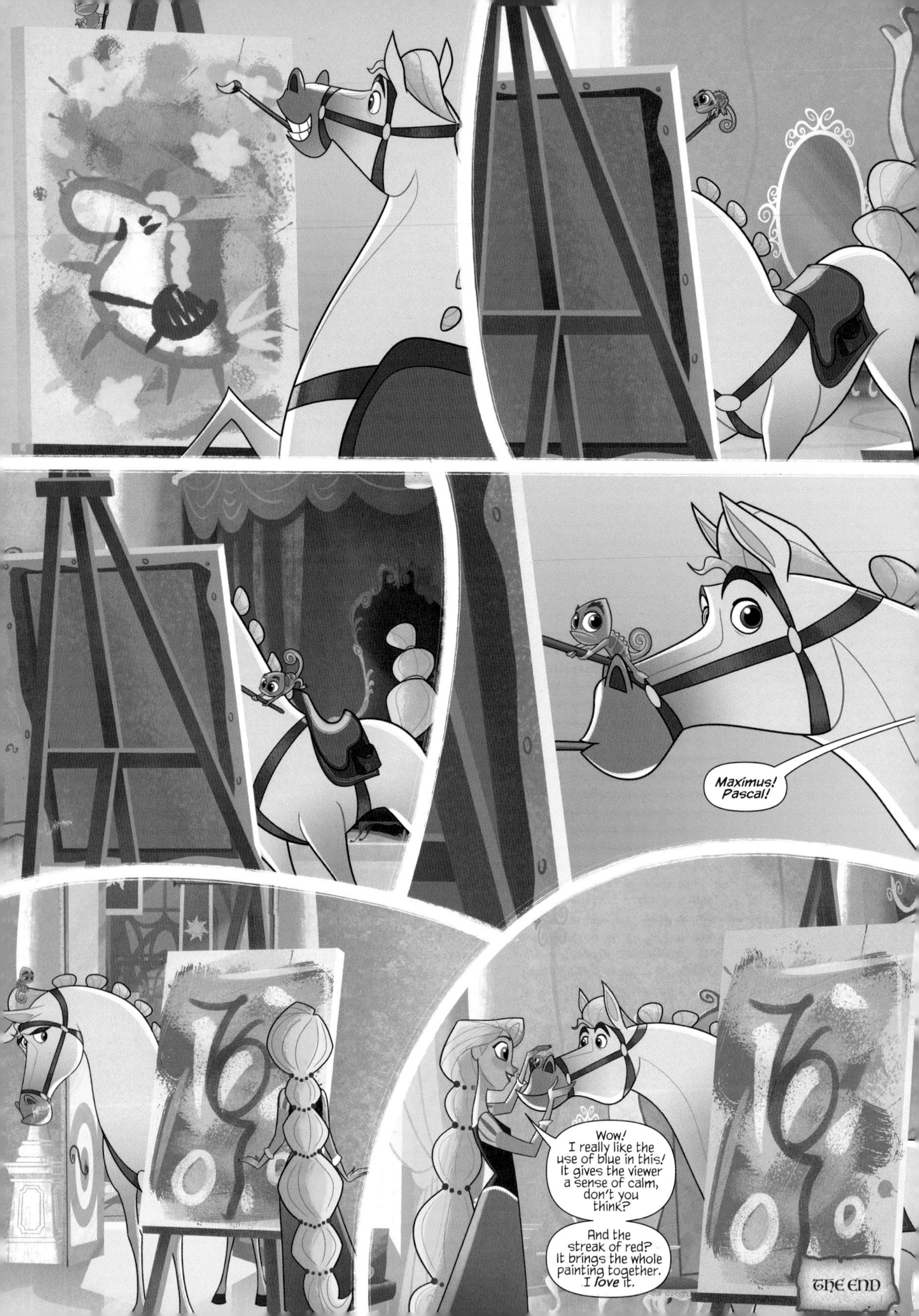
Maximus!
Pascal!
Wow! I really like the use of blue in this! It gives the viewer a sense of calm, don't you think?
And the streak of red? It brings the whole painting together. I *love* it.
THE END

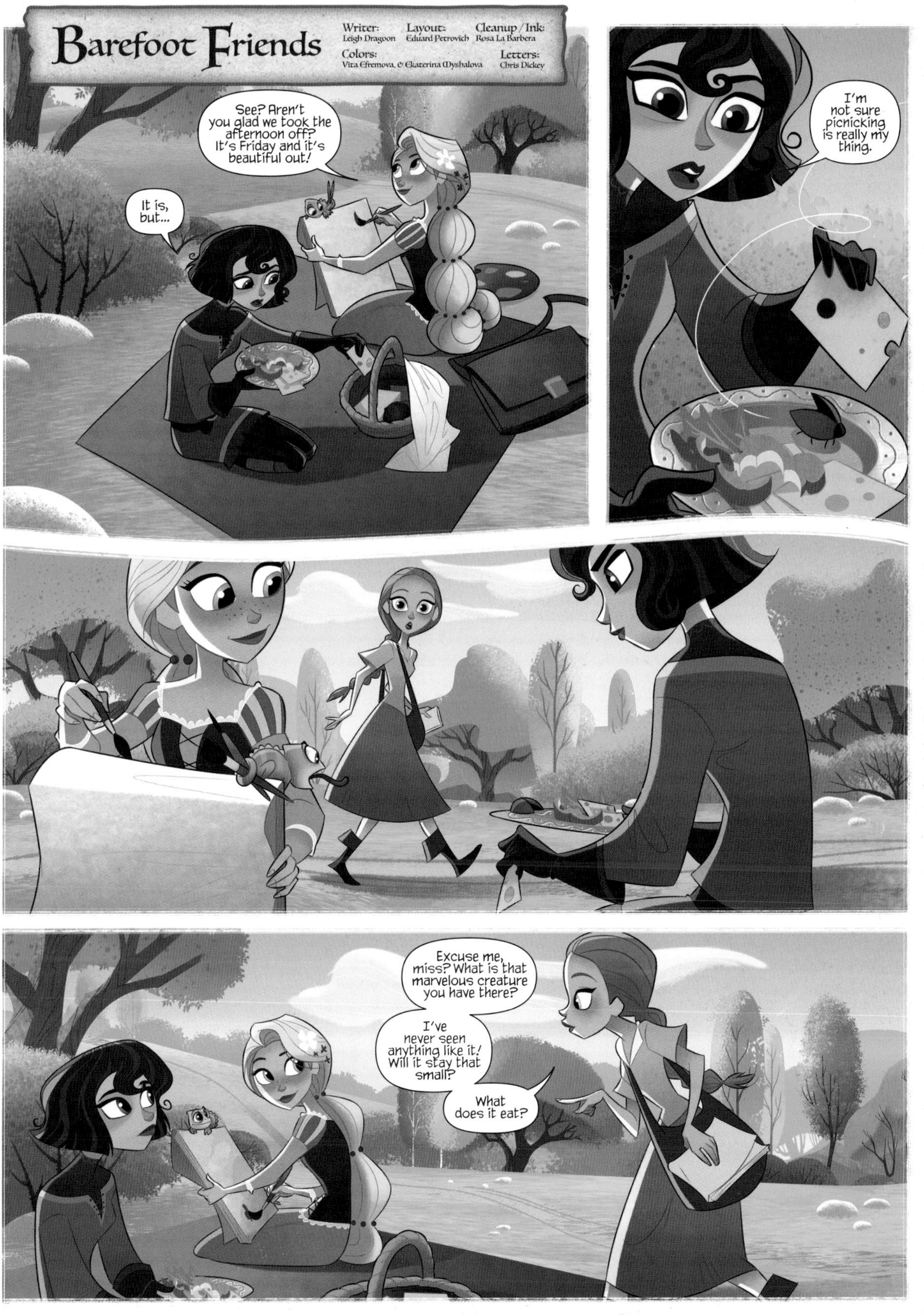
Barefoot Friends
Writer: Leigh Dragoon
Layout: Eduard Petrovich
Cleanup / Ink: Rosa La Barbera
Colors: Vita Efremova, & Ekaterina Myshalova
Letters: Chris Dickey
See? Aren't you glad we took the afternoon off? It's Friday and it's beautiful out!
It is, but...
I'm not sure picnicking is really my thing.
Excuse me, miss? What is that marvelous creature you have there?
I've never seen anything like it! Will it stay that small?
What does it eat?

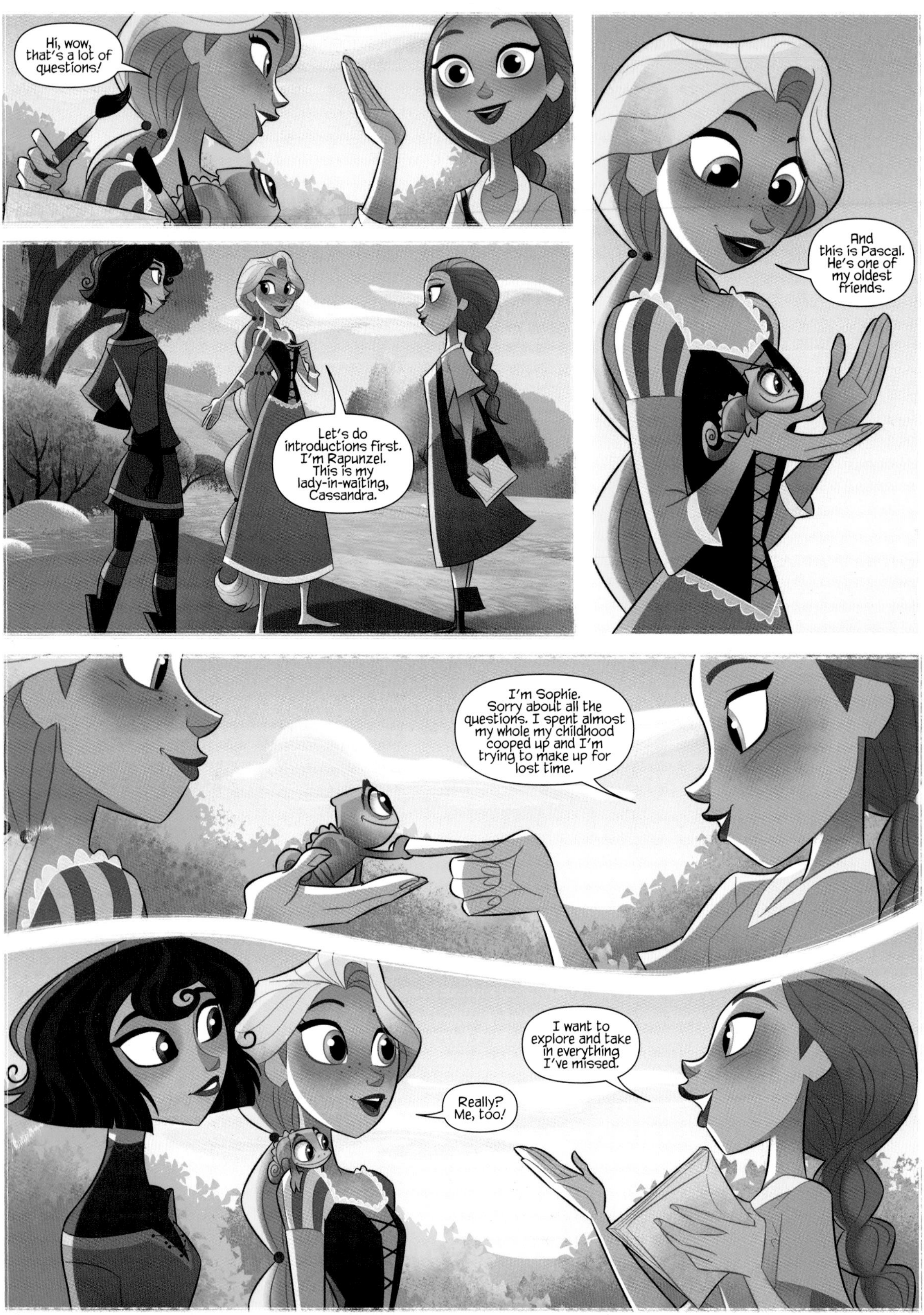
Hi, wow, that's a lot of questions!
Let's do introductions first. I'm Rapunzel. This is my lady-in-waiting, Cassandra.
And this is Pascal. He's one of my oldest friends.
I'm Sophie. Sorry about all the questions. I spent almost my whole my childhood cooped up and I'm trying to make up for lost time.
I want to explore and take in everything I've missed.
Really? Me, too!

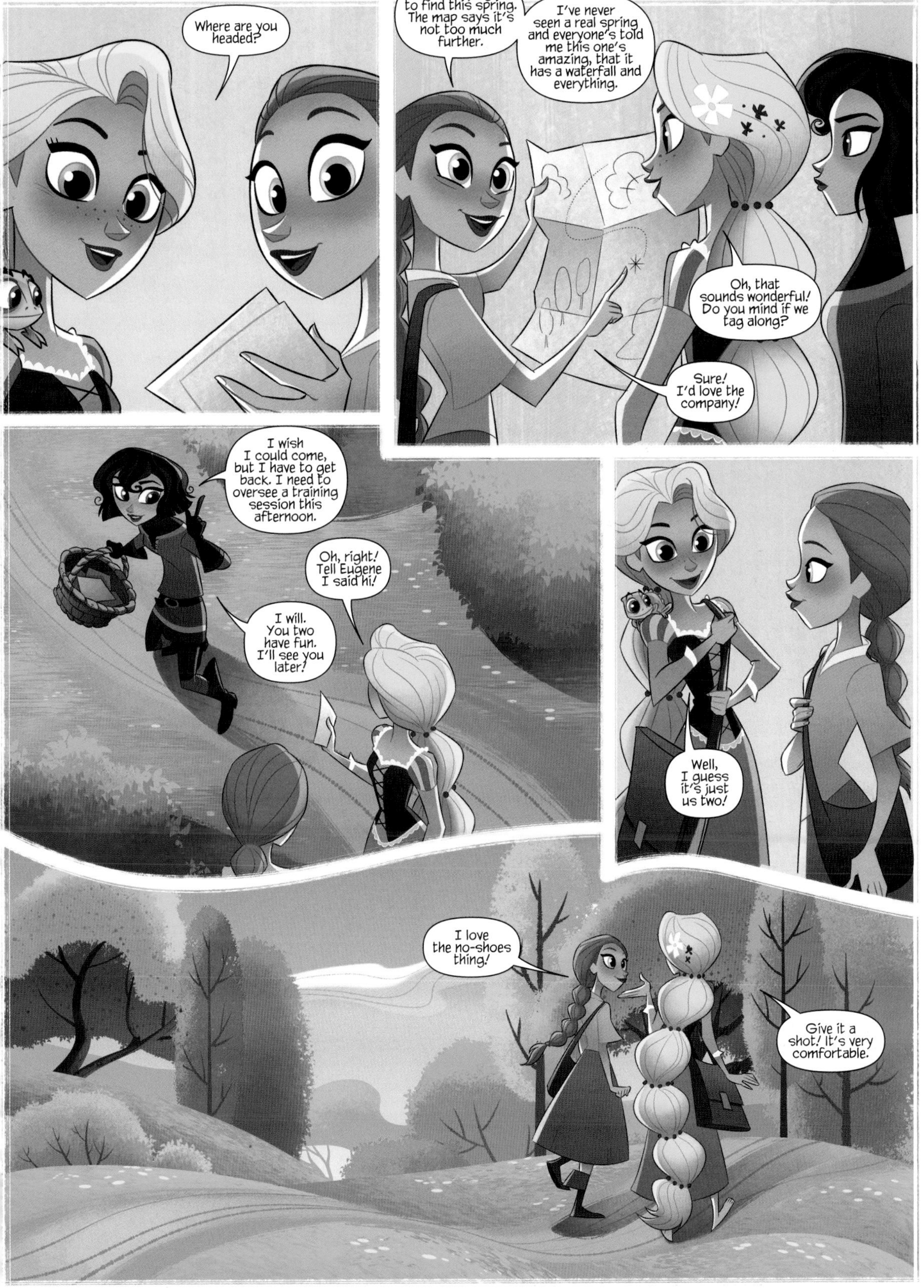
Where are you headed?
I'm trying to find this spring. The map says it's not too much further.
I've never seen a real spring and everyone's told me this one's amazing, that it has a waterfall and everything.
Oh, that sounds wonderful! Do you mind if we tag along?
Sure! I'd love the company!
I wish I could come, but I have to get back. I need to oversee a training session this afternoon.
Oh, right! Tell Eugene I said hi!
I will. You two have fun. I'll see you later!
Well, I guess it's just us two!
I love the no-shoes thing!
Give it a shot! It's very comfortable.

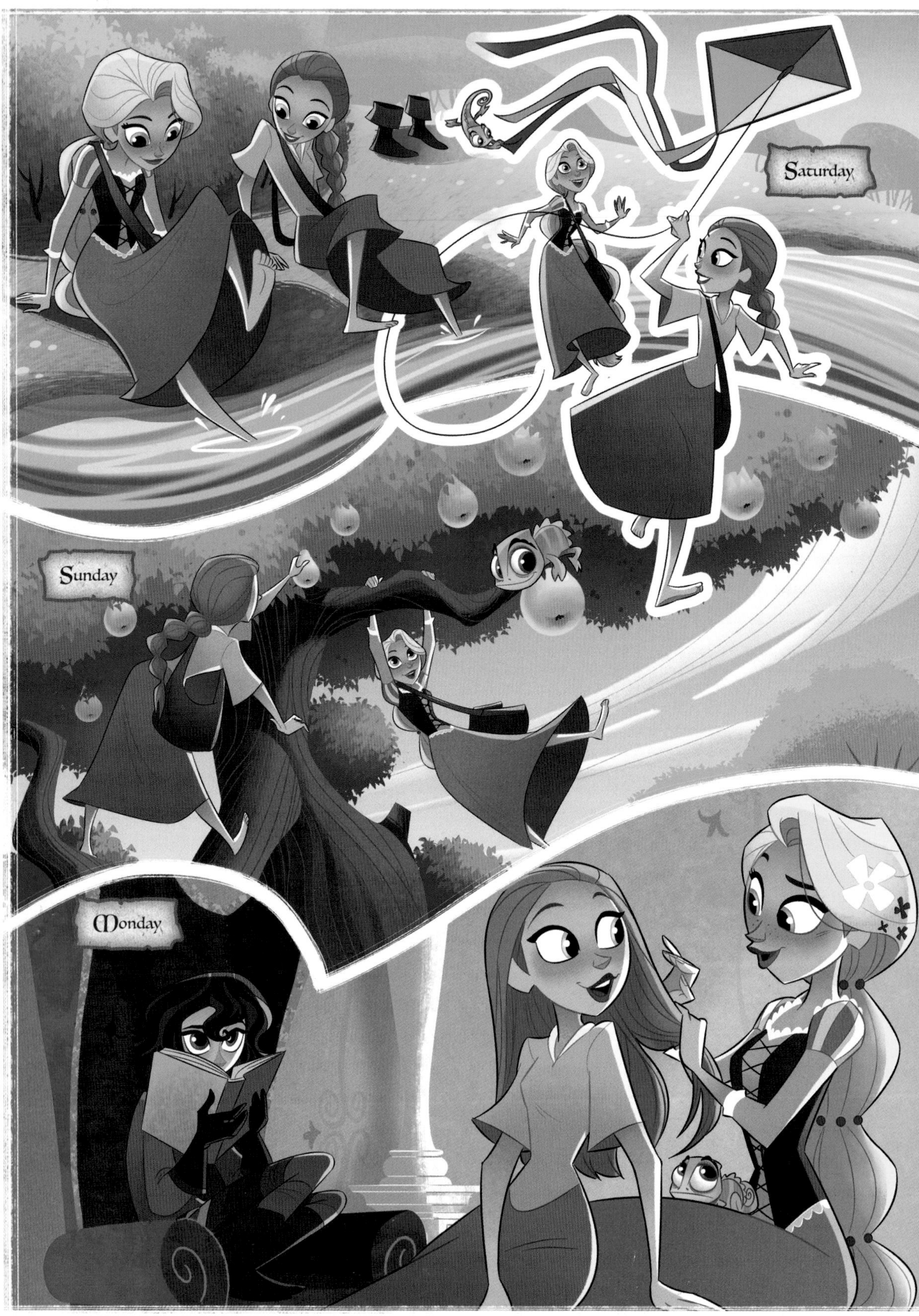
Saturday
Sunday
Monday

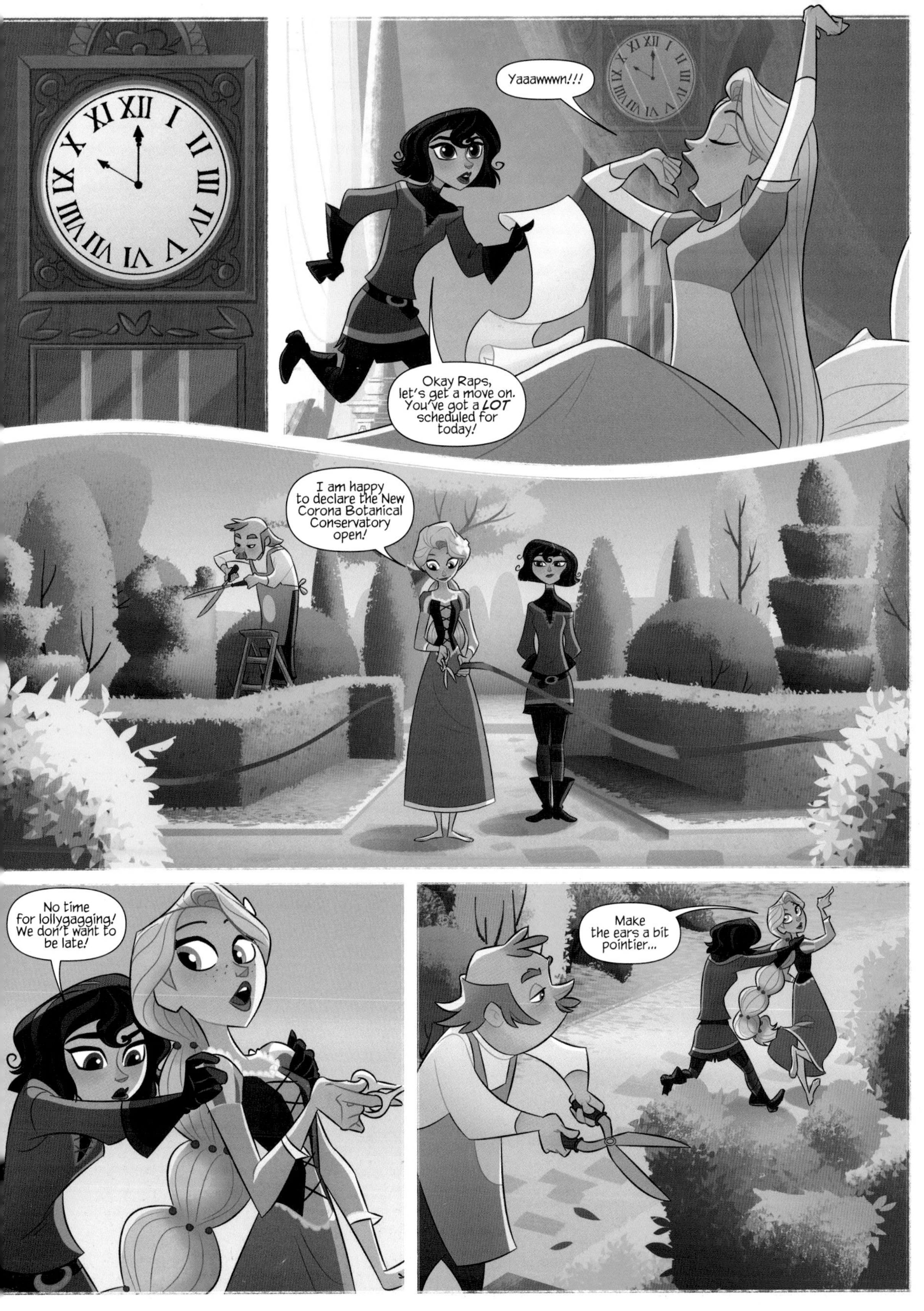

Yaaawwwn!!!
Okay Raps, let's get a move on. You've got a LOT scheduled for today!
I am happy to declare the New Corona Botanical Conservatory open!
No time for lollygagging! We don't want to be late!
Make the ears a bit pointier...

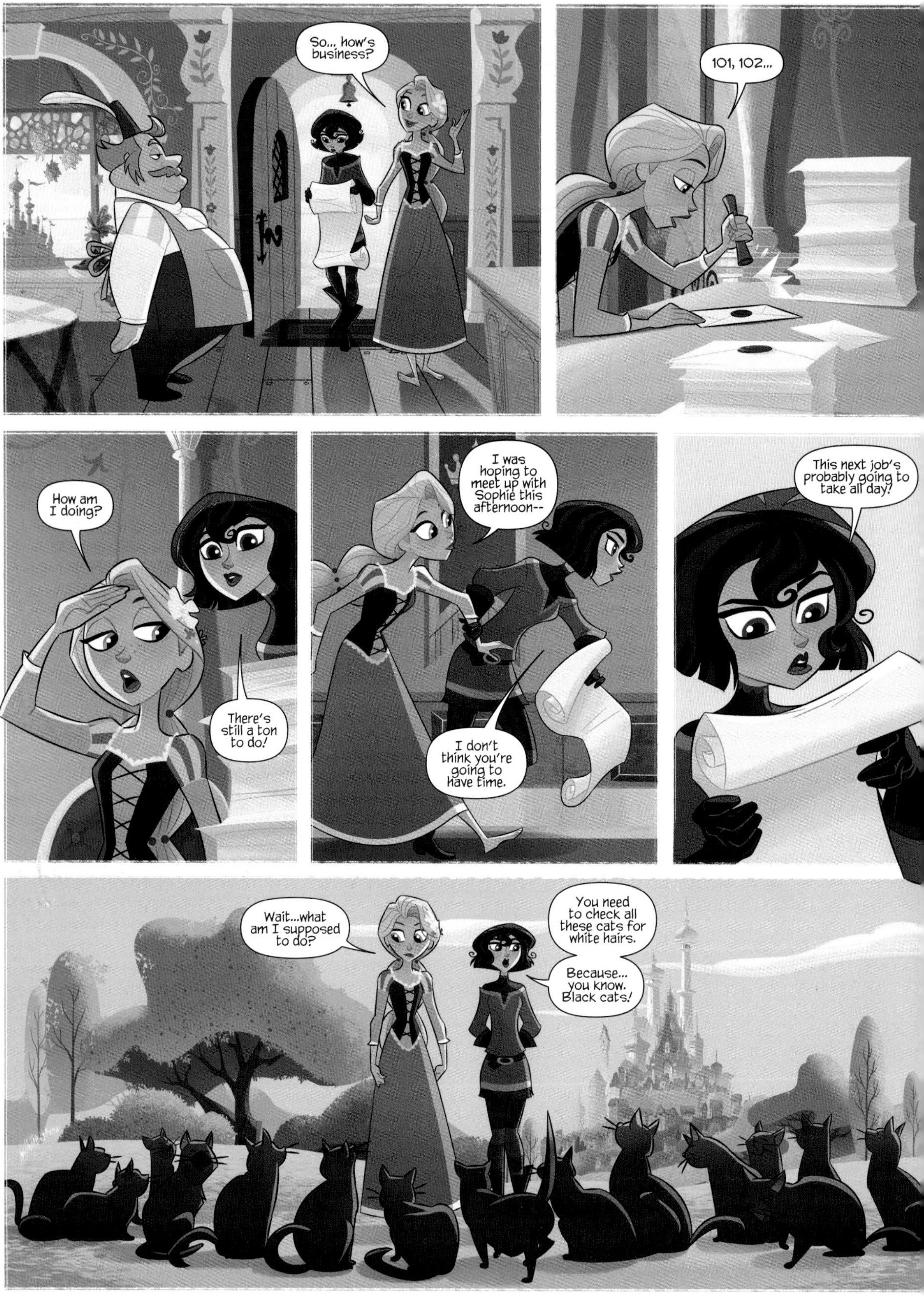

So... how's business?
101, 102...
How am I doing?
There's still a ton to do!
I was hoping to meet up with Sophie this afternoon--
I don't think you're going to have time.
This next job's probably going to take all day!
Wait...what am I supposed to do?
You need to check all these cats for white hairs.
Because... you know. Black cats!

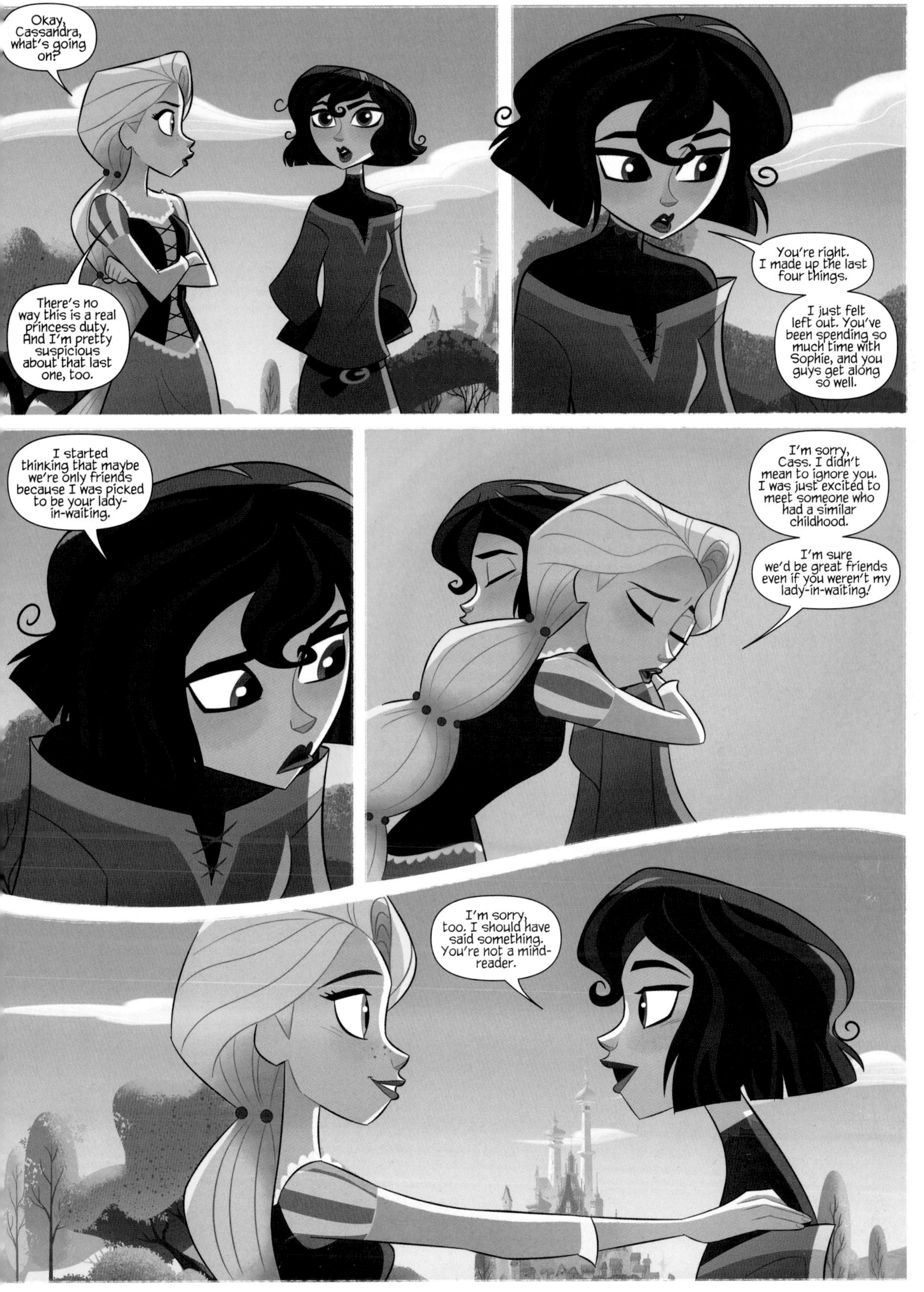
Okay, Cassandra, what's going on?
There's no way this is a real princess duty. And I'm pretty suspicious about that last one, too.
You're right. I made up the last four things.
I just felt left out. You've been spending so much time with Sophie, and you guys get along so well.
I started thinking that maybe we're only friends because I was picked to be your lady-in-waiting.
I'm sorry, Cass. I didn't mean to ignore you. I was just excited to meet someone who had a similar childhood.
I'm sure we'd be great friends even if you weren't my lady-in-waiting!
I'm sorry, too. I should have said something. You're not a mind-reader.

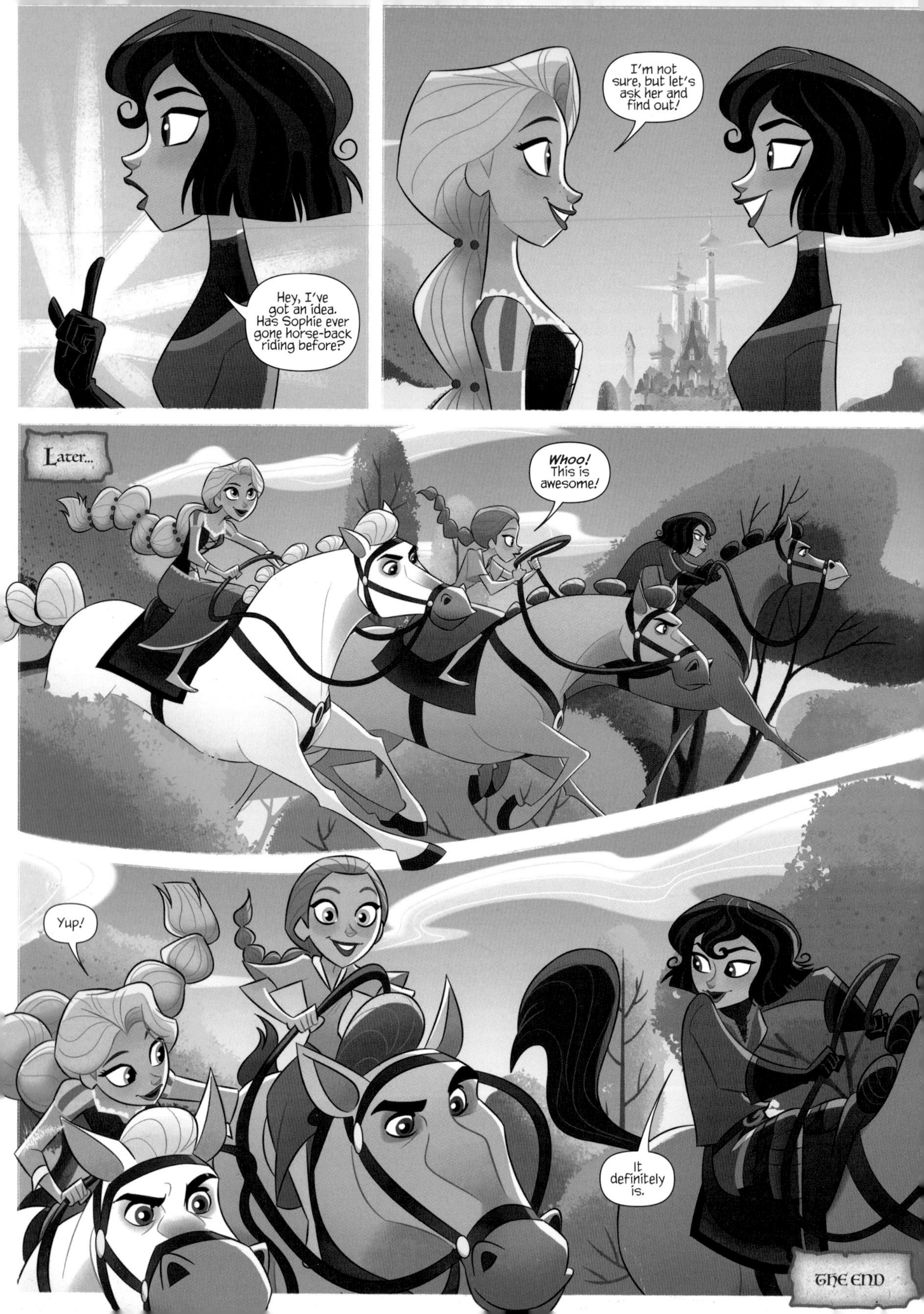

Hey, I've got an idea. Has Sophie ever gone horse-back riding before?
I'm not sure, but let's ask her and find out!
Later...
Whoo! This is awesome!
Yup!
It definitely is.
THE END

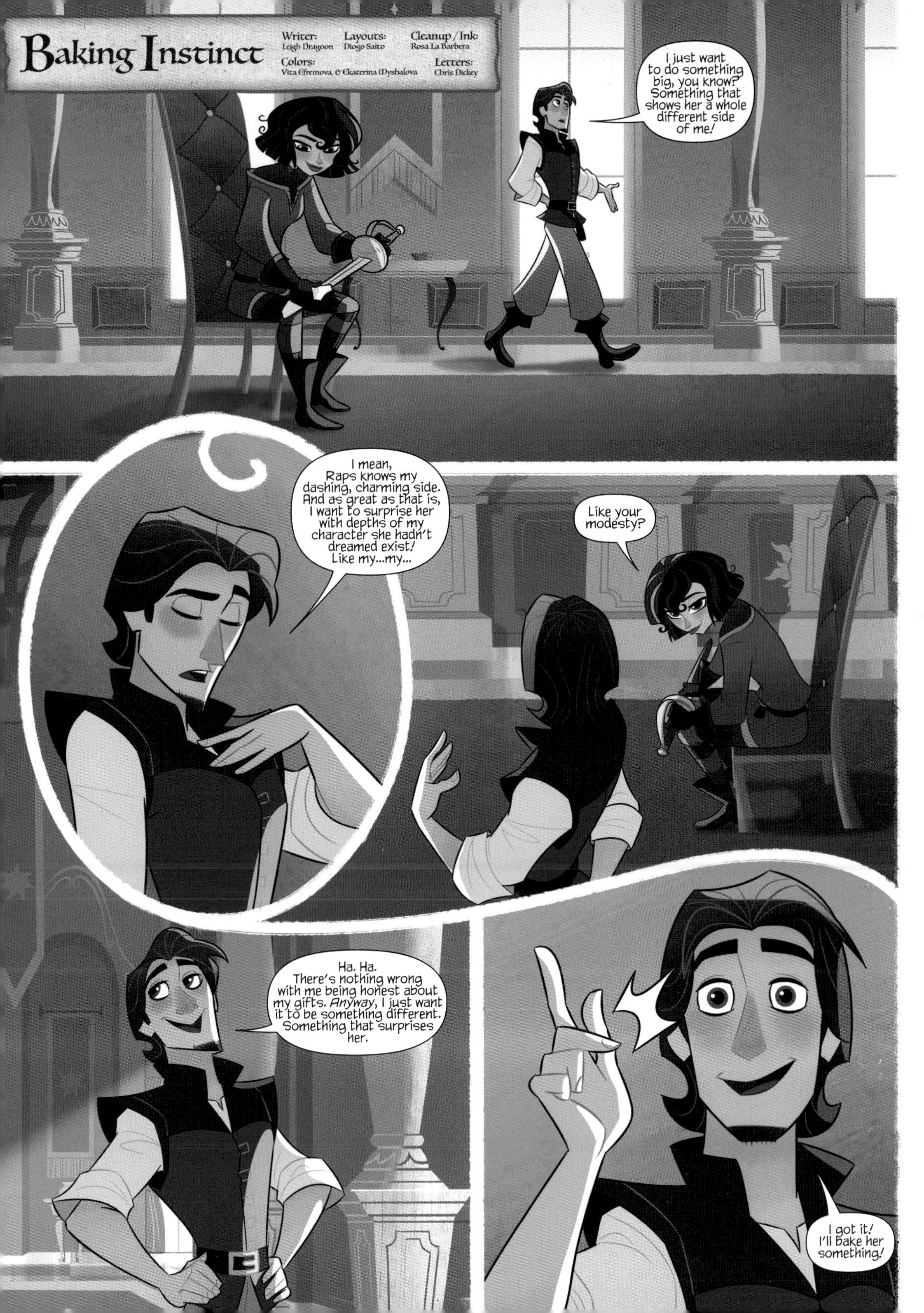

Baking Instinct
Writer: Leigh Dragoon
Layouts: Diogo Saito
Cleanup / Ink: Rosa La Barbera
Colors: Vita Efremova, & Ekaterina Myshalova
Letters: Chris Dickey
I just want to do something big, you know? Something that shows her a whole different side of me!
I mean, Raps knows my dashing, charming side. And as great as that is, I want to surprise her with depths of my character she hadn't dreamed exist! Like my...my...
Like your modesty?
Ha. Ha. There's nothing wrong with me being honest about my gifts. *Anyway*, I just want it to be something different. Something that surprises her.
I got it! I'll bake her something!

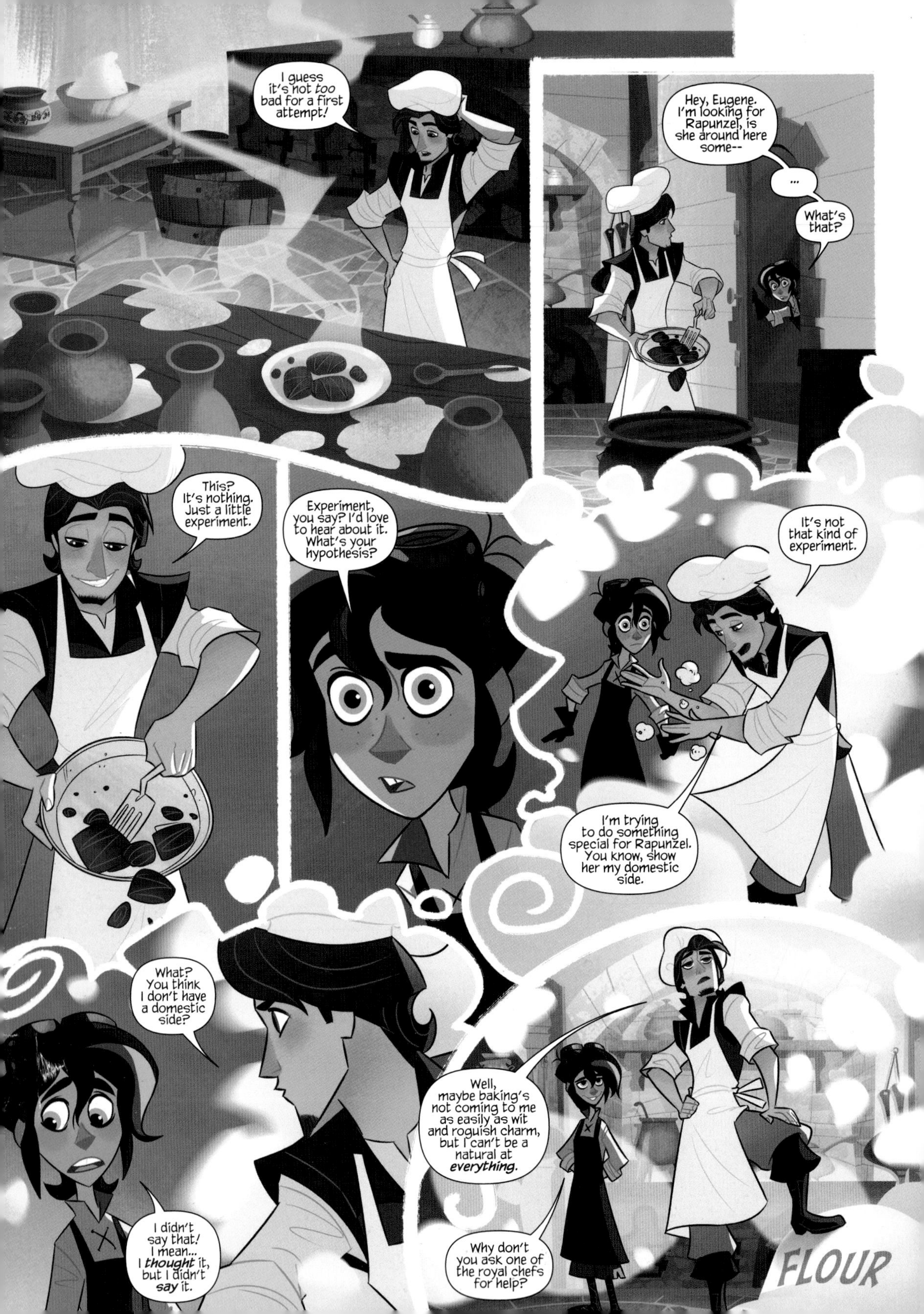
I guess it's not *too* bad for a first attempt!
Hey, Eugene. I'm looking for Rapunzel, is she around here some--
...
What's that?
This? It's nothing. Just a little experiment.
Experiment, you say? I'd love to hear about it. What's your hypothesis?
It's not that kind of experiment.
I'm trying to do something special for Rapunzel. You know, show her my domestic side.
What? You think I don't have a domestic side?
I didn't say that! I mean... I ***thought*** it, but I didn't ***say*** it.
Well, maybe baking's not coming to me as easily as wit and roguish charm, but I can't be a natural at ***everything***.
Why don't you ask one of the royal chefs for help?
FLOUR

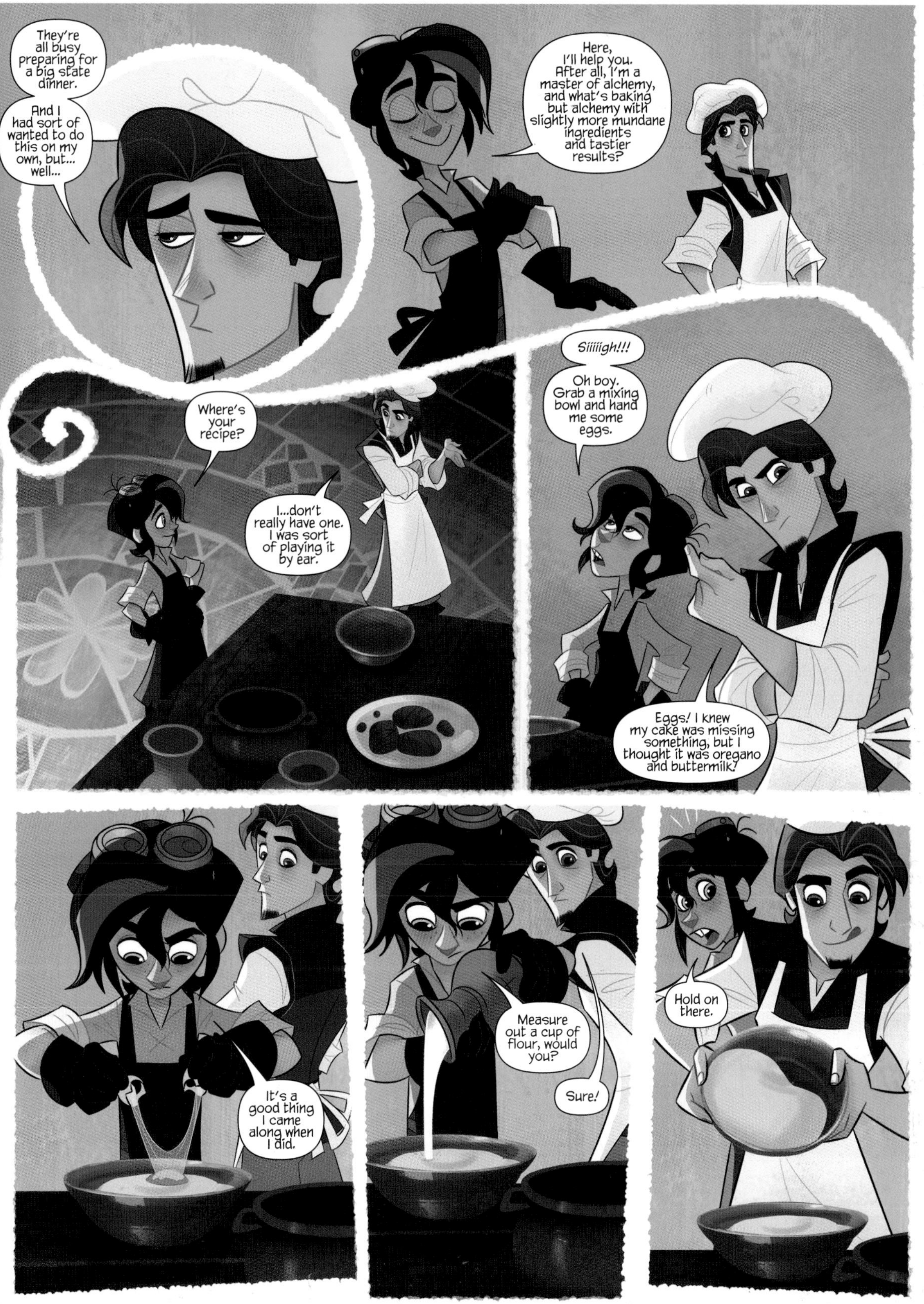
They're all busy preparing for a big state dinner.
And I had sort of wanted to do this on my own, but... well...
Here, I'll help you. After all, I'm a master of alchemy, and what's baking but alchemy with slightly more mundane ingredients and tastier results?
Where's your recipe?
I...don't really have one. I was sort of playing it by ear.
Siiiiigh!!!
Oh boy. Grab a mixing bowl and hand me some eggs.
Eggs! I knew my cake was missing something, but I thought it was oregano and buttermilk!
It's a good thing I came along when I did.
Measure out a cup of flour, would you?
Sure!
Hold on there.

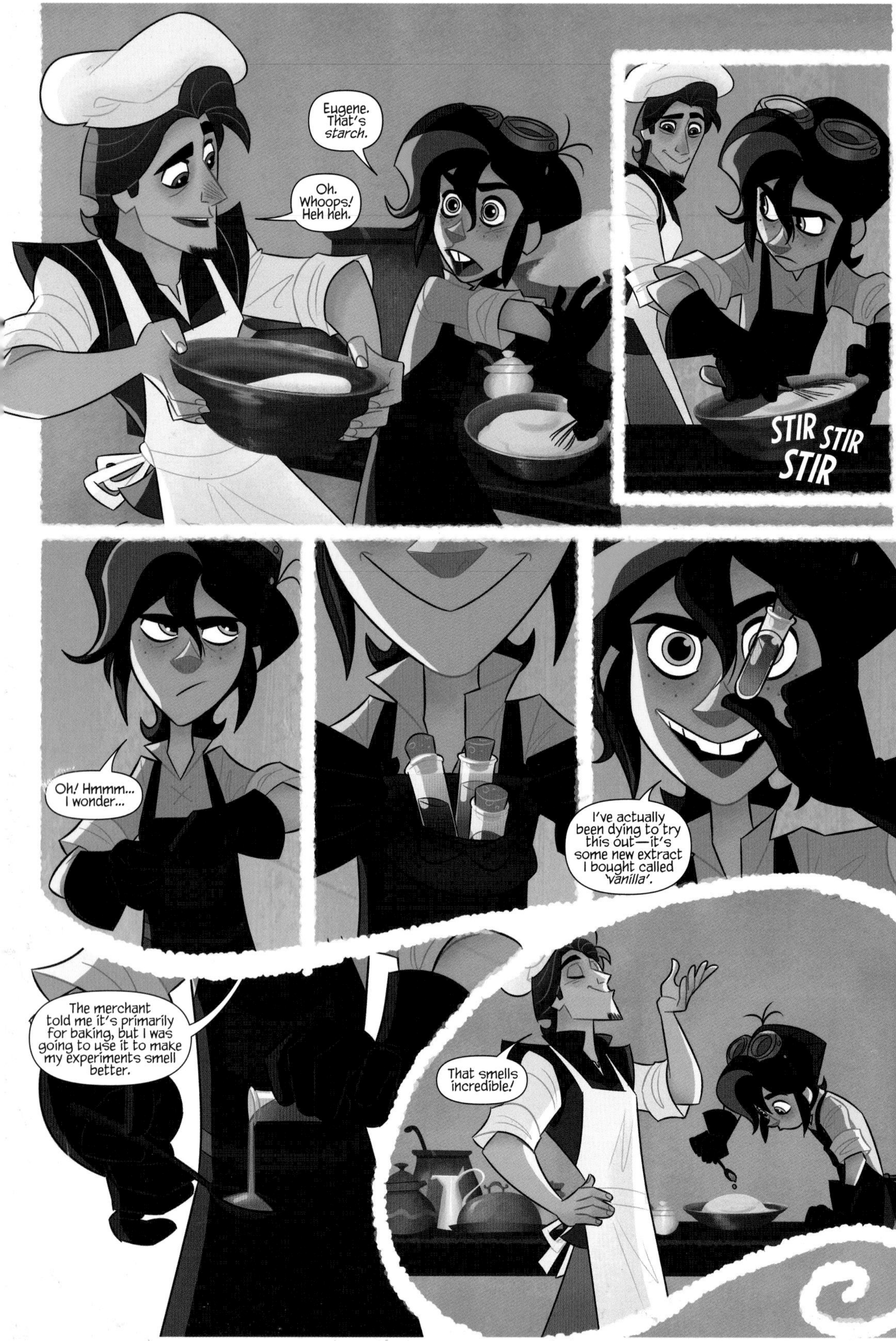
Eugene. That's *starch.*
Oh. Whoops! Heh heh.
STIR STIR STIR
Oh! Hmmm... I wonder...
I've actually been dying to try this out—it's some new extract I bought called *'vanilla'*.
The merchant told me it's primarily for baking, but I was going to use it to make my experiments smell better.
That smells incredible!

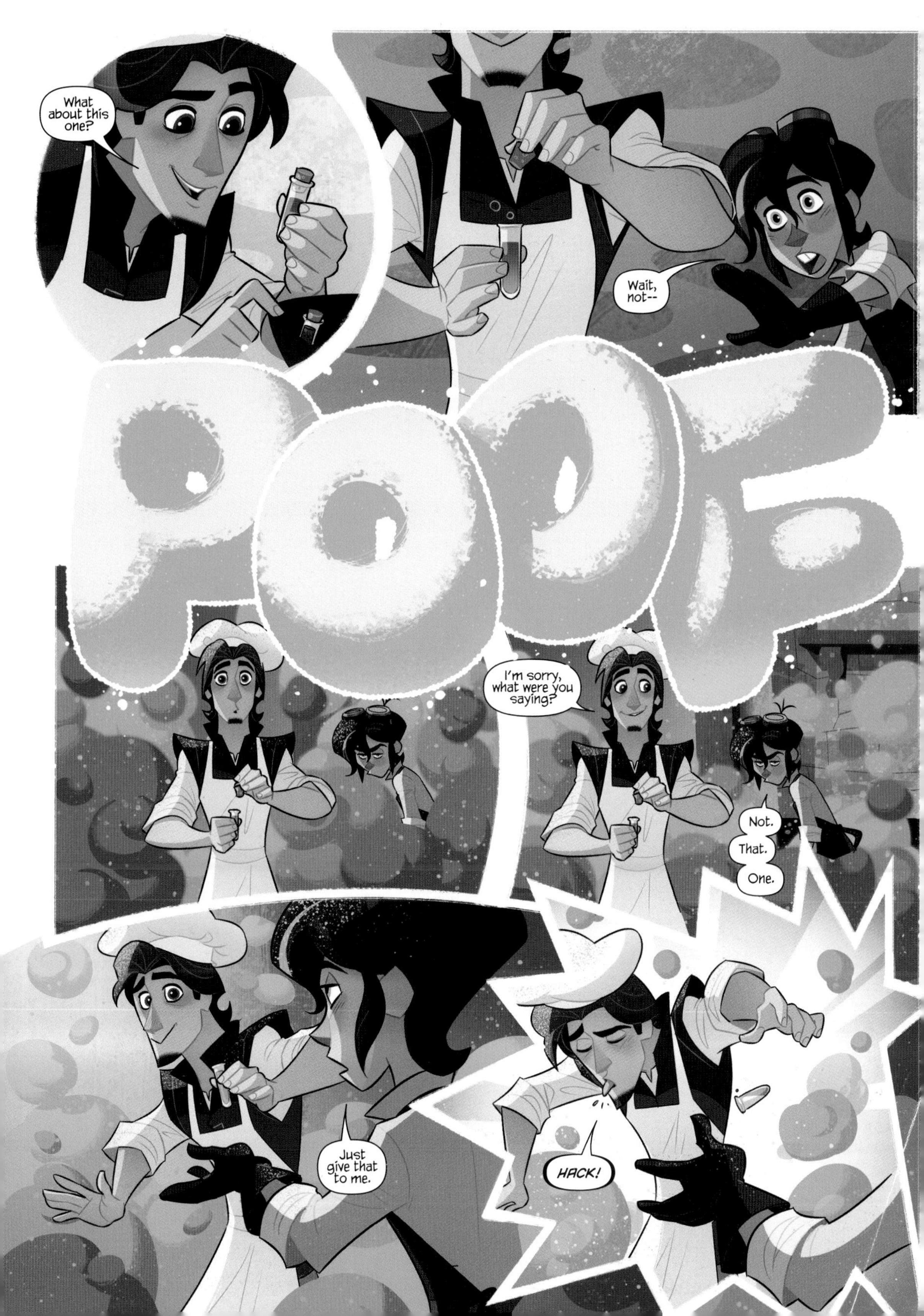
What about this one?
Wait, not--
POOF
I'm sorry, what were you saying?
Not.
That.
One.
Just give that to me.
HACK!

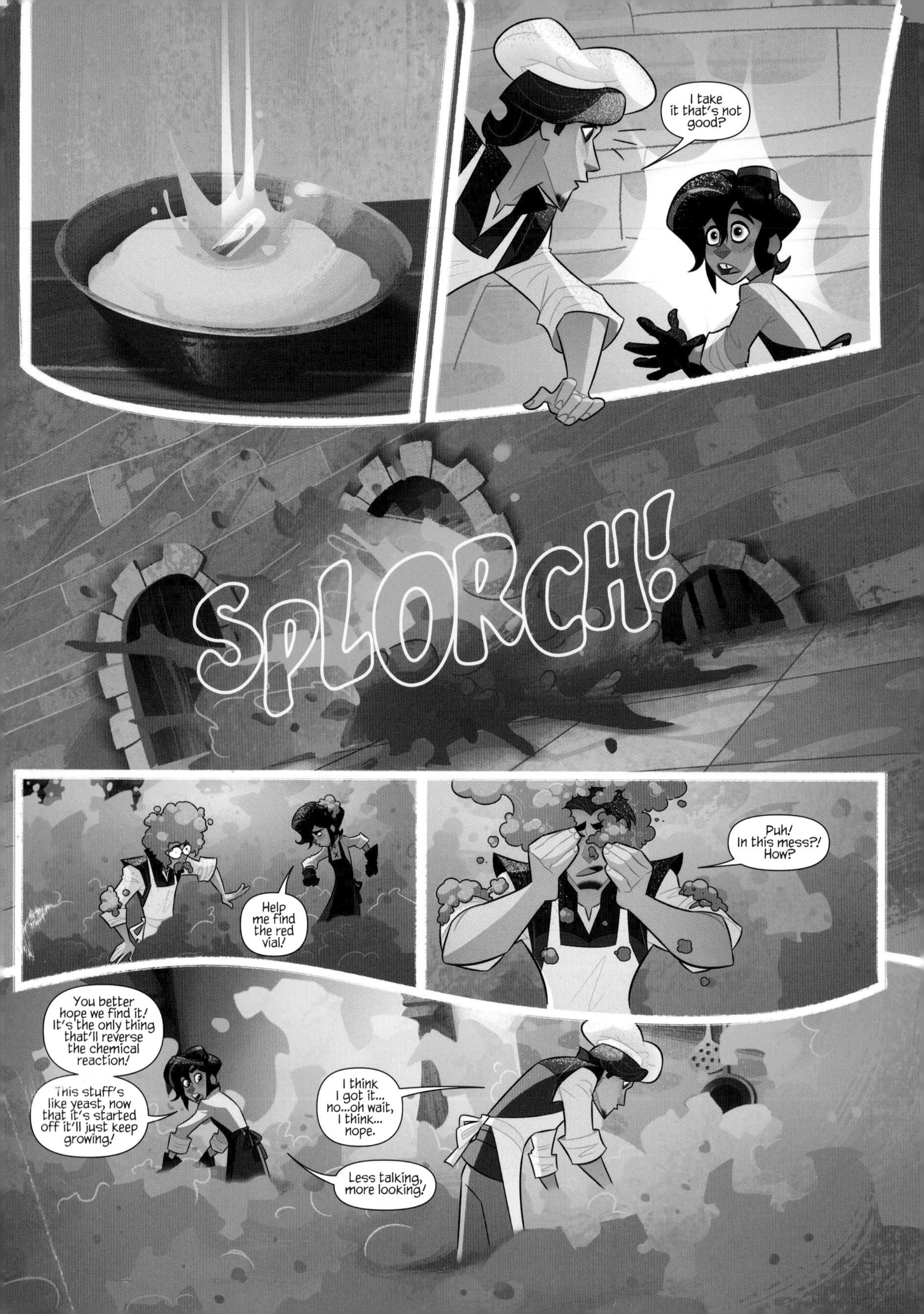
I take it that's not good?
SPLORCH!
Help me find the red vial!
Puh! In this mess?! How?
You better hope we find it! It's the only thing that'll reverse the chemical reaction!
This stuff's like yeast, now that it's started off it'll just keep growing!
I think I got it... no...oh wait, I think... nope.
Less talking, more looking!

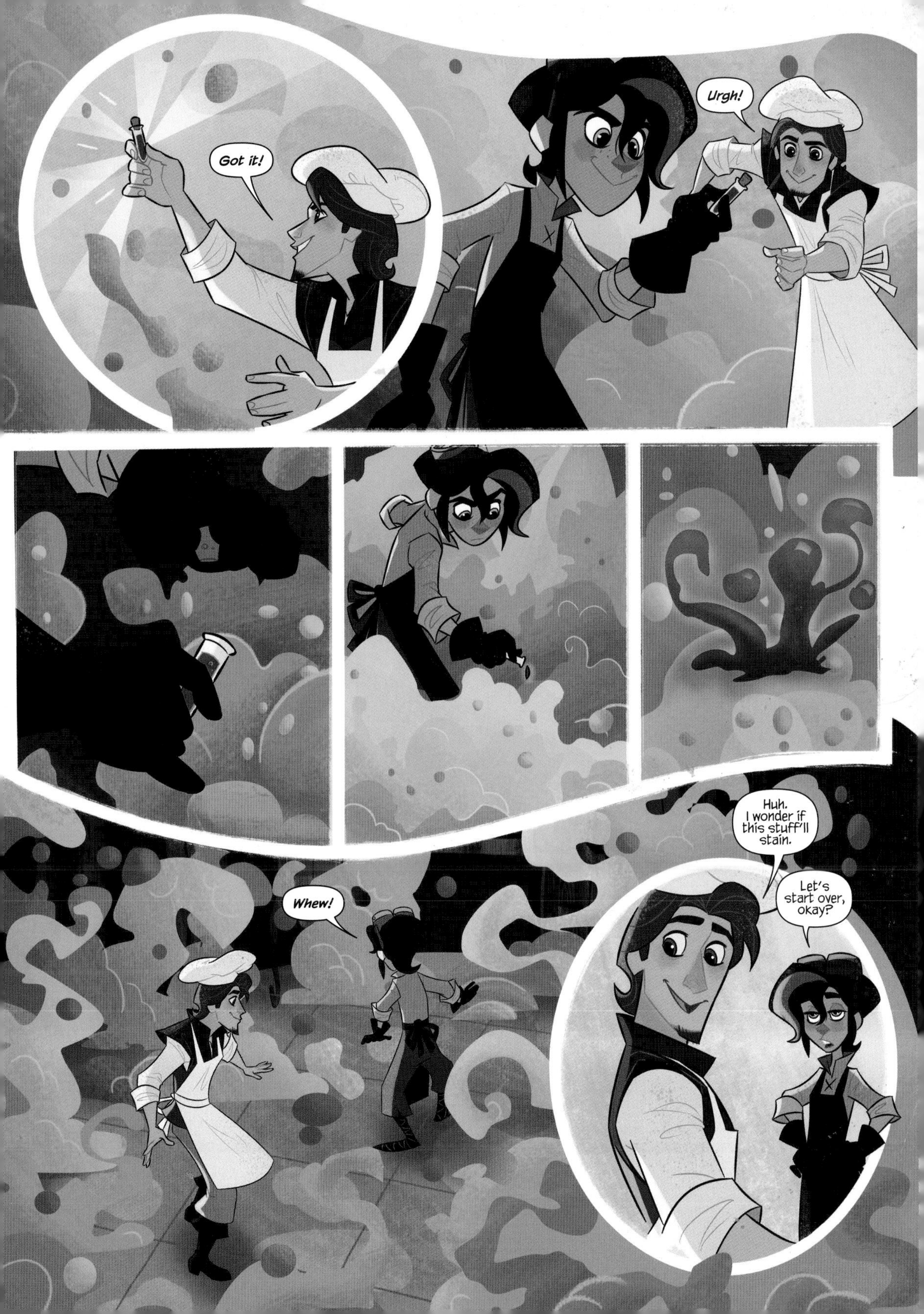
Got it!
Urgh!
Whew!
Huh. I wonder if this stuff'll stain.
Let's start over, okay?

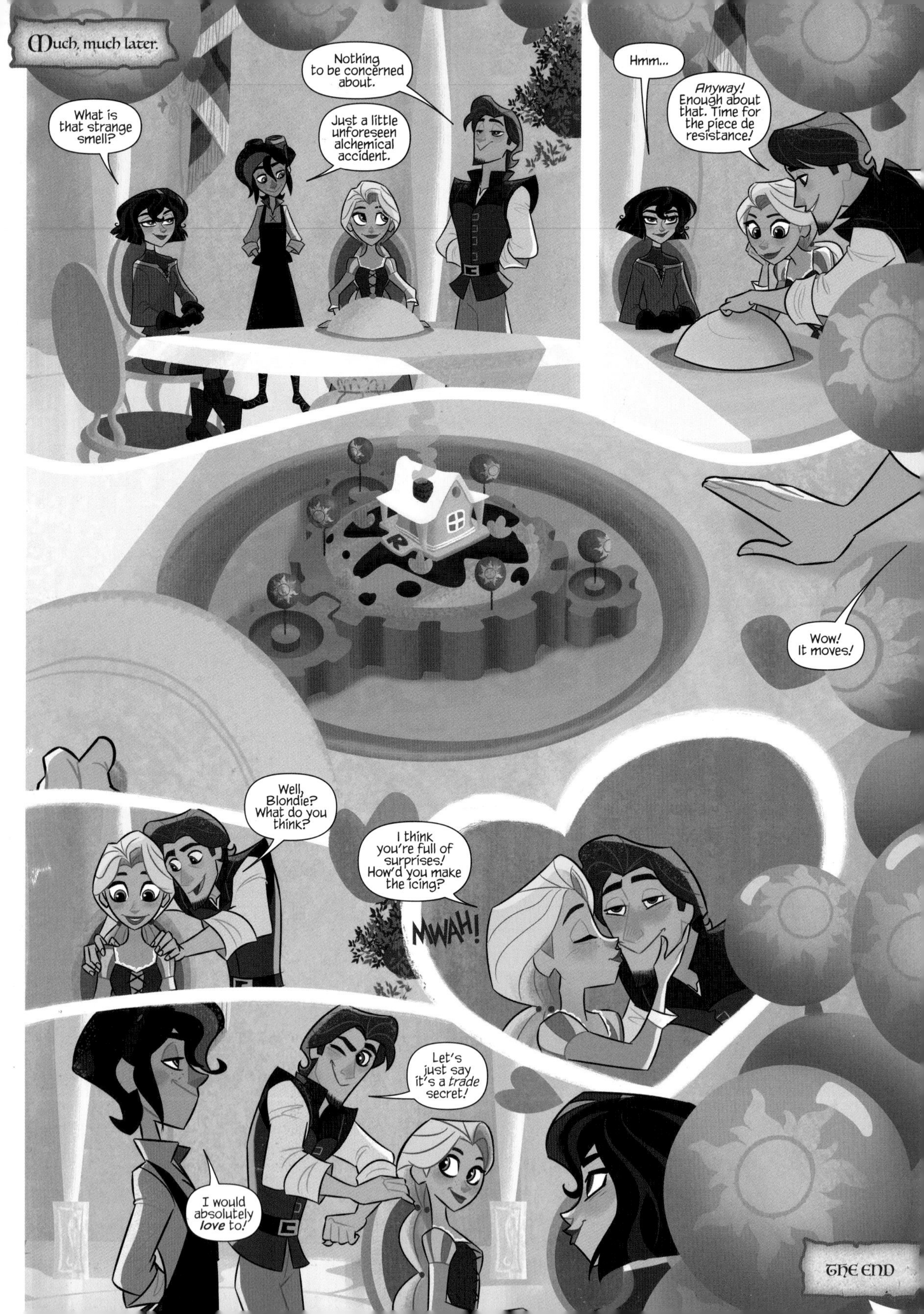
Much, much later.
What is that strange smell?
Nothing to be concerned about.
Just a little unforeseen alchemical accident.
Hmm...
Anyway! Enough about that. Time for the piece de resistance!
Wow! It moves!
Well, Blondie? What do you think?
I think you're full of surprises! How'd you make the icing?
MWAH!
Let's just say it's a trade secret!
I would absolutely love to!
THE END

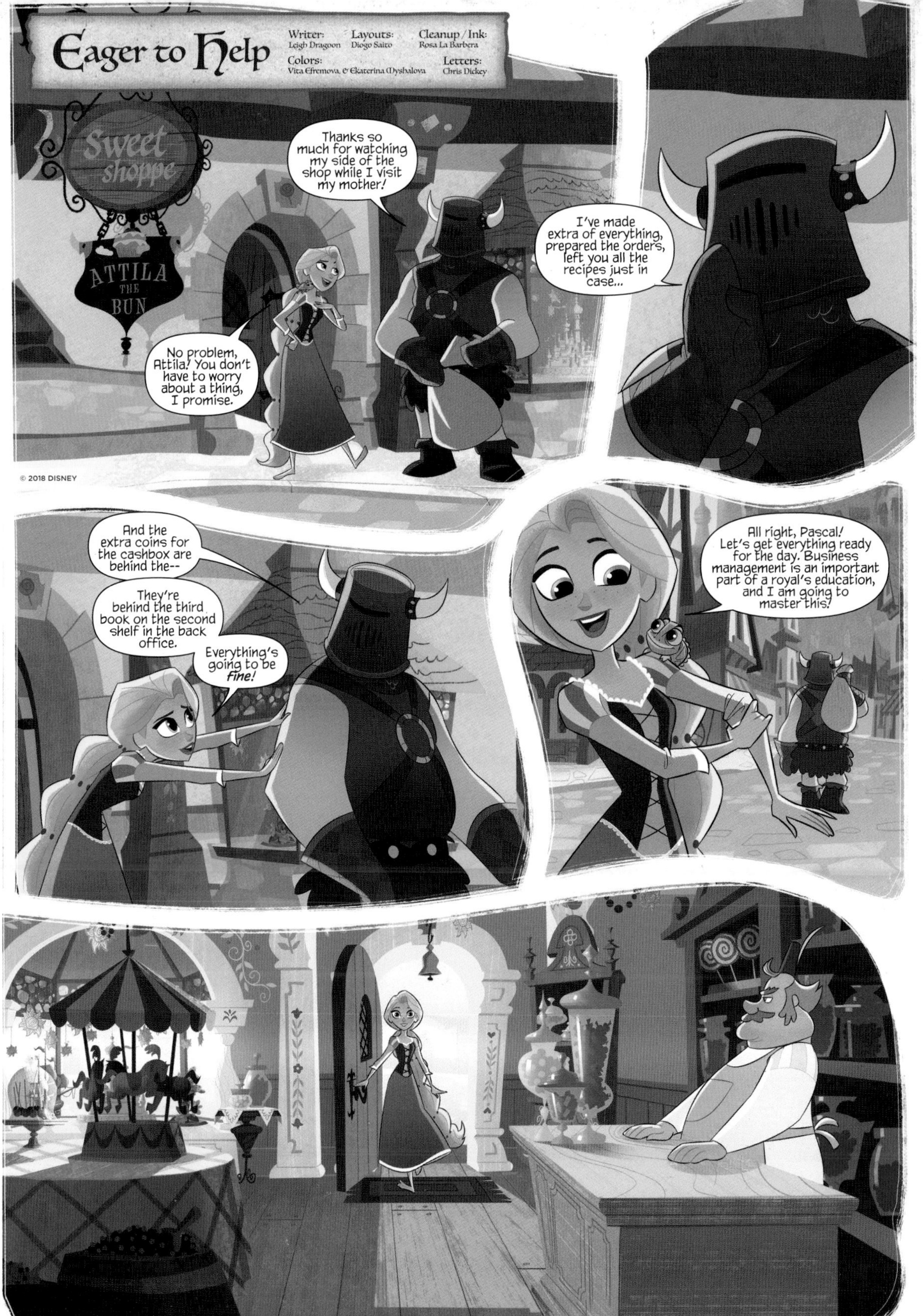
Eager to Help
Writer: Leigh Dragoon
Layouts: Diogo Saito
Cleanup / Ink: Rosa La Barbera
Colors: Vita Efremova, & Ekaterina Myshalova
Letters: Chris Dickey
Sweet shoppe
ATTILA THE BUN
Thanks so much for watching my side of the shop while I visit my mother!
No problem, Attila! You don't have to worry about a thing, I promise.
I've made extra of everything, prepared the orders, left you all the recipes just in case...
And the extra coins for the cashbox are behind the--
They're behind the third book on the second shelf in the back office.
Everything's going to be *fine!*
All right, Pascal! Let's get everything ready for the day. Business management is an important part of a royal's education, and I am going to master this!

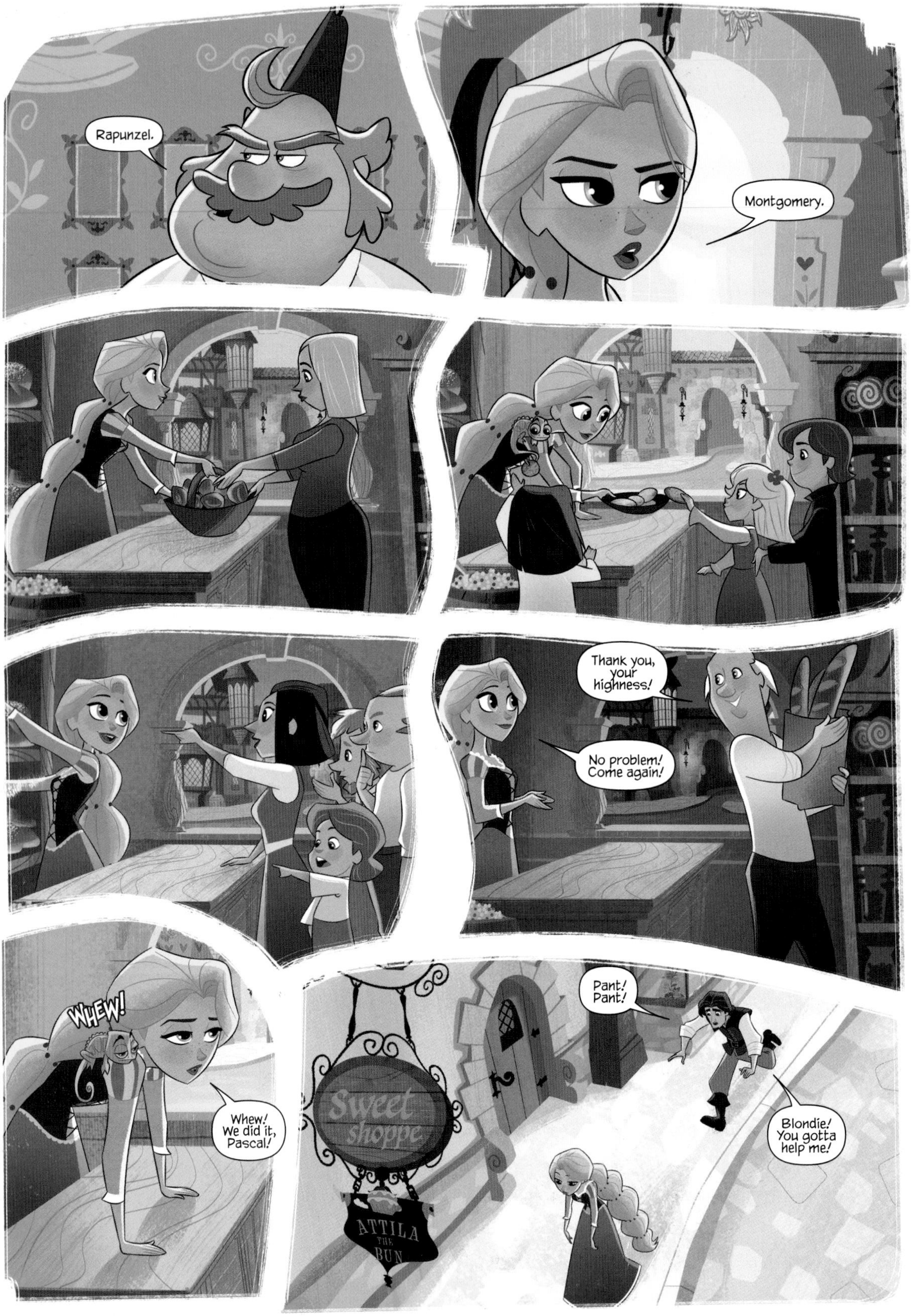
Rapunzel.
Montgomery.
Thank you, your highness!
No problem! Come again!
WHEW!
Whew! We did it, Pascal!
Sweet shoppe
ATTILA THE BUN
Pant! Pant!
Blondie! You gotta help me!

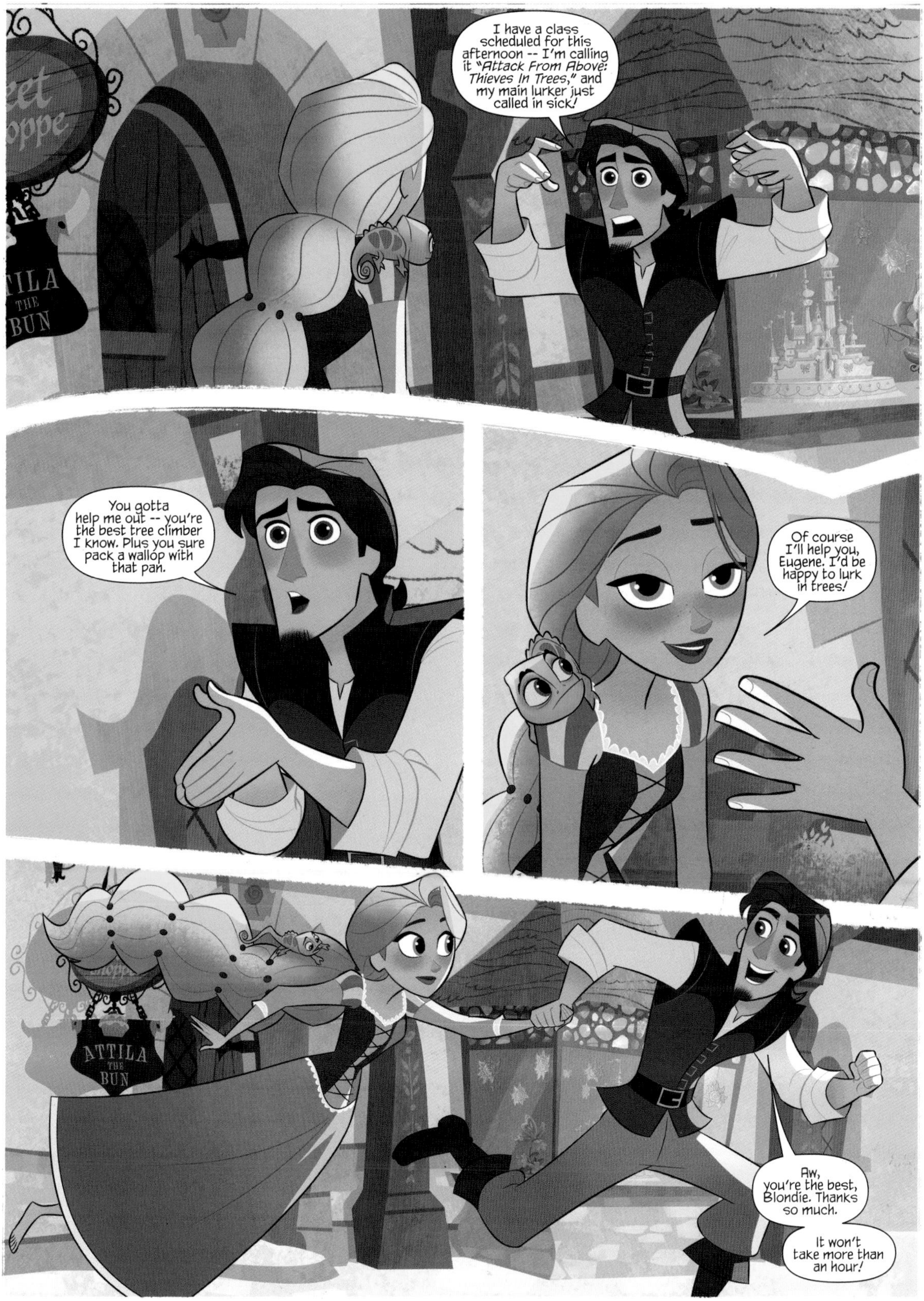

I have a class scheduled for this afternoon -- I'm calling it *"Attack From Above: Thieves In Trees,"* and my main lurker just called in sick!
ATTILA THE BUN
You gotta help me out -- you're the best tree climber I know. Plus you sure pack a wallop with that pan.
Of course I'll help you, Eugene. I'd be happy to lurk in trees!
ATTILA THE BUN
Aw, you're the best, Blondie. Thanks so much.
It won't take more than an hour!

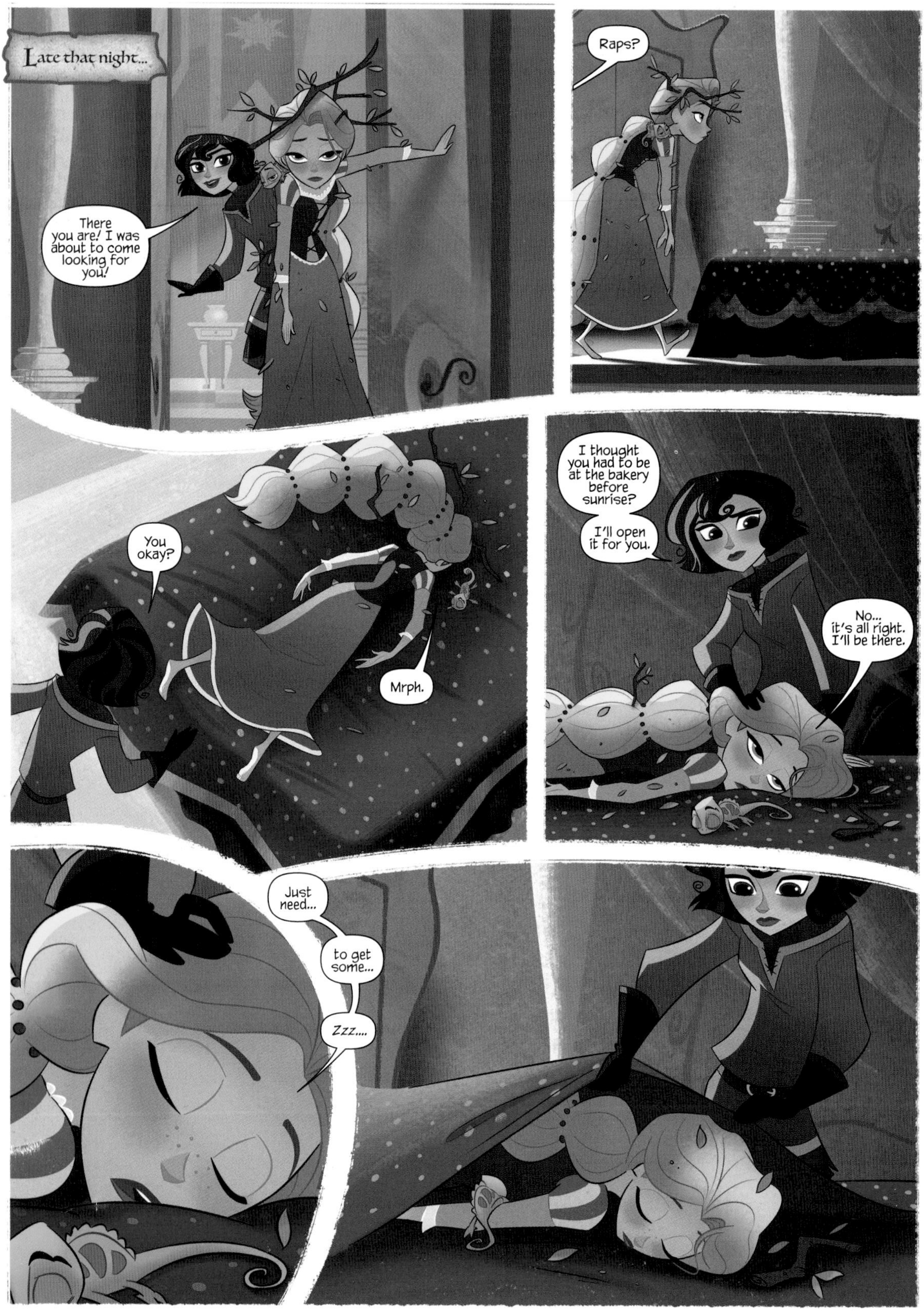
Late that night...
There you are! I was about to come looking for you!
Raps?
You okay?
Mrph.
I thought you had to be at the bakery before sunrise?
I'll open it for you.
No... it's all right. I'll be there.
Just need...
to get some...
Zzz....

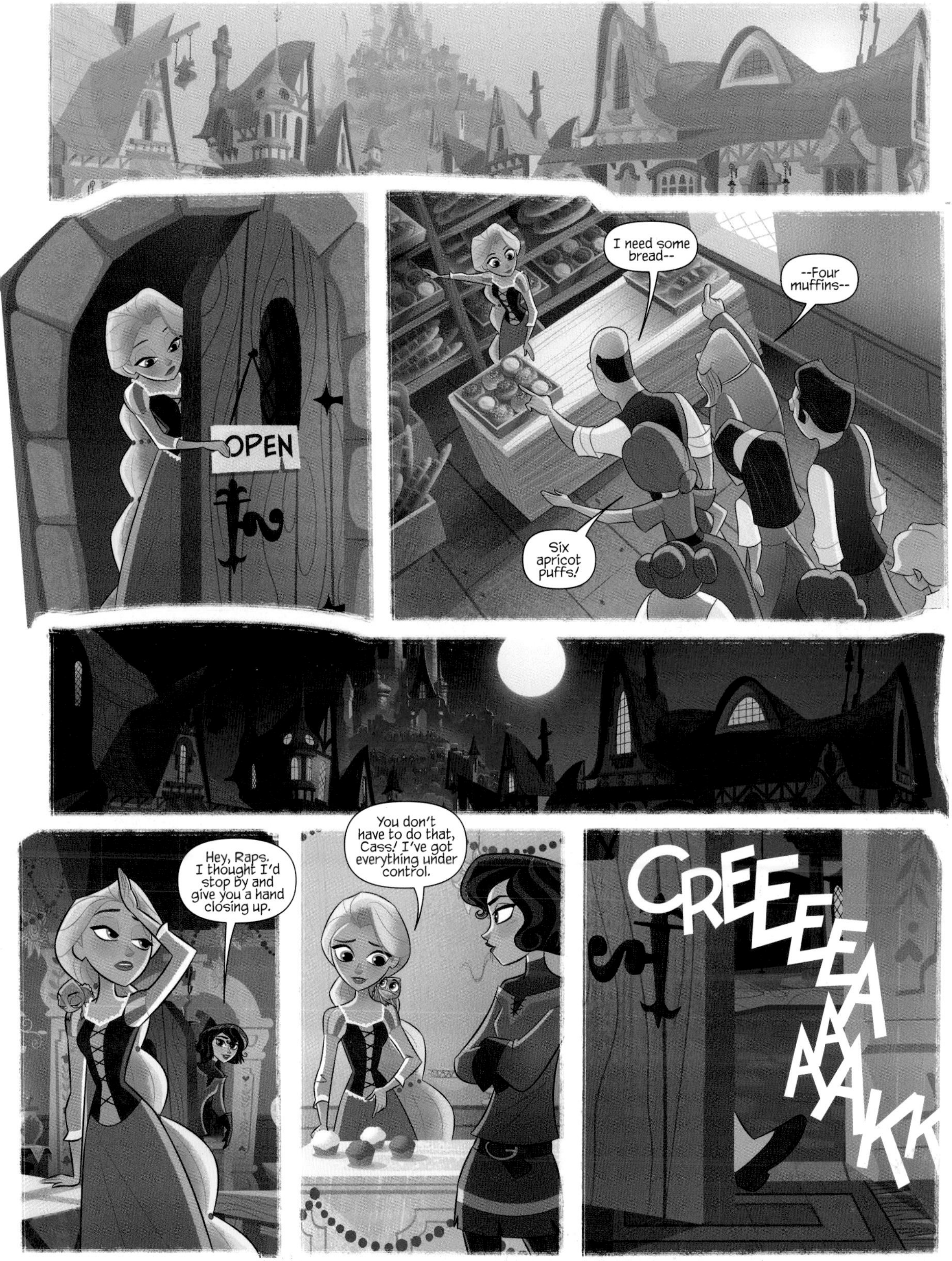
OPEN
I need some bread--
--Four muffins--
Six apricot puffs!
Hey, Raps. I thought I'd stop by and give you a hand closing up.
You don't have to do that, Cass! I've got everything under control.
CREEEEAAAAKKK

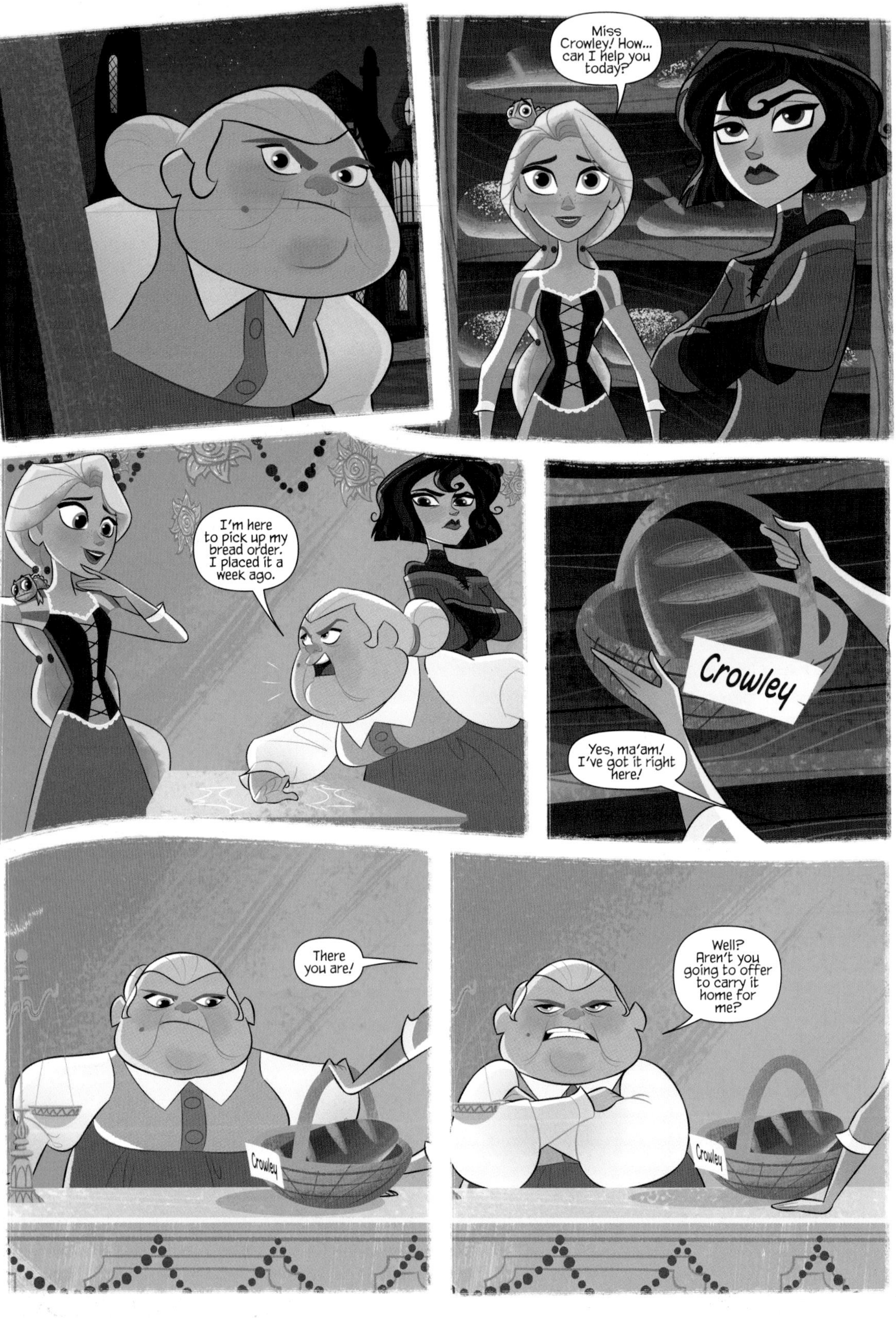
Miss Crowley! How... can I help you today?
I'm here to pick up my bread order. I placed it a week ago.
Crowley
Yes, ma'am! I've got it right here!
There you are!
Crowley
Well? Aren't you going to offer to carry it home for me?
Crowley

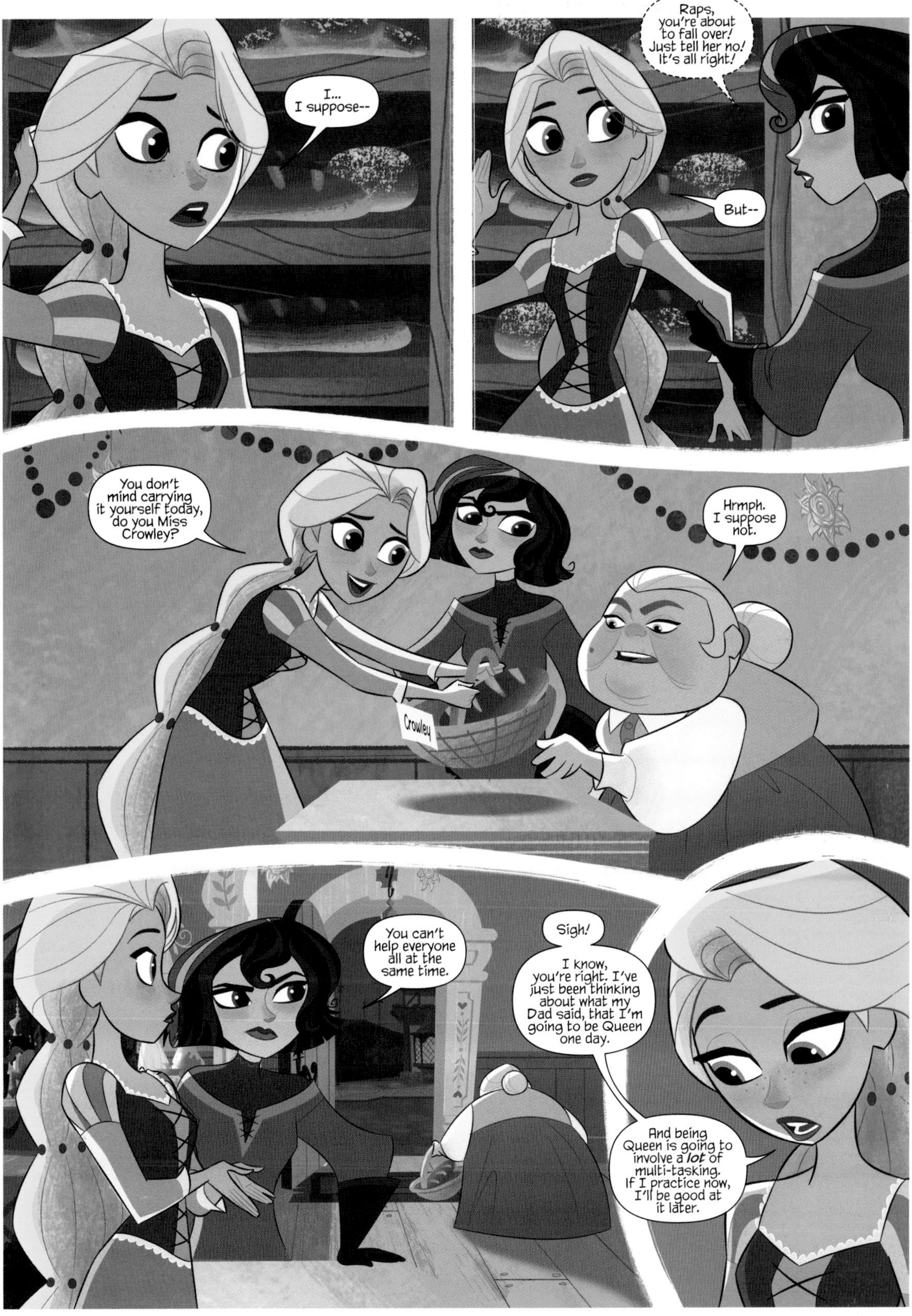

I... I suppose--
Raps, you're about to fall over! Just tell her no! It's all right!
But--
You don't mind carrying it yourself today, do you Miss Crowley?
Hrmph. I suppose not.
Crowley
You can't help everyone all at the same time.
Sigh!
I know, you're right. I've just been thinking about what my Dad said, that I'm going to be Queen one day.
And being Queen is going to involve a *lot* of multi-tasking. If I practice now, I'll be good at it later.

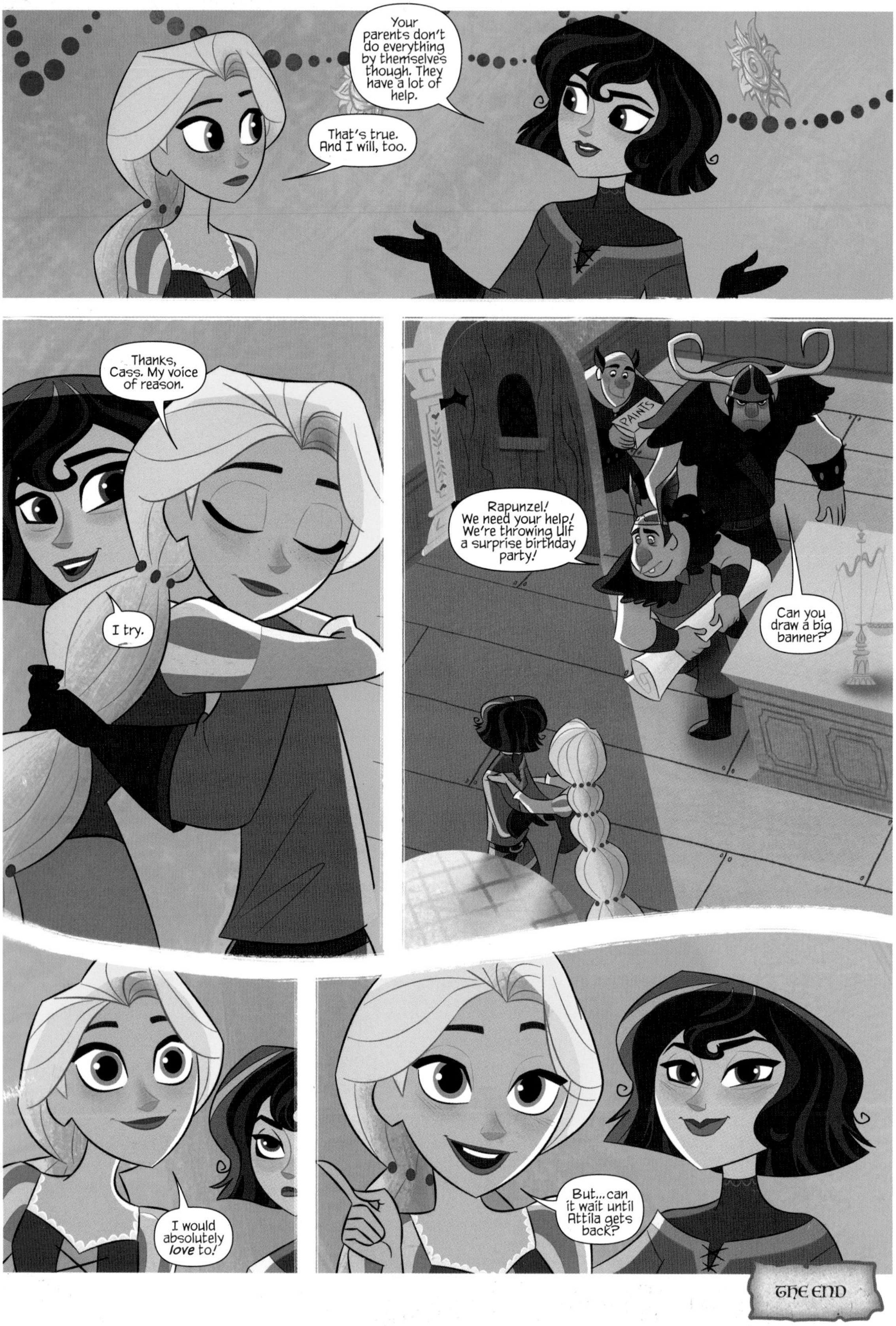

Your parents don't do everything by themselves though. They have a lot of help.
That's true. And I will, too.
Thanks, Cass. My voice of reason.
I try.
Rapunzel! We need your help! We're throwing Ulf a surprise birthday party!
PAINTS
Can you draw a big banner?
I would absolutely *love* to!
But...can it wait until Attila gets back?
THE END

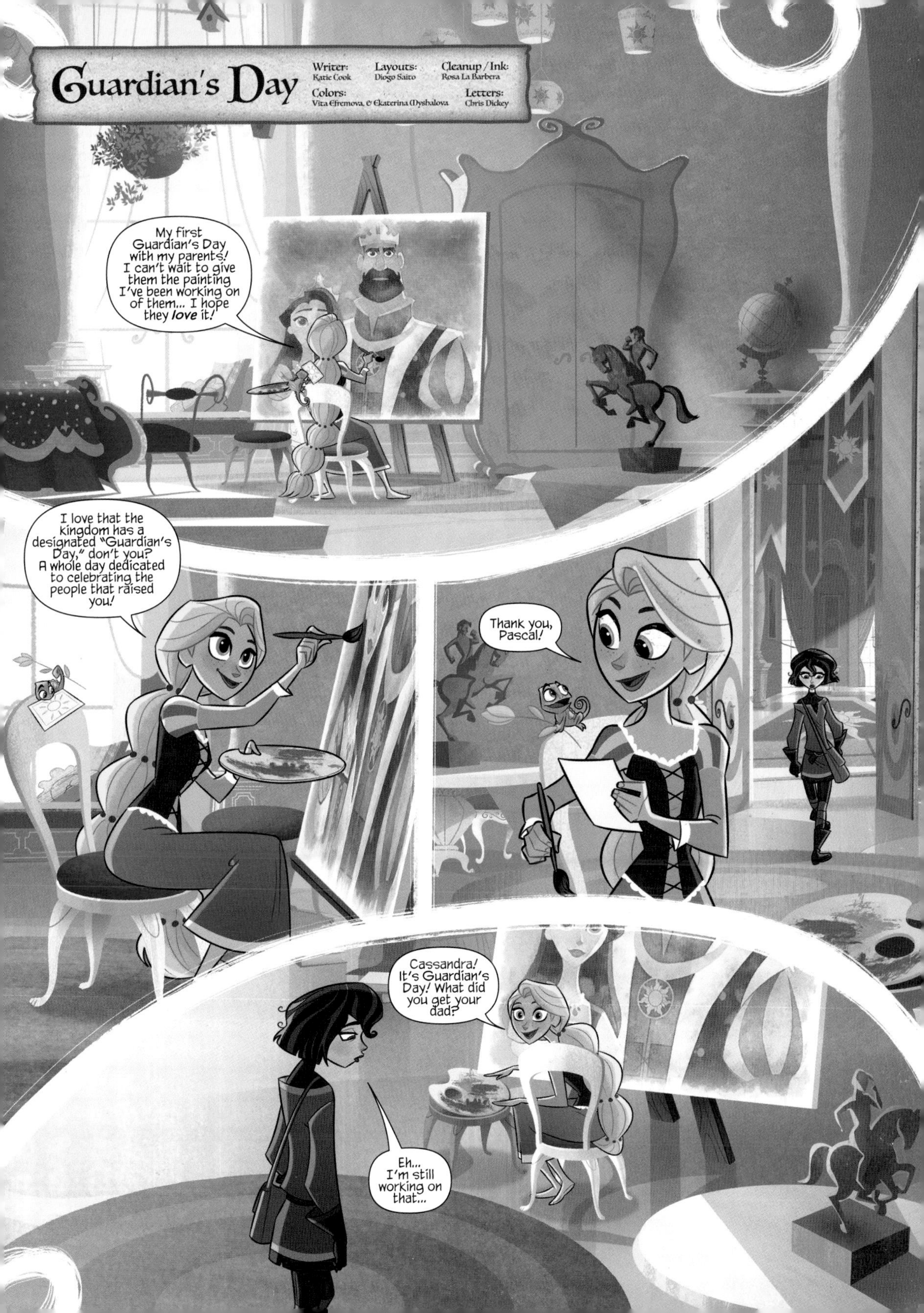
Guardian's Day
Writer: Katie Cook
Layouts: Diogo Saito
Cleanup / Ink: Rosa La Barbera
Colors: Vita Efremova, & Ekaterina Myshalova
Letters: Chris Dickey
My first Guardian's Day with my parents! I can't wait to give them the painting I've been working on of them... I hope they *love* it!
I love that the kingdom has a designated "Guardian's Day," don't you? A whole day dedicated to celebrating the people that raised you!
Thank you, Pascal!
Cassandra! It's Guardian's Day! What did you get your dad?
Eh... I'm still working on that...

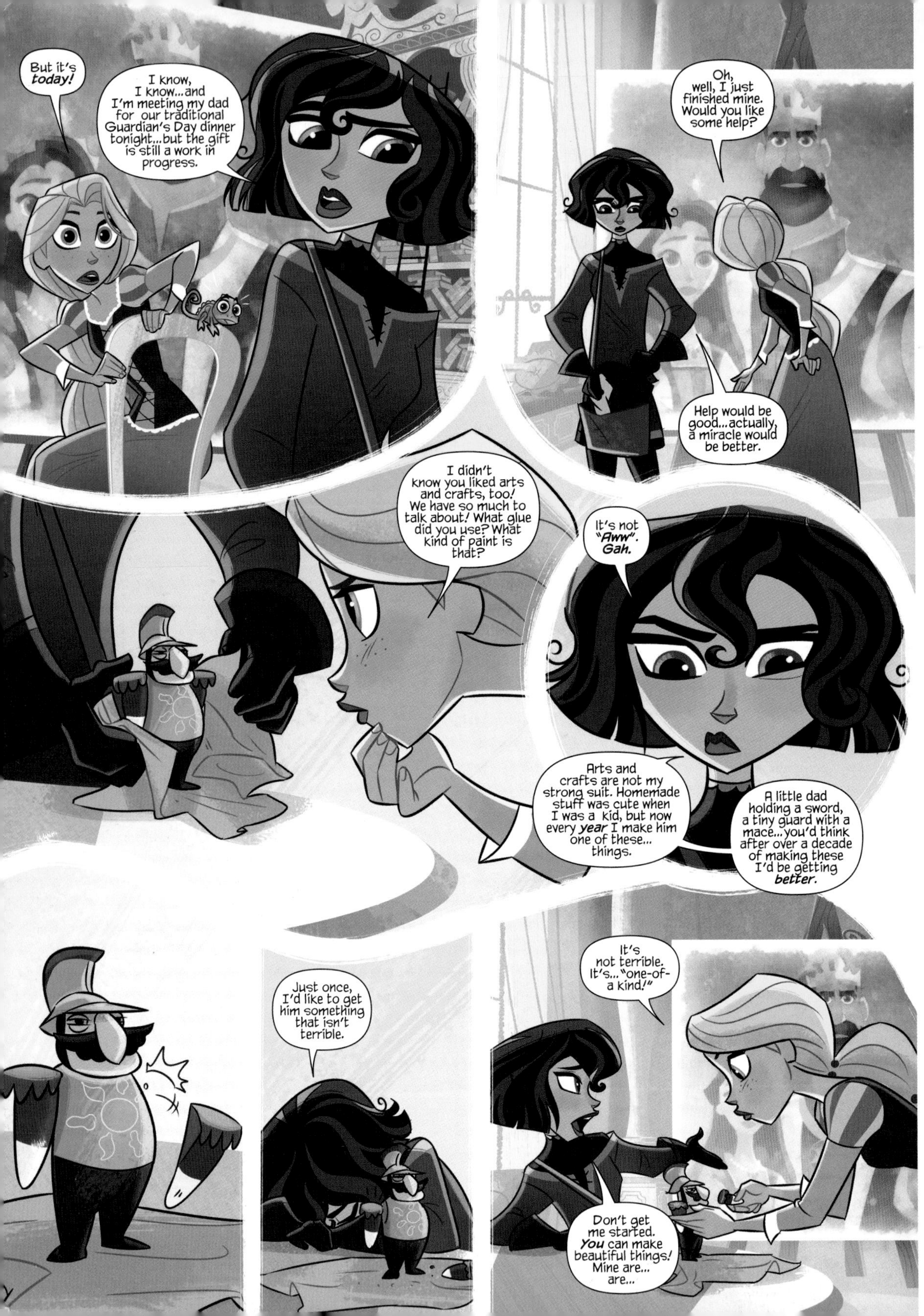

But it's *today!*
I know, I know...and I'm meeting my dad for our traditional Guardian's Day dinner tonight...but the gift is still a work in progress.
Oh, well, I just finished mine. Would you like some help?
Help would be good...actually, a miracle would be better.
I didn't know you liked arts and crafts, too! We have so much to talk about! What glue did you use? What kind of paint is that?
It's not "Aww". Gah.
Arts and crafts are not my strong suit. Homemade stuff was cute when I was a kid, but now every *year* I make him one of these... things.
A little dad holding a sword, a tiny guard with a mace...you'd think after over a decade of making these I'd be getting *better*.
Just once, I'd like to get him something that isn't terrible.
It's not terrible. It's..."one-of-a kind!"
Don't get me started. *You* can make beautiful things! Mine are... are...

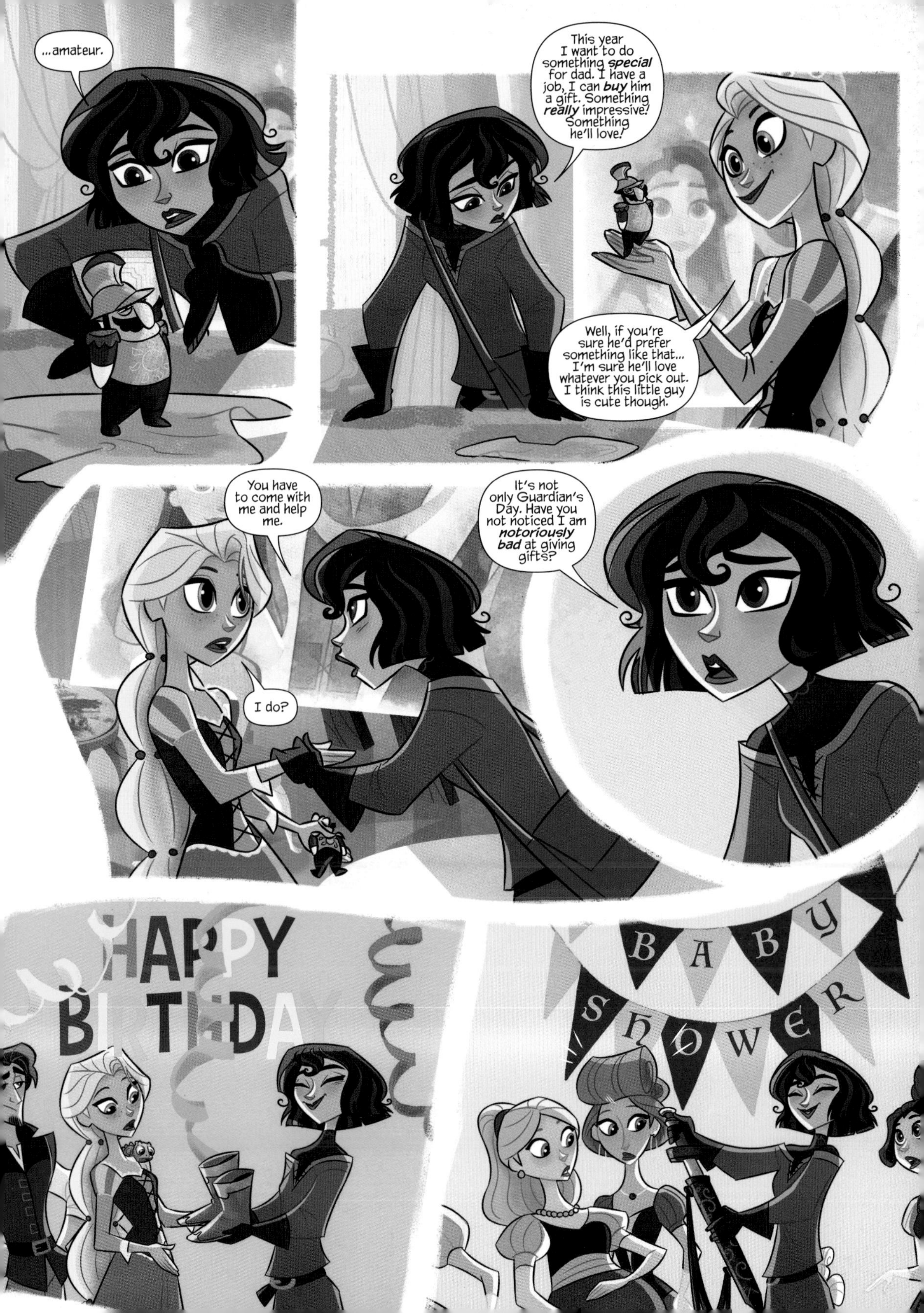
...amateur.
This year I want to do something *special* for dad. I have a job, I can *buy* him a gift. Something *really* impressive! Something he'll love!
Well, if you're sure he'd prefer something like that... I'm sure he'll love whatever you pick out. I think this little guy is cute though.
You have to come with me and help me.
I do?
It's not only Guardian's Day. Have you not noticed I am *notoriously bad* at giving gifts?
HAPPY BIRTHDAY
BABY SHOWER

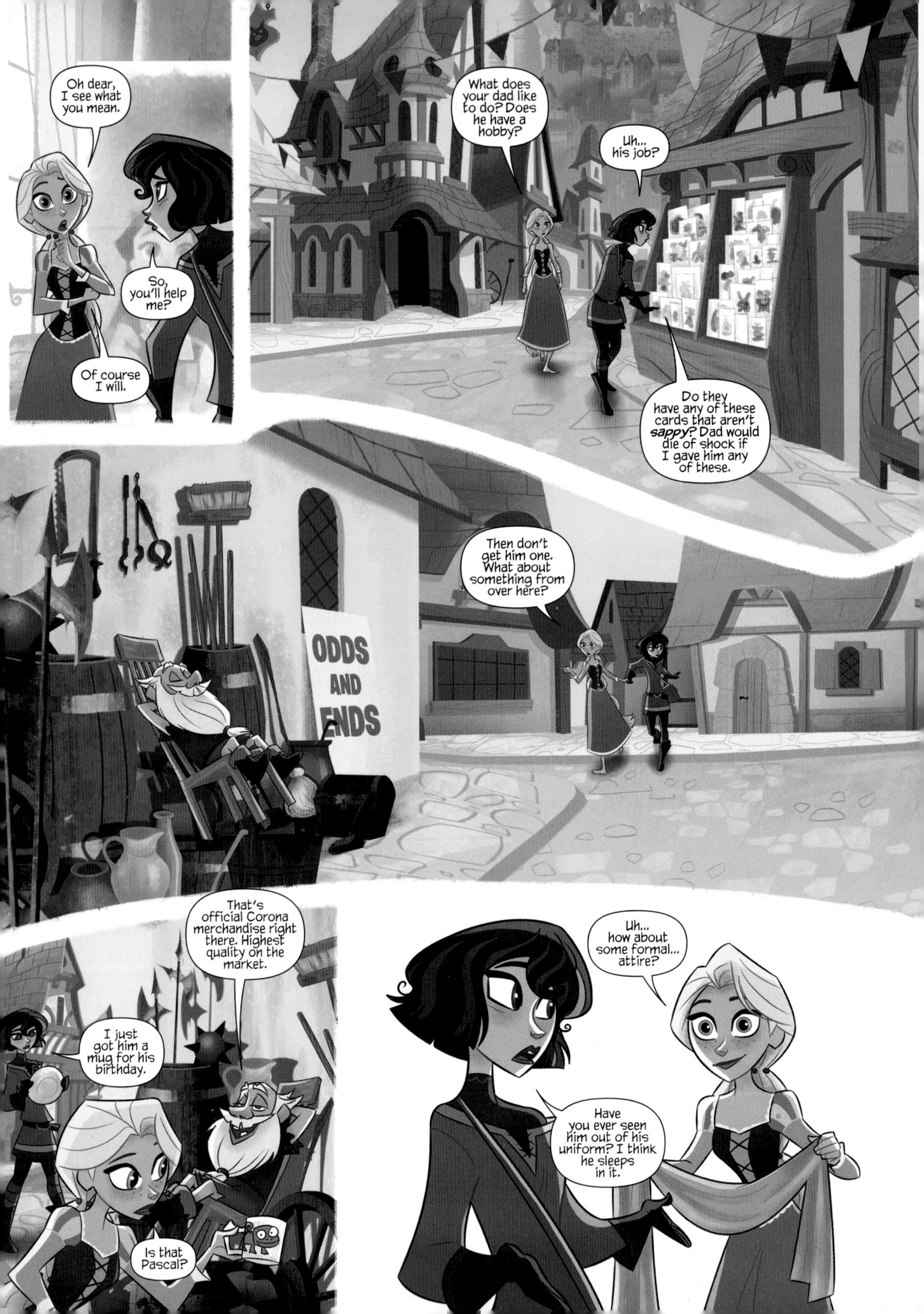
Oh dear, I see what you mean.
So, you'll help me?
Of course I will.
What does your dad like to do? Does he have a hobby?
Uh... his job?
Do they have any of these cards that aren't *sappy*? Dad would die of shock if I gave him any of these.
Then don't get him one. What about something from over here?
ODDS AND ENDS
That's official Corona merchandise right there. Highest quality on the market.
I just got him a mug for his birthday.
Is that Pascal?
Uh... how about some formal... attire?
Have you ever seen him out of his uniform? I think he sleeps in it.

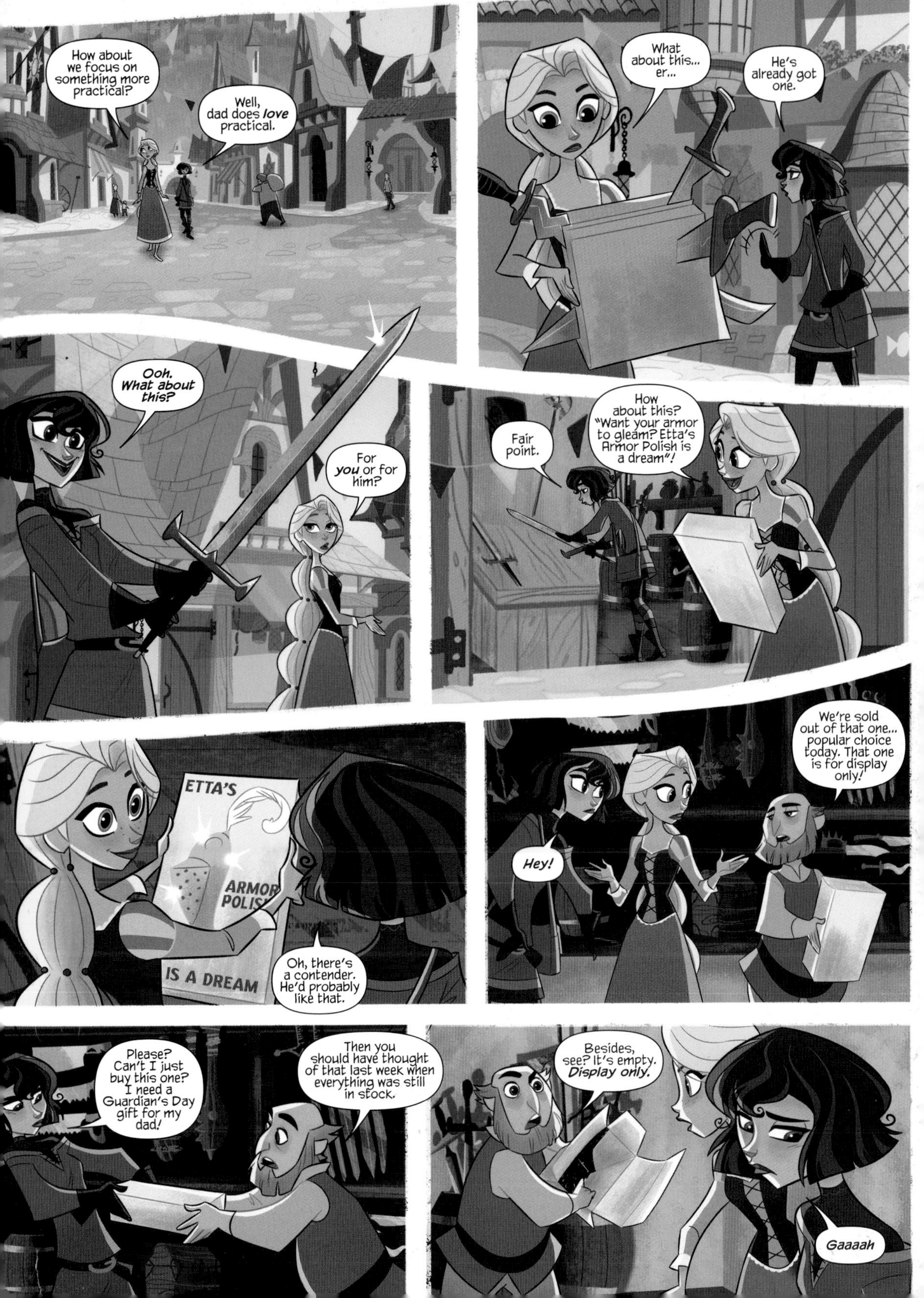
How about we focus on something more practical?
Well, dad does *love* practical.
What about this... er...
He's already got one.
Ooh. What about this?
For *you* or for him?
Fair point.
How about this? "Want your armor to gleam? Etta's Armor Polish is a dream"!
ETTA'S
ARMOR POLISH
IS A DREAM
Oh, there's a contender. He'd probably like that.
We're sold out of that one... popular choice today. That one is for display only!
Hey!
Please? Can't I just buy this one? I need a Guardian's Day gift for my dad!
Then you should have thought of that last week when everything was still in stock.
Besides, see? It's empty. *Display only.*
Gaaaah

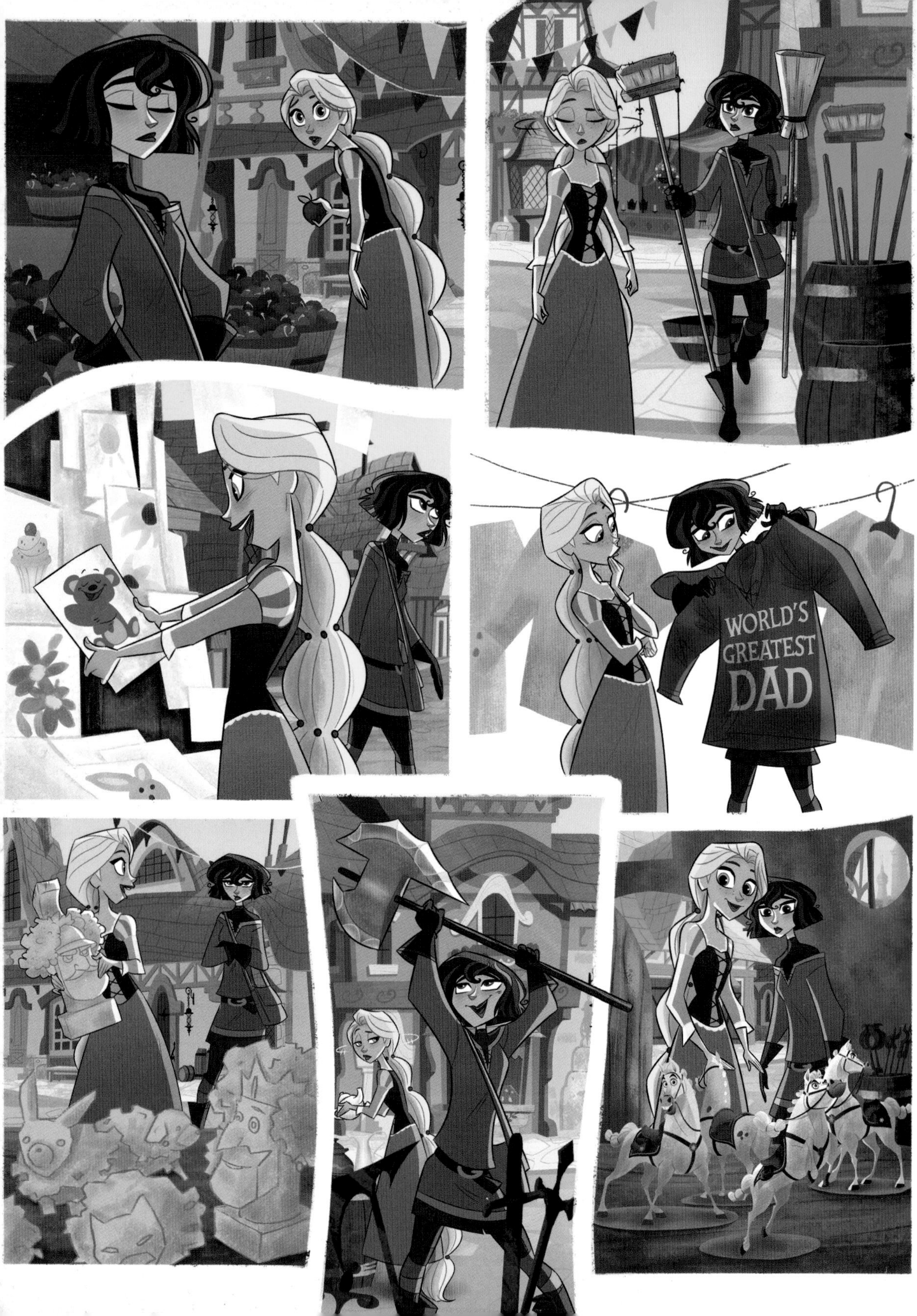
WORLD'S
GREATEST
DAD

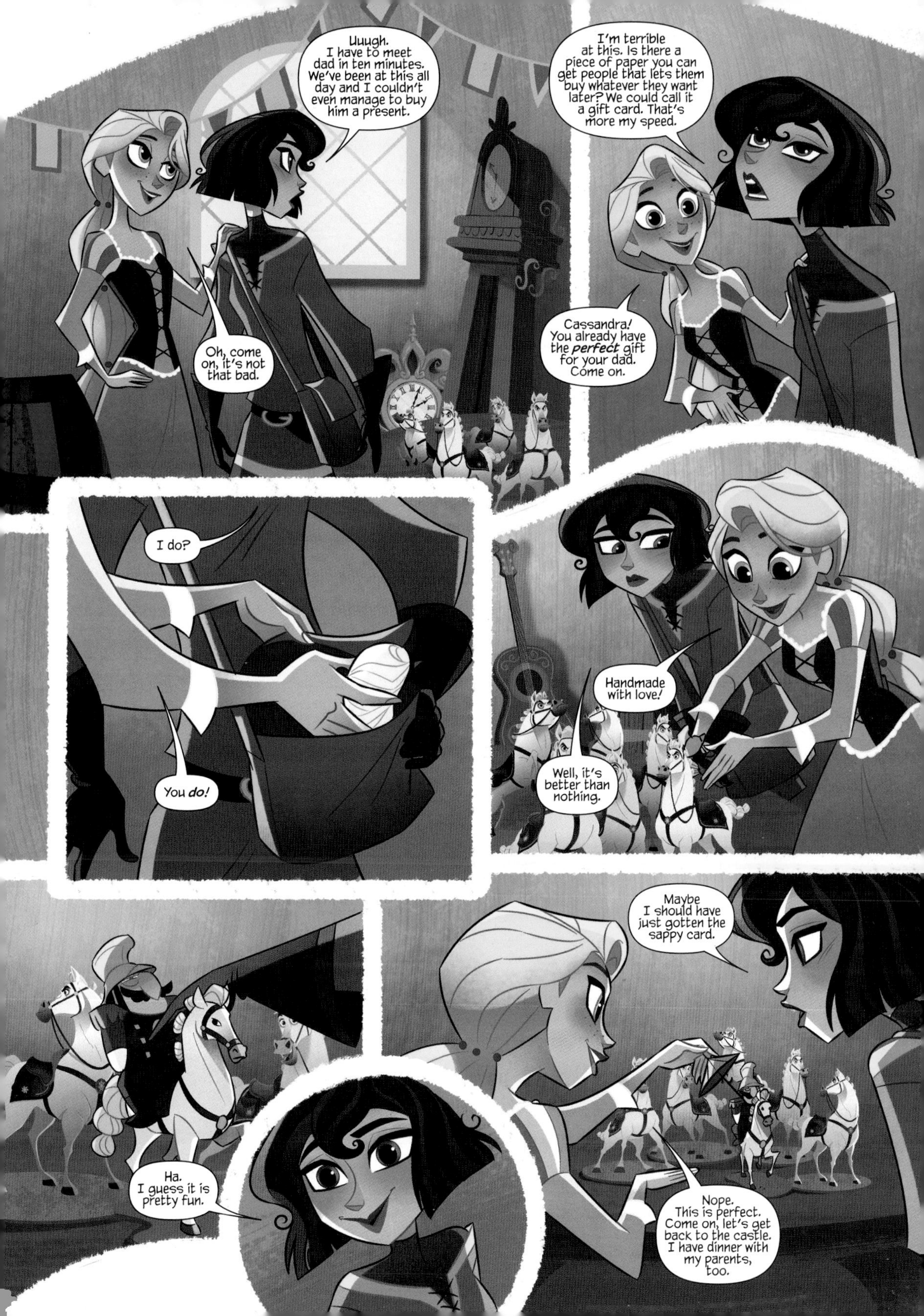

Uuugh. I have to meet dad in ten minutes. We've been at this all day and I couldn't even manage to buy him a present.
Oh, come on, it's not that bad.
I'm terrible at this. Is there a piece of paper you can get people that lets them buy whatever they want later? We could call it a gift card. That's more my speed.
Cassandra! You already have the *perfect* gift for your dad. Come on.
I do?
You *do!*
Handmade with love!
Well, it's better than nothing.
Ha. I guess it is pretty fun.
Maybe I should have just gotten the sappy card.
Nope. This is perfect. Come on, let's get back to the castle. I have dinner with my parents, too.

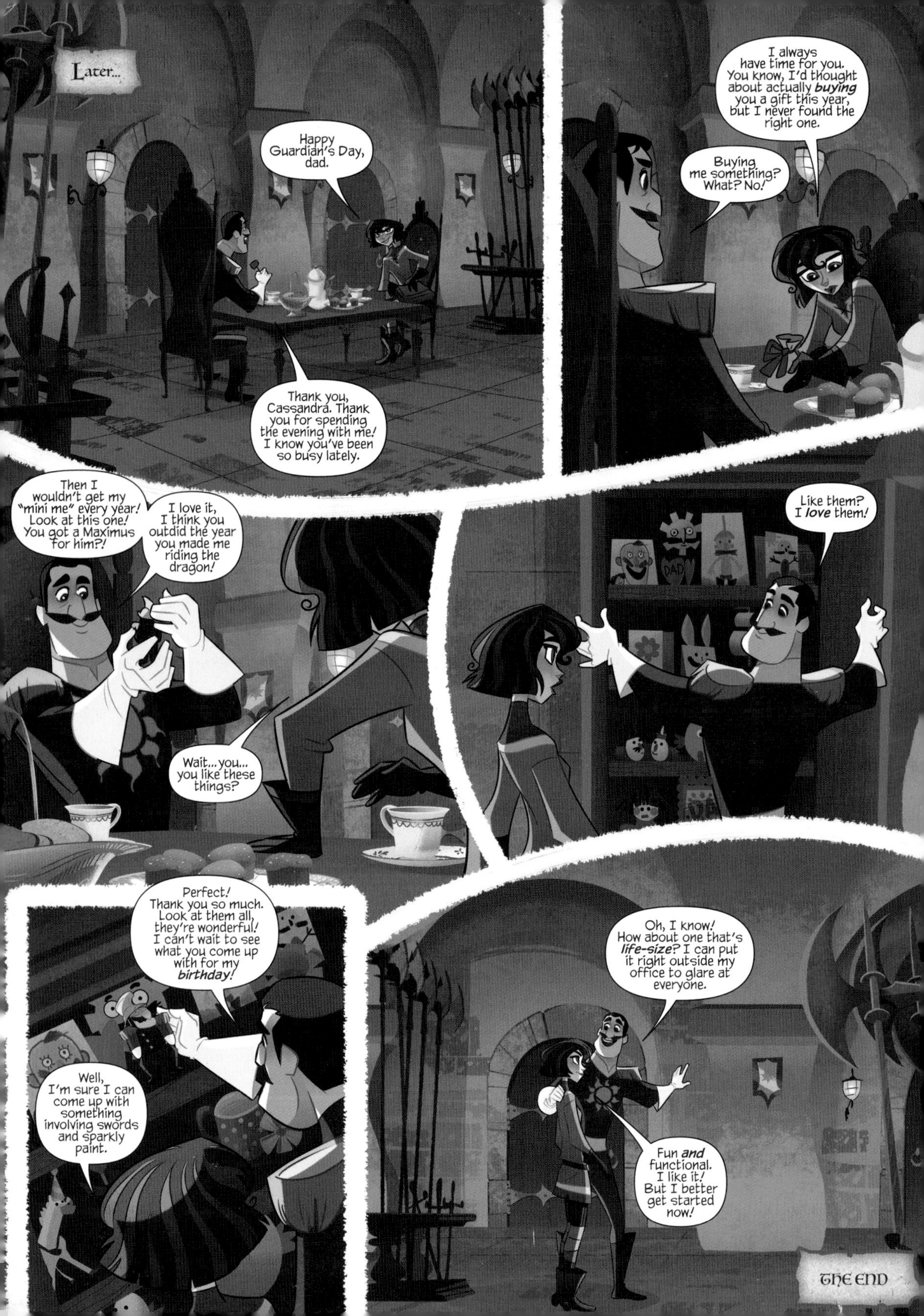
Later...
Happy Guardian's Day, dad.
Thank you, Cassandra. Thank you for spending the evening with me! I know you've been so busy lately.
I always have time for you. You know, I'd thought about actually *buying* you a gift this year, but I never found the right one.
Buying me something? What? No!
Then I wouldn't get my "mini me" every year! Look at this one! You got a Maximus for him?!
I love it, I think you outdid the year you made me riding the dragon!
Wait... you... you like these things?
Like them? I *love* them!
DAD
Perfect! Thank you so much. Look at them all, they're wonderful! I can't wait to see what you come up with for my *birthday*!
Well, I'm sure I can come up with something involving swords and sparkly paint.
Oh, I know! How about one that's *life-size*? I can put it right outside my office to glare at everyone.
Fun *and* functional. I like it! But I better get started now!
THE END

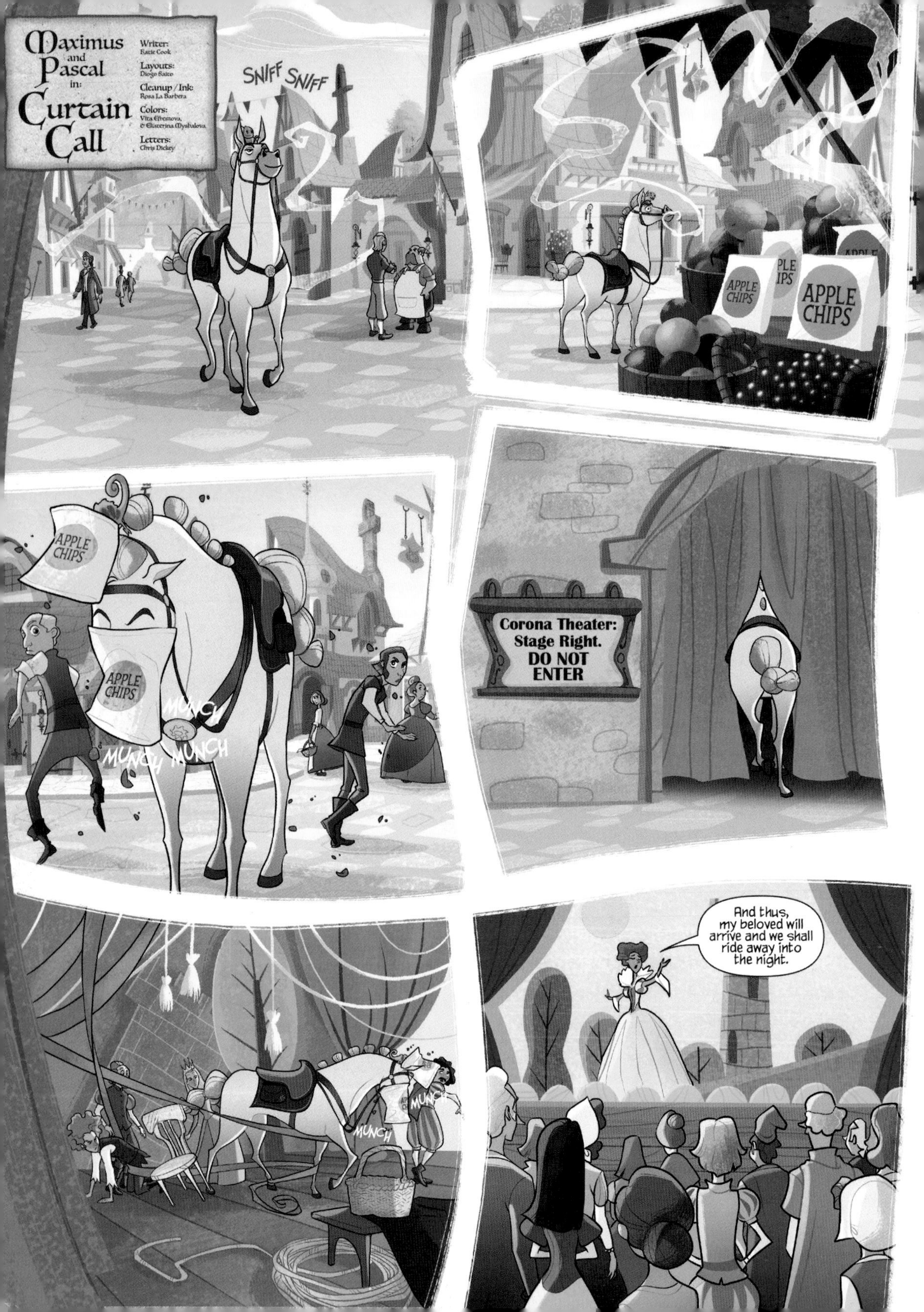
Maximus and Pascal in: Curtain Call
Writer: Katie Cook
Layouts: Diogo Saito
Cleanup / Ink: Rosa La Barbera
Colors: Vita Efremova, & Ekaterina Myshalova
Letters: Chris Dickey
SNIFF SNIFF
APPLE CHIPS
APPLE CHIPS
APPLE CHIPS
APPLE CHIPS
MUNCH
MUNCH MUNCH
Corona Theater: Stage Right. DO NOT ENTER
MUNCH
MUNCH
And thus, my beloved will arrive and we shall ride away into the night.

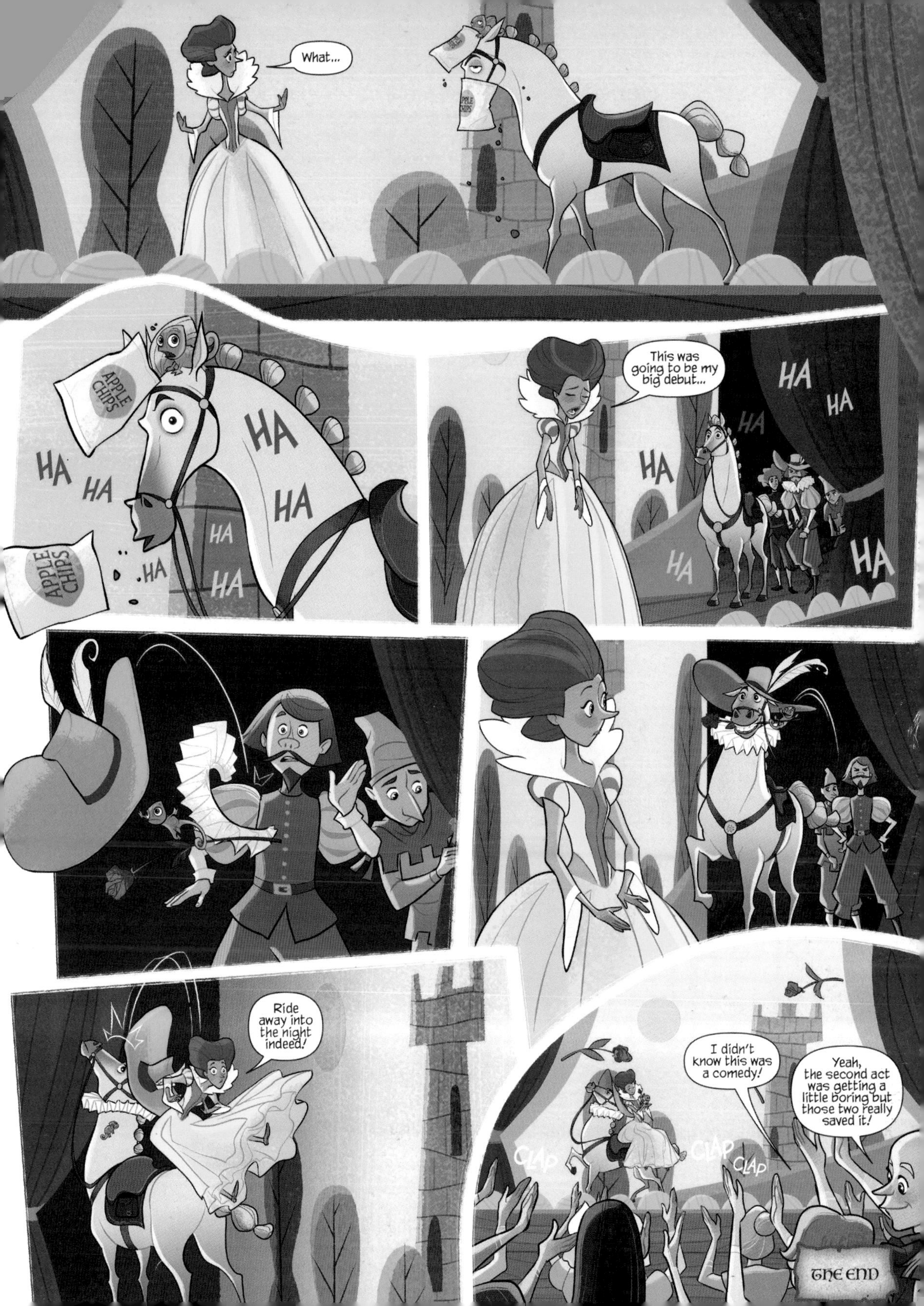
What...
APPLE CHIPS
APPLE CHIPS
HA HA HA HA HA HA .HA
This was going to be my big debut...
HA HA HA HA HA HA
Ride away into the night indeed!
I didn't know this was a comedy!
Yeah, the second act was getting a little boring but those two really saved it!
CLAP CLAP CLAP
THE END

Art by Disney Storybook Art Team

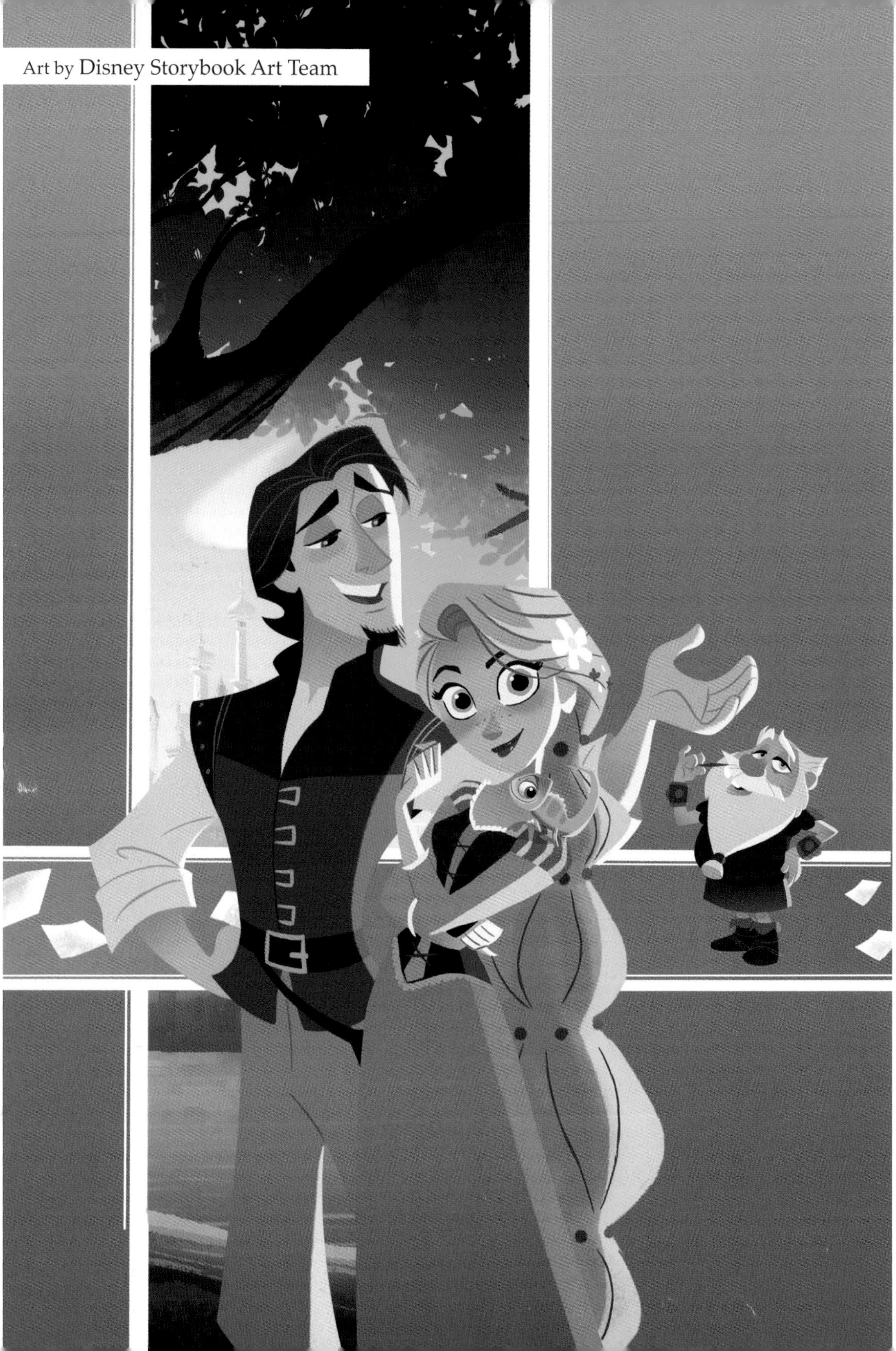

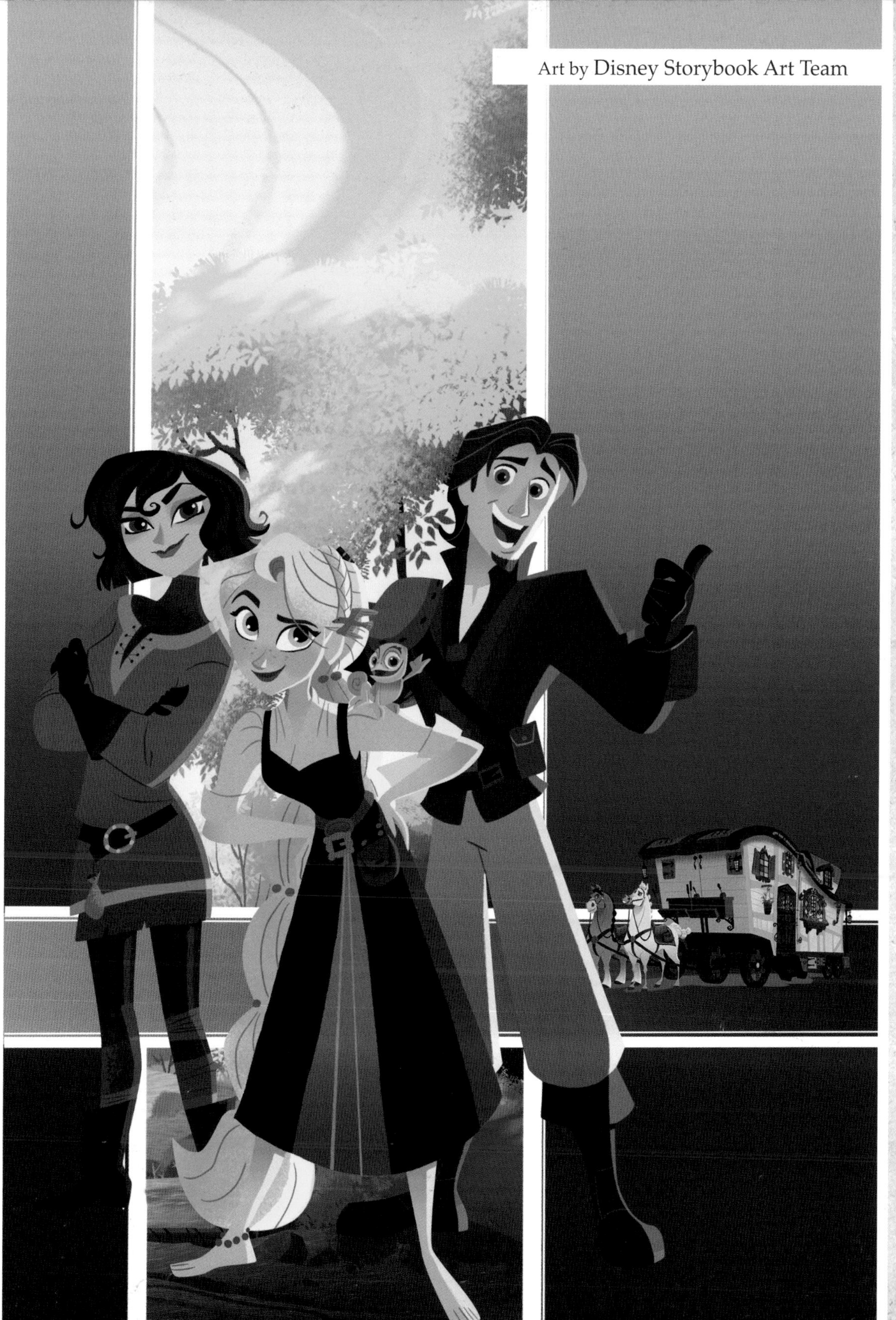

Art by Disney Storybook Art Team

Art by Eduard Petrovich, Rosa La Barbera, and Monica Catalano, Colors by Tomato Farm Color Team

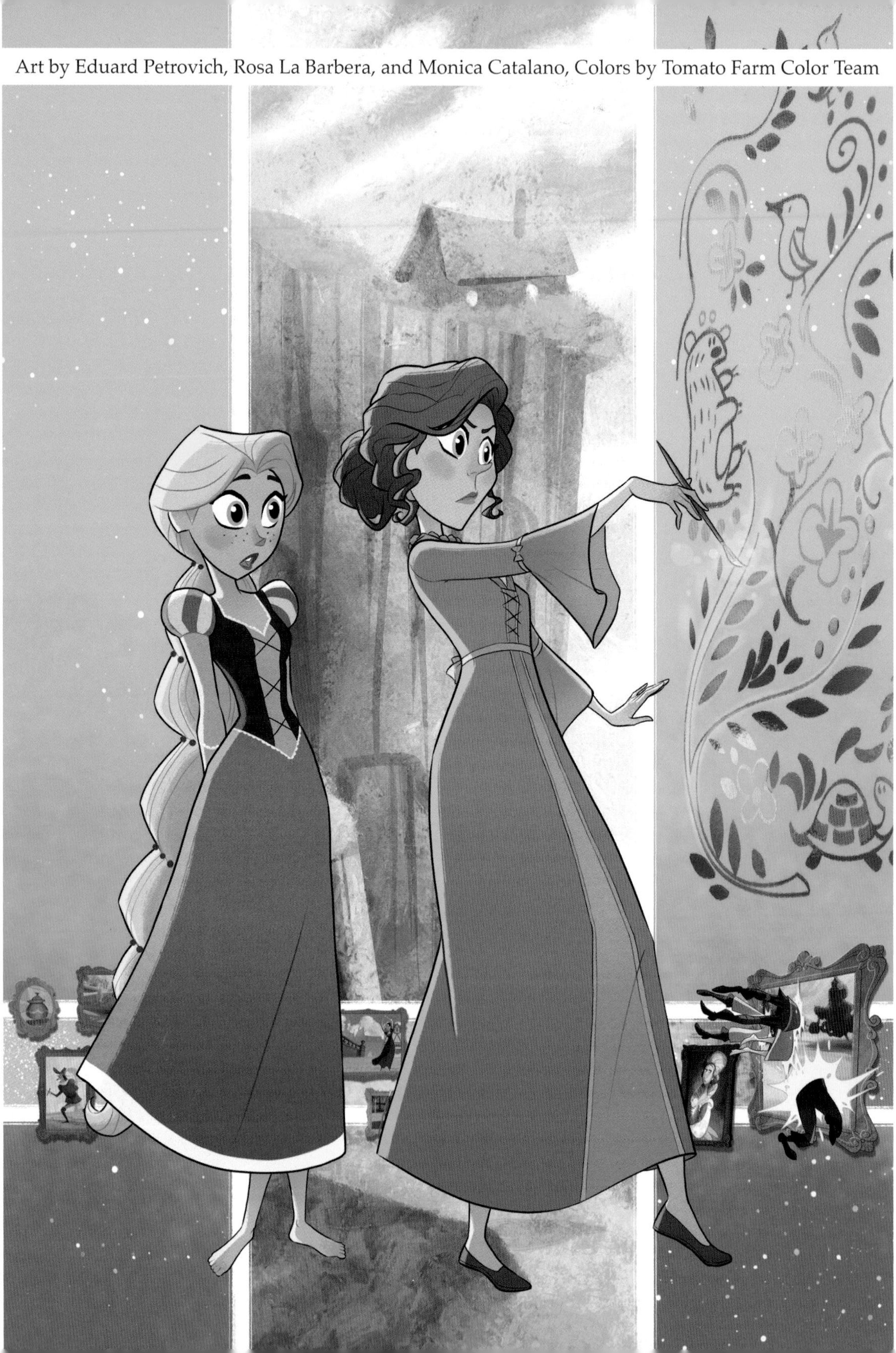

Art by Gabby Zapata

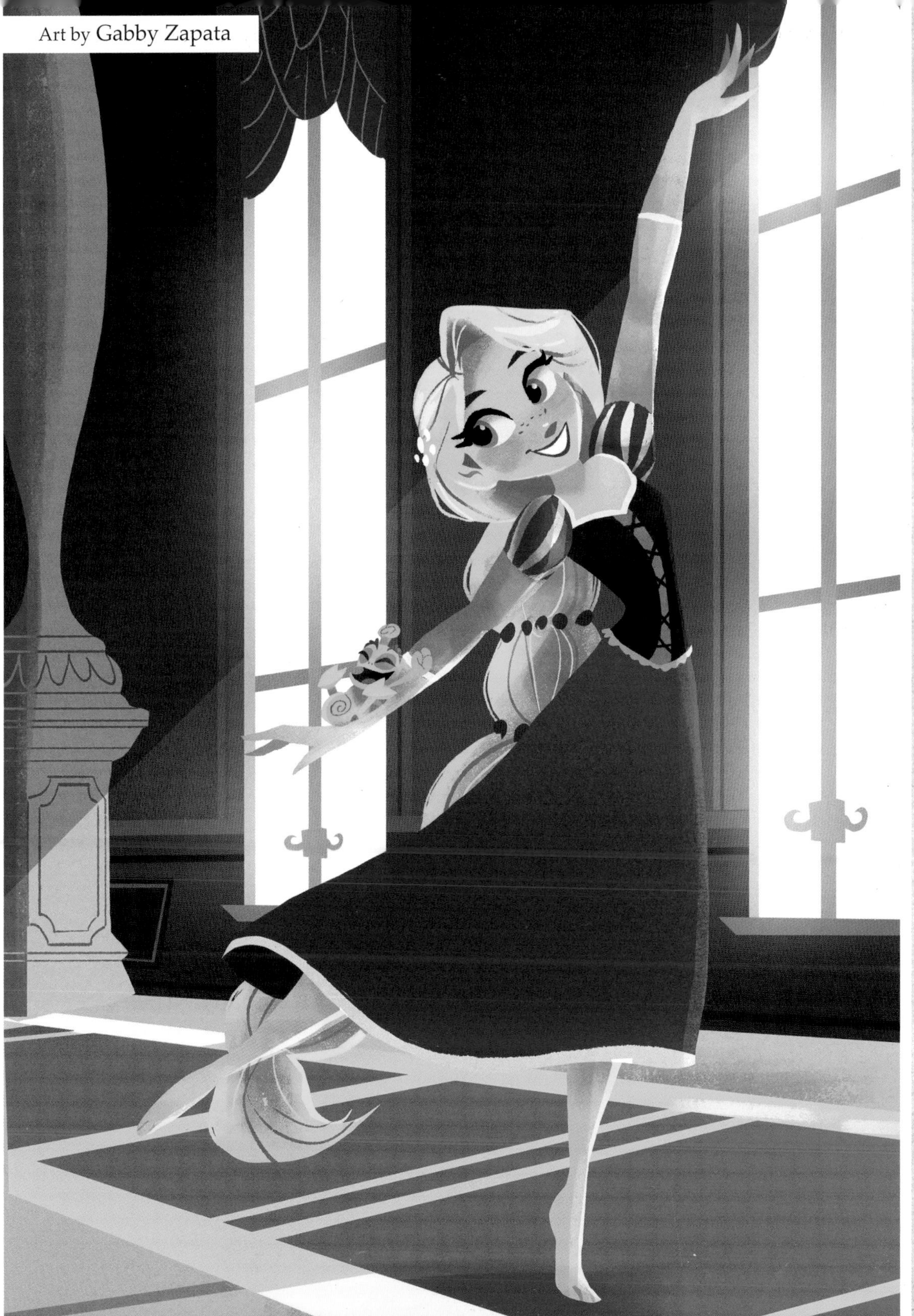

Art by Gabby Zapata

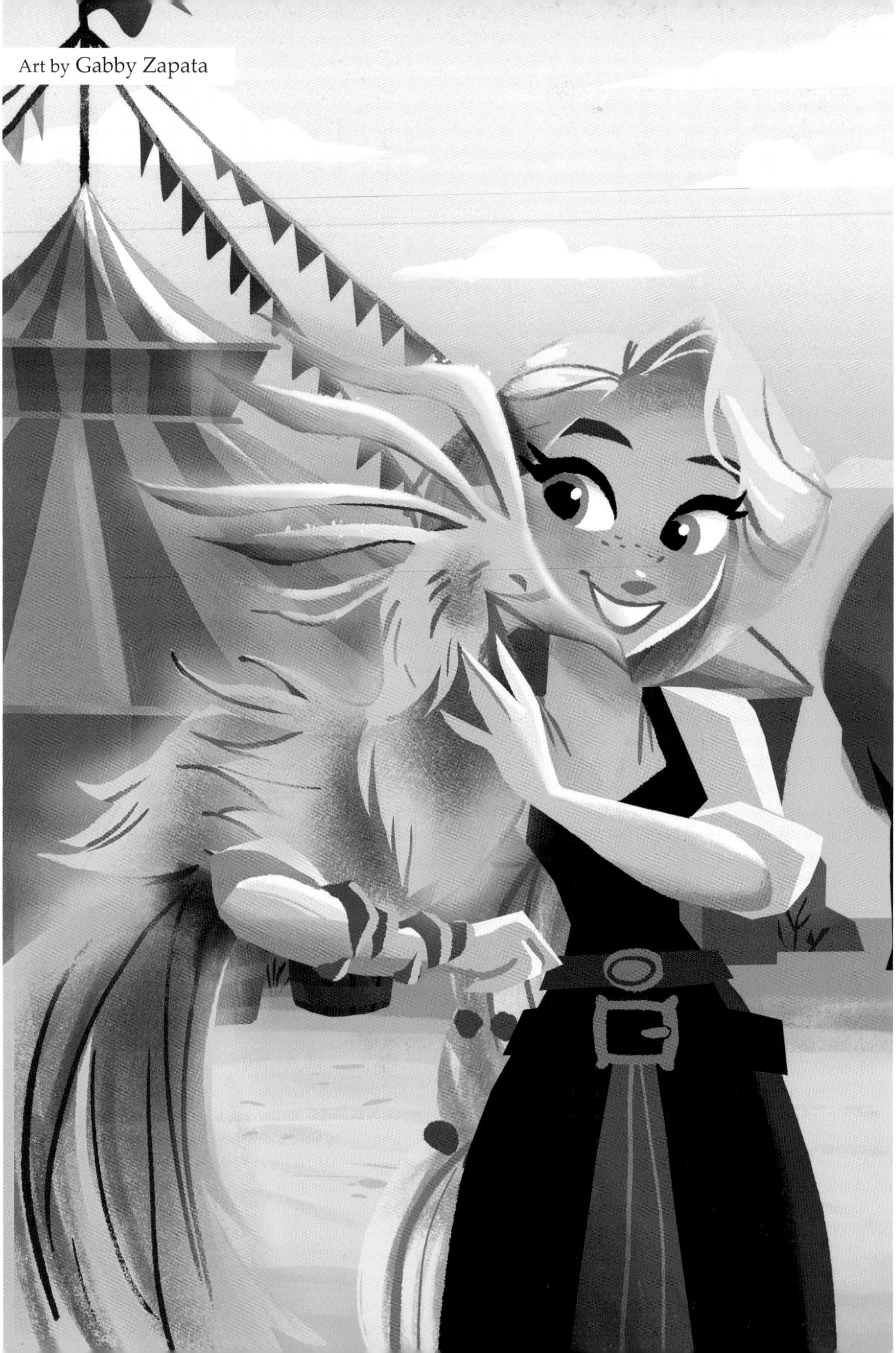

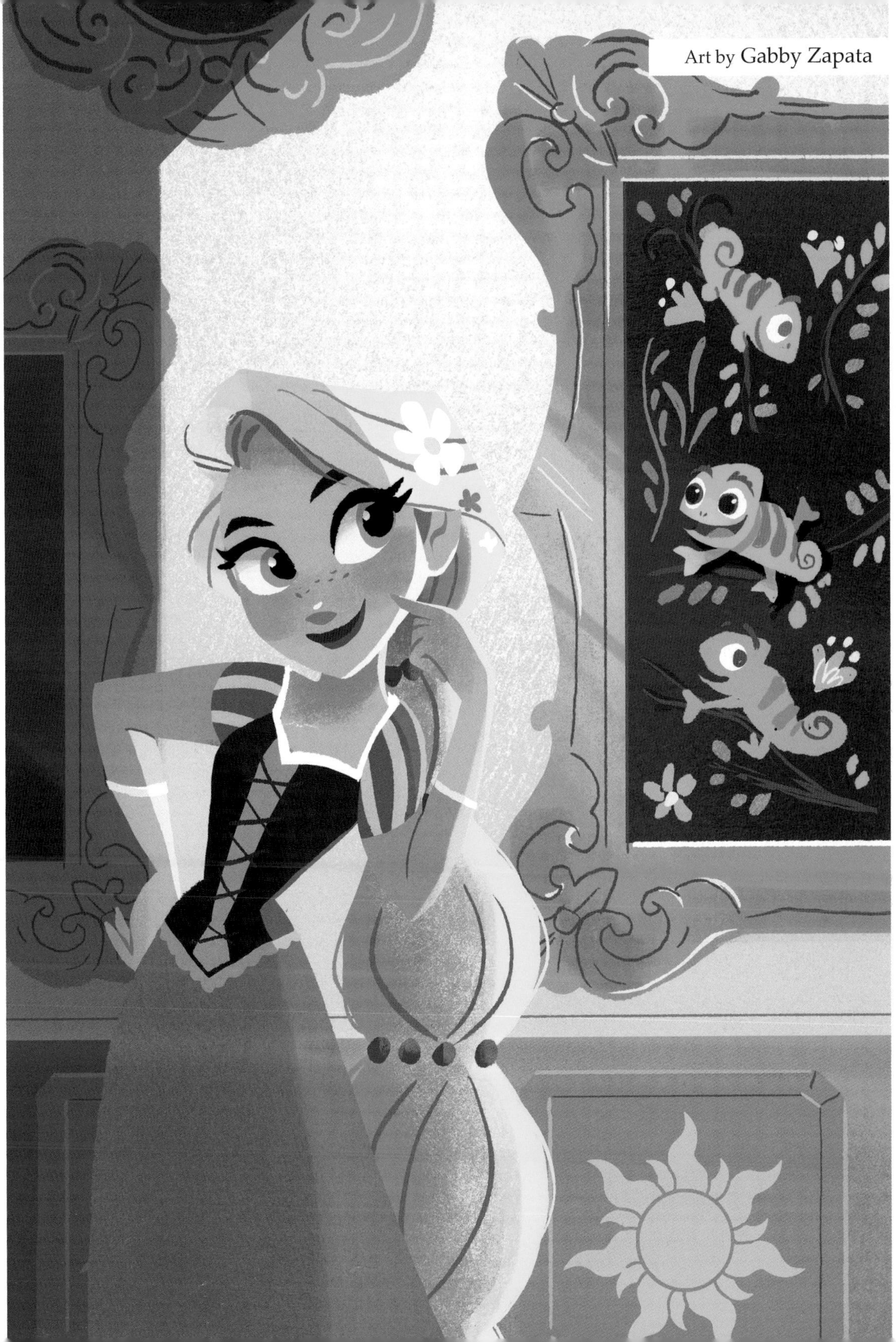

Art by Gabby Zapata

Art by Disney Storybook Art Team

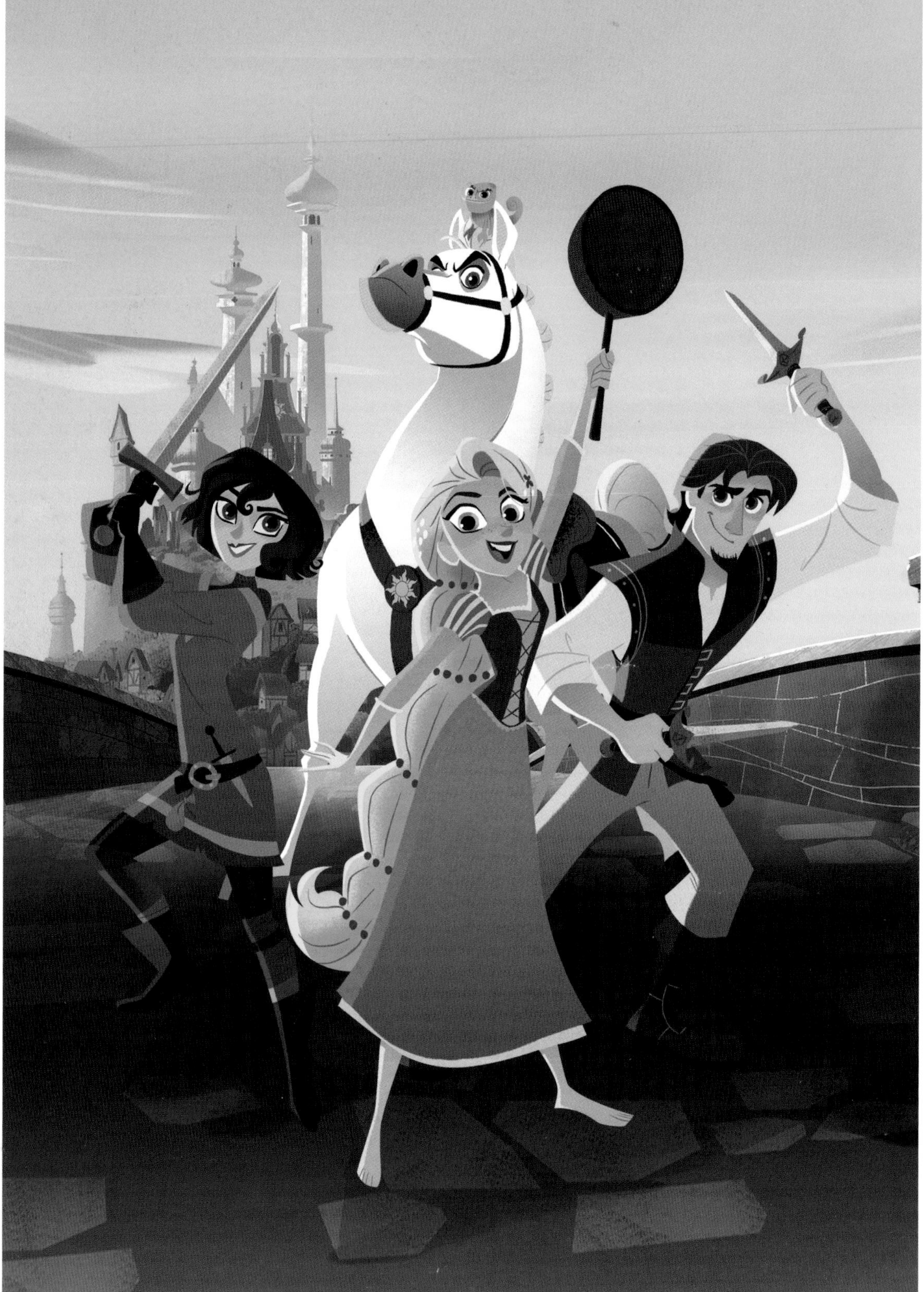

Art by Disney Storybook Art Team

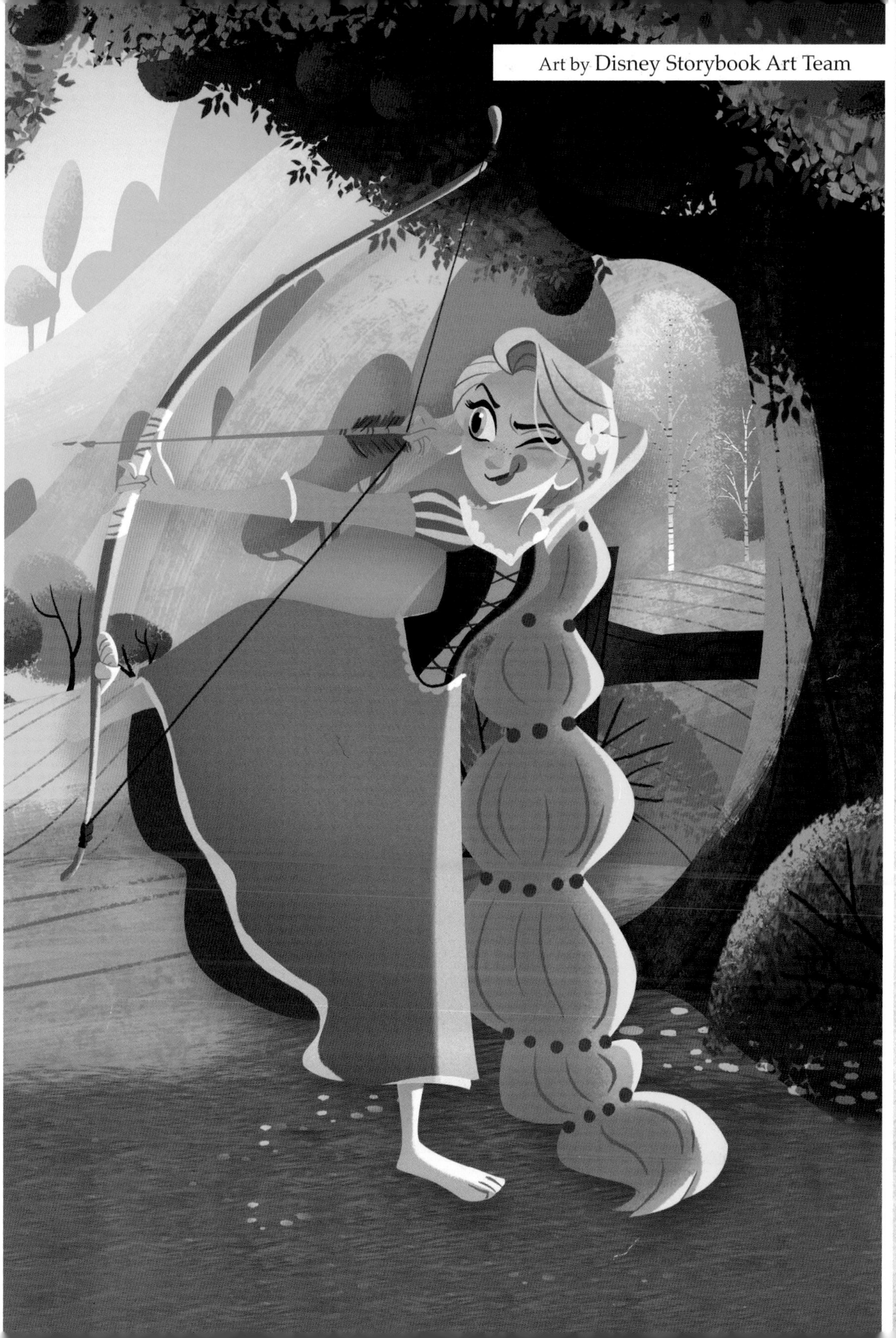